"THIS IS EARTHFORCE COMMANDER IVANOVA
TO SUSPECTED RAIDER SHIPS. CUT YOUR
ENGINES OR I WILL ATTACK."

There was no response. Then it was all or nothing. The raiders continued their flight toward the jump point, and Alpha Wing's formation, a fusion-powered spearpoint, flung itself at its targets, phased plasma guns fully charged, closing in.

But the targets weren't blind or helpless. As soon as they detected the Earthforce fighters bearing down on them, the raiders reacted, a half-dozen of the small wing-shaped fighters peeling off to engage their pursuers.

"Lock on target. Fire."

Superheated plasma shot from her guns, intercepted by the transport's defensive weapons. From the formation around her came more fire as Alpha Wing engaged the enemy. A raider ship bore down on her from straight ahead, but Ivanova had it in her sights, fired, and had the savage satisfaction of seeing the incandescent gases of its death-explosion fill her screen. Another raider took a hit, spun crazily for a brief instant, then disintegrated into flying debris. . . .

Look for VOICES, BABYLON 5 BOOK #1,
in your local bookstore

ACCUSATIONS

a BABYLON 5 Novel

Lois Tilton

Based on the series by
J. Michael Straczynski

(This story takes place after the
events in *The Coming of Shadows*
and before *All Alone in the Night*)

A Dell Book

Published by
Dell Publishing
a division of
Bantam Doubleday Dell Publishing Group, Inc.
1540 Broadway
New York, New York 10036

ISBN: 0-440-22058-0

Printed in the United States of America

Published simultaneously in Canada

May 1995

10 9 8 7 6 5 4 3 2 1

RAD

To the Bulging Groupmind
And to Don, who Came Through

CHAPTER 1

Observation Dome, Babylon 5: When it was quiet, with no ships departing or approaching the station, an observer could look out through the curved windows and see the stars glowing silently against the black backdrop of space. At such times it might be possible to contemplate the infinity of the cosmos and wonder at humanity's place among the sentient races of the universe.

But such peaceful meditation was rarely possible in the Observation Dome. This was the Control Center of Babylon 5, and Commander Susan Ivanova was intent on her console, not contemplating the view from the window. The surface of the large curved control console was black, as space was black, but its data screens glowed in vivid electronic hues as the figures constantly flickered and changed. On the central screen, icons represented the ships filling the station's traffic lanes, pulling away from the station, coming in to dock. One in particular was highlighted: a crippled cargo transport coming in, three days behind schedule, with damage to its stabilizers that predicted an interesting docking experience to come.

Ivanova stood with hands clasped behind her back, considering the computer-projected trajectory of the incoming freighter on the screen. The colors of the lighted displays played across her face, its skin pulled taut by her tightly braided hair.

Then she ordered crisply, "Centauri transport *Gonfalion,* this is Babylon Control. Your trajectory is erratic. I'm ordering you to cut your engines. We're going to tow you in. Do not, repeat *not* attempt to dock under your own power. Do you read me, *Gonfalion*?"

The face of the alien pilot on the communications screen did not look happy on hearing this order. There would be towing charges added to the station's usual docking fees. But the fines for noncompliance would certainly be a lot stiffer yet. "Acknowledged, Babylon Control. I'm cutting power to the thrusters now."

The scan technician checking her own instruments confirmed, "Their engines are shutting down, Commander."

Ivanova acknowledged with a short nod. Still intently watching the screen, she ordered, "Get a couple of shuttles out there to tow her into cargo bay eight. Divert all incoming traffic away from that traffic lane. Give them plenty of room."

It was a slow and tricky job, to lock grapples onto a ship the size of an interstellar freighter and maneuver it into the narrow chute of the station's docking bay. Ivanova would oversee the operation from here at her console, as insurance against something else going wrong. Not that she mistrusted the skill of the station's pilots, but there was only one desirable outcome and an infinite number of disastrous ones. Under such circumstances, she preferred not to rely on luck. It was the Russian in her coming out, she sometimes said.

There were other, smaller annoyances trying to claim her attention: the communications screen on her console now showed three more new messages waiting in the queue. Ivanova already knew what most of them were about. In the corridors outside the sanctuary of the Observation Dome, where they weren't allowed entry, prowled a small pack of shipping factors, insurance agents, hopeful salvage operators, and others who wanted news of the damaged freighter and its cargo. But they'd just have to wait until the ship was safely docked. She had no time and less inclination to deal with them now.

On the screen, the shuttles were closing in on the mass of the cargo ship, deploying grapples.

"Got it, Control," the pilot of shuttle A reported. "Locked on."

"Well done," Ivanova commended her.

"Commander," Communications broke in, "there's another message. Sender says it's urgent and personal."

"If it's personal, then it can wait," Ivanova said curtly. Several months ago, such a message would have instantly aroused concern about her father, dying in a hospital on Earth, but that phase of her life was over now. Mother, brother, now father, all of them dead, and there was no one else she could think of who might be calling her on a matter both personal and urgent enough to interfere with duty.

Now both shuttles had the cargo ship fast, and Ivanova ordered, "All right, take her in."

There was one tense moment after that when a departing Narn fighter cut too close to the crippled ship's path, but Ivanova instantly ordered it, "Narn fighter 42, reduce your speed and return to your assigned traffic lane."

The maneuver had been deliberate, Ivanova suspected. The Narn and the Centauri had been at war intermittently for over a century, and the hostilities between them were always close to the surface, even here on Babylon 5, this station whose very reason for existence was peace between all sentient races. Lately, with war between them now breaking out in earnest, that goal was seeming further and further remote, but for the moment, the balance of power held, precariously. And it was simple common-sense self-preservation to obey the instructions of the traffic controller on a station as crowded with ships as this one was now.

The rest of the docking maneuvers were uneventful, even tedious, and from time to time Ivanova's thoughts wandered to the waiting message: urgent and personal. Who could have sent it to her? What could they want?

With the crisis finally averted, she returned control of traffic operations to the technicians on duty, then after a slight hesitation, she queried the computer for the name of the sender of that one particular message.

"The sender's name is J. D."

"J. D.?" she wondered aloud. "Just J. D.?"

"There is no other name or identification with the message."

But Ivanova had already remembered. Ortega. J. D. Ortega. But what was he doing here on Babylon 5? And what urgent business could he have with her? As far as she knew, Ortega had gone back home to Mars, turning down a career in Earthforce, choosing to go back to the mines while Ivanova went on to be promoted full commander before she was thirty. His face was coming back to her now: the blue-black curly hair, the warm smile.

There hadn't been anything between the two of them. It would have been wrong for a number of reasons: J. D. was her flight instructor, he was fiercely loyal to his wife back home on Mars. Ivanova remembered how he kept her picture with him all the time—what was her name? Constanzia? Ivanova had always suspected that it was for Constanzia's sake that he'd left Earthforce. It was hard to imagine him down in the red cavern of some Martian mine instead of the freedom of a Starfury.

But he'd taught her everything she knew about flying. Yes, she remembered.

"Let's see the message," she finally ordered the computer.

"Playing message now."

The face that appeared on her communications screen was and was not J. D.'s. His father, maybe, or a brother, she thought at first. This was an older face, with the laugh lines deeper and somehow not so much like laughter. Ivanova had to suppress a sudden urge to stare at her own face in the mirror surface of her console. *Have we changed so much? Has it been so long? Ten years?*

But the voice was the same. The message was brief, hurried. "Susan, I'm in trouble. They say you're Number Two here on this station. I don't know anyone else who might be able to help. There's something I have to tell you. Please, meet me in the Alpha Wing ready room at 20:00 hours."

"J. D.?" Ivanova asked aloud, but it was the computer that responded: "End of message."

20:00 hours. Ivanova thought quickly. She'd be off duty by then. Of course she'd meet him. But what kind of trouble was he in? Why did he seem so nervous, even fearful? What was wrong?

"Computer, what time is it now?"
"21:55 hours."
Ivanova stood up, paced the width of the room, sat down again. The ready room was empty, which it usually was at this hour, when Alpha Wing was off duty. She'd been here almost two hours, first watching the news on the wall screens, then reading a few of the old newspapers lying around the place, finally resorting to a holographic game that she found under a seat cushion, sending a tiny image of a Starfury zipping around the room on the tail of a Minbari fighter. It probably ought to be confiscated, she thought. Earth was at peace with the Minbari now, it couldn't do any good to go bringing up the war again, especially here on Babylon 5 where running into a real Minbari fighter was a frequent occurrence. On the other hand, it was a fairly good game.

She was still in uniform, her hair pulled back into the braid she usually wore on duty, contributing an edge to the headache she could feel now, throbbing above her temples. Almost two hours! Where was J. D.? Her concern had progressed from "Why doesn't he show up on time?" to "What's keeping him?" and by now to "What's happened to him?"

"Computer, what time is it now?"

"22:02 hours."

More than two hours. And in all that time, no one had come into the room. Only one other person had been here at all, a large man with Oriental features who'd come out of the rest room and brushed past her just after she entered the main waiting room.

So what had happened to J. D.? In his message, he'd said he was in trouble. Had seemed afraid. Hard to believe that J. D. Ortega could have any enemies at all, let alone here on Babylon 5, where he'd never set foot until—

Until when? How long *had* he been on the station? Why hadn't he contacted her until now?

"Computer, when did J. D. Ortega arrive on the station?"

"Station registry shows there have been eight individuals named Ortega arriving at Babylon 5 since it first went on-line. None of them had the initials J. D."

"What? That's impossible!"

There was a computer console at a battered table in one corner, and Ivanova went to it now and queried the registry again. A list of names scrolled down the screen. It was true. *Ortega, J. D.* wasn't listed.

Now, that was wrong, just plain very wrong. If J. D. was somewhere on the station, he had to be in the registry. She called up his message again and queried its origin.

"Message was sent from Gray 18 at 13:08 hours."

So he was on the station. That *was* J. D. Ortega's face on the screen. His voice: "I'm in trouble."

Ivanova was starting to wonder just what kind of trouble. "Something's going on," she said to herself in a low voice. But maybe the registry was the wrong place to be looking.

"Computer, search all files for the name J. D. Ortega," she ordered.

The response wasn't quite what she'd wanted to hear. "This file is restricted."

Ivanova scowled. She input her password, identifying herself as the station's executive officer.

"Password is valid. Security clearance is valid. Accessing file: J. D. Ortega."

And there was his image on the screen, but this time it was flagged for all Earth Alliance Security Forces: FUGITIVE ALERT. RED LEVEL. WANTED FOR SUSPICION OF TERRORISM AND CONSPIRACY.

J. D. Ortega? A terrorist? A part of Ivanova's universe shifted on its foundations. No, that was impossible, it couldn't be true, it had to be some kind of error. Mistaken identity. But the face on the screen—it *was* J. D.'s.

Shaken and anxious, she touched her personal communications link to switch it on. "Garibaldi? This is Ivanova."

With relief, she heard the familiar voice of Babylon 5's security chief answering, "Ivanova? What's up?"

"I know you're not on duty—"

"Hey, there's no rest for the wicked, and that's me. Spill it, Ivanova."

But that was harder than it sounded. Ivanova started to explain, "Earlier today I got a message from an old friend. My old flight instructor. He asked me to meet him in the Alpha Wing ready room at 20:00 hours. I've waited all that time. He never showed."

Garibaldi's voice was amused. "Stood you up, huh? You want security to track down your date for you?"

Ivanova shook off the remark. Michael Garibaldi was notorious for his bad jokes, but she wasn't in the mood for him to start now.

"In his message, he said he was in trouble." She hesitated. Was this betraying J. D.? "When he didn't show up after more than two hours, I queried the computer. First, it said there was no record of him in the station registry. Then . . . it said there was an alert out for him. On suspicion of terrorism."

Garibaldi's voice was suddenly serious. "What's your friend's name?"

"J. D. Ortega."

There was a pause. Then Garibaldi said grimly, "I think you'd better meet me in Security Central, Commander."

He was waiting for her, waiting in his usual swivel chair, surrounded by banks of screens and instrumentation that took up half the space in the office. Garibaldi's gray Earthforce uniform was, as usual, not quite as crisp as a career officer's might be. He'd been around a long while and come to believe that results were what counted, not image. Ivanova had come to learn that he usually got the results.

On the main console, a file was displayed on a data screen. Garibaldi waved Ivanova over to it. "Is this your friend?" he asked her. "Does he come from Mars Colony?"

With a slight feeling of reluctance, she nodded. "That's J. D."

"It looks like your friend Ortega's gone and gotten himself involved in Mars Colony politics. Separatist politics, the Free Mars movement. Earth Central put out the alert for him ten days ago."

"No." She shook her head, reading through the file, stunned by the revelations. "No, Garibaldi, this can't be right. Not J. D. You don't *know* him—how he is. I mean, his wife, his family mean everything to him. He gave up his career for them, so he could stay home on Mars. He went back to work for the mines. He wouldn't . . ."

Ivanova's voice trailed off, silenced by what she was reading. "Do you have him in the lockup? Is that where he is?"

Garibaldi shook his head. "Until now, I had no idea he might even be on Babylon 5. This was just a general alert, sent out to all Earth Alliance security officers. Tell me, how well do you know this guy? He was your flight instructor? Have you seen him since then? Met with him recently?"

"No, not since he left Earthforce. That was before I took the assignment on Io. Where I served under Captain Sheridan the first time." She paused abruptly, looked at Garibaldi with an altered expression, suddenly aware that this was an interrogation. Then she went on in the same controlled voice she used at the command console. "I haven't seen him since then. A few messages, the kind of thing you send on the holidays. The last few years, no, nothing. I don't think I've thought of him in the last few years—until today."

Garibaldi said quietly, "I think you'd better show me that message you got today."

Ivanova felt a strange sensation of being torn in half. J. D. had come to her for help. But she had no choice, not as an Earthforce officer. And besides, she realized at once that Garibaldi didn't really need to ask her permission. As head of station security, he had access to almost any message he wanted to see. "Of course," she said quickly, covering up the momentary hesitation.

This time, viewing the message on the screen, she couldn't help seeing J. D. Ortega's expression as furtive, the face of a man on the run. "I'm in trouble," he was saying. That was certainly an understatement, Ivanova thought.

"That's him," she confirmed it again, shaking her head. "I just can't understand it. Not J. D."

"But we do know," Garibaldi reminded her, "that he

managed to get onto Babylon 5 and send at least one message without being identified. That's what worries me. How did he manage to get onto the station without triggering the alert? And if he could do that, what else was he involved in? We've got no idea how long he's been on the station. Or if someone's been hiding him. If we have a branch of the Free Mars organization on Babylon 5, that's a problem.''

Ivanova wasn't quite ready to give up. "But if he was a terrorist, then why would he come to me for help? He must have known my position on the station. If he was involved in Free Mars, why not go to them? Maybe they're the ones who were after him. He said he was in trouble.''

"I'd certainly like to know, too. Which means we have to take him in for questioning. Whenever he contacts you again.''

Wordlessly, she agreed. But there was still that gnawing doubt.

Ortega's face was still displayed on the screen. *J. D.? What kind of trouble are you in? What happened? Where were you tonight?*

CHAPTER 2

The distress signal was going out on all frequencies, to all ships in Epsilon Sector as well as Babylon 5. On the communications screen in the station's Observation Dome, the pilot's frantic face was sweating as he sent, "Mayday! Mayday! We're under attack! Raiders closing in fast! We need help out here! This is the transport ship *Cassini*, coordinates Red 470 by 13 by 16! Mayday! Mayday!"

Captain John Sheridan was at the command console. Instantly, he ordered, "Commander Ivanova, scramble Alpha Wing! We've got raiders! Red 470 by 13 by 16! That's out by the secondary transit point in Section 13!"

Ivanova was already heading at a run for the Cobra bays where her fighter stood prepped and ready to go, while in the Observation Dome Sheridan continued to deal with the endangered transport ship. The main force of raider ships had been eliminated last year, but there were still small pockets, independent units functioning alone. "*Cassini*, this is Babylon Control, we have a fighter wing scrambling now. Are you hit? What weapons do you have? Can you hold them off till we get there?"

"We're trying to make it back to the jump gate," the desperate pilot reported. "It's our only chance; we can't run from them. There's too many of them and they're too fast! But I don't know if we'll make it. They've got us cut off. They were on us almost as soon as we came through the gate. Waiting for us! It was a setup!"

"Try to hold on, *Cassini*, help is on the way!" But when he turned away from the communications screen,

Sheridan's expression was grim. He knew, as the transport's pilot had to, that there wasn't much hope of Ivanova reaching the endangered ship before it was too late. After Alpha Wing came out of hyperspace into Section Red 13, the fighters would still have almost three hours in normal space before they could reach the transfer jump point where the transport had been ambushed, even at a Starfury's maximum acceleration.

The Cobra bay doors stood open wide, ready. C&C had already cleared them for immediate launch, priority. Ivanova ran quickly through her preflight check. "Alpha Wing, ready for drop?"

With all nine ships signaling readiness, "Prepare to launch. On my mark, Alpha Wing. Let's go! Drop!"

The cradle swung down, and the F23 Starfury dropped free of the station, falling out into space in the curved trajectory imparted by the station's spin. Then Ivanova fired the thrusters, and the fighter blasted away from Babylon 5. One by one, the rest of Alpha Wing joined in behind her, falling into formation as they accelerated toward the jump gate.

Ivanova's hands were tight on the fighter's controls, as if she could propel the ship by the sheer force of will. Time was the crucial element in these situations—time to launch the fighters, to get to the jump point, even more time to reach the endangered ship once they were through. Through her command helmet, she was monitoring Sheridan's exchange with the *Cassini*'s pilot, and she could already tell the situation wasn't good. The transport was too far away, the raiders were too close on its tail. By the time Alpha flight got there, it might already be too late.

Too often, lately, they'd been too late. Angrily, Ivanova thrust away the memory of what they'd found on those occasions.

Ahead was the jump gate, the permanent hyperspace installation maintained by Babylon 5. "This is Alpha Leader, prepare for jump," Ivanova ordered, heading for the gate's center at the head of the fighter wing. As her Starfury entered the gate, an immense power surge opened the hyperspace vortex, warping space, time, light, pulling the ship in and through. Simultaneously it disappeared into the jump point's infinite black center and into the dark red nightmare of hyperspace, and emerged from the blue-shifted funnel of energy into Section Red 13, light-years from Babylon 5 in normal space. One by one, in order, the rest of Alpha Wing followed, taking up formation again behind Ivanova.

"This is Alpha Leader, let's get to that transport! Maximum burn," she ordered. "ETA to the *Cassini*'s last recorded position 166 minutes. Warm up your weapons. Let's be ready for the raiders when we get there!"

But when she tried to raise the transport to report that she was on the way, there was no response. "Any transmissions from the *Cassini*?"

"Negative," reported Alpha Two, Gordon Mokena, her wingman and the designated scan/communications ship for the mission.

Damn, she said under her breath. Not good, not good at all.

She opened up a direct subspace tachyon channel to Babylon 5. "Babylon Control, this is Ivanova, we're out in 13, and I can't raise the *Cassini*. Are you still in contact? Do you have a current fix on their position?"

Sheridan's voice responded, "Ivanova, we lost contact with the *Cassini* about the time you went through the jump gate. Their last reported position was 470 by 13 by 18. They were trying to make it back through the jump gate."

Grimly, Ivanova made the course correction, just as if there were still a realistic odds on the transport's survival. There was no question of turning back. You had to see it through, no matter how bad it looked. For the chance that some other ship might come onto the scene and manage to chase off the raiders. For the chance of saving a survivor. And if all that failed, for the chance of revenge, of getting just one raider ship in your sights and seeing it disintegrate, lit by the brief flare as its fuel went up with the oxygen from its ruptured tanks.

Vengeance was supposed to be something you left to the Lord, or so she'd been taught as a child, but Ivanova didn't care. She wanted those raiders.

Sometimes it seemed they would never be able to stamp them out. Wipe out one nest of them, another would pop up in a different sector of space. The more trade grew between the stars, the more the opportunities for piracy, the more the profits in it, feeding the black market. *Humans and aliens—greed seems to be one thing we have in common,* Ivanova thought grimly.

The raiders were typically hit-and-run operators, snatching what was valuable from the transports they hit, killing the crews, and abandoning their victims to the cold void of space. They had started out as opportunistic pirates, roaming the shipping routes and hitting whatever random targets they came across, but after the destruction of their main force, they were becoming more desperate. These days, they didn't like to leave their profits to chance. The remaining pirate consortiums operated from mother ships large enough to create their own jump points in space. And they preferred to choose their targets in advance, relying on bribes to obtain cargo manifests and routing schedules. There didn't seem to be any information that wasn't for sale if the price was high enough.

Angrily, Ivanova diverted her mind from this train of thought by querying the computer for the current ETA at the *Cassini*'s position.

"ETA for coordinates 470 by 13 by 18 is twenty-four minutes."

Close enough. She opened her command channel. "This is Alpha Leader, all ships activate long-range scan," she ordered. "Let's see if we can pick them up out there."

For several minutes she watched the screen while the scan turned up nothing. Then Alpha Two reported in: "I'm getting something! Looks like raiders! Four . . . no, I think five of them!"

"I'm getting more! They've got another ship with them! Something big, like a transport!" Alpha Five announced.

"Location?"

Both pilots sent the coordinates and other scan data. The data matched with what Ivanova's own instruments were picking up. The raiders were obviously heading for the Red 13 jump point. Then they didn't come from a jump-capable carrier.

"What about the *Cassini*?" Ivanova asked, but there was still no communication from the ship they were trying to save.

At their current acceleration, the raiders would be at the jump point in less than fourteen minutes. They were close, but the transport they were escorting was clearly slowing them down. Alpha Wing's Starfuries, with thrusters on maximum burn, could make it there in twelve minutes. But what about the *Cassini*? Had the raiders captured the freighter, taken her in tow?

Then, from Alpha Two: "Commander, I'm picking up a mass of about 850K tonnes at 470 by 13 by 18. Reading just mass, no acceleration, no life sign."

The *Cassini*. Ivanova knew it. Her worst-case outcome, realized again.

Now it was decision time. "Alpha Two, Six, Ten—

check it out. If it's the transport . . . you know what to do.

"The rest of you, close up formation. Activate weapons. We're going to cut those bastards off at the jump point and burn them down."

As the three designated Starfuries pivoted out of the main formation, the remaining fighters closed up as ordered, following Ivanova's thruster flares on an intercepting course, to reach the jump gate before the raiders and their hijacked cargo. If she could do it, cut them off at the jump gate, the raiders were already hot ash, with nowhere to run. The Starfuries were faster, and there was no sanctuary in empty space, no safety but engines and firepower, and Alpha Wing had the raider ships outgunned. Their situation would be as hopeless as the transport *Cassini* had been when they attacked it.

Ivanova's voice over the command channel never lost its clipped, cool tones, her orders were by the book, her hands on the controls were steady, but there was a tightness in her jaw, a look in her eyes that promised no mercy on the raiders once she got them in her sights.

Because it was procedure, she opened a wide-band comm channel. "This is Earthforce Commander Ivanova to suspected raider ships. Cut your engines or I will attack."

There was no response. Then it was all or nothing. The raiders continued their flight toward the jump point, and Alpha Wing's formation, a fusion-powered spearpoint, flung itself at its targets, phased plasma guns fully charged, closing in.

But the targets weren't blind or helpless. As soon as they detected the Earthforce fighters bearing down on them, the raiders reacted, a half-dozen of the small wing-shaped fighters peeling off to engage their pursuers. On her screen, Ivanova could see the transport and its remaining escort begin to increase acceleration as they raced for the safety of the jump gate.

Whatever was in that transport, whatever they were guarding, had to be valuable if the raiders were willing to risk themselves to save it. "This is Alpha Leader. Three, Four, Nine, Twelve—engage their rear guard. The rest of you stay with me. We're going to take out that transport. Open fire as soon as you're in range."

The larger ship was not, she could see clearly now, the *Cassini,* but a leaner, faster type of freighter, designed for the rapid loading of stolen cargo and a fast escape, and undoubtedly armed. A fleeting thought passed through Ivanova's mind that the raiders had been well prepared to grab this cargo, whatever it was. But she had no time to think of anything but the coming fight as soon as the ready indicator on her weapons system finally showed the closest fighter in range.

"Lock on target. Fire."

Superheated plasma shot from her guns, intercepted by the transport's defensive weapons. From the formation around her came more fire as Alpha Wing engaged the enemy. A raider ship bore down on her from straight ahead, but Ivanova had it in her sights, fired, and had the savage satisfaction of seeing the incandescent gases of its death-explosion fill her screen. Another raider took a hit, spun crazily for a brief instant, then disintegrated into flying debris.

Ivanova's command channel was filled with voices.

Raider at ten o'clock.

I've got him, Ten!

I've lost an engine, Alpha Leader. I'm falling back.

About twenty degrees away and behind them, Ivanova's tactical screen showed the smaller formation of Starfuries led by Alpha Three engaging the raiders' rear defenders. Around her, the main body of Alpha Wing was in pursuit of the rest, taking out the raider fighters one by one. With some part of her brain she was aware of all this activity, tracking it, making the correct responses. But most of her attention was focused on the raider transport, the rapidly decreasing distance between it and the jump point, and the slower rate with which she was inexorably closing the gap between them. The transport ship was well armed. As it fired one of its rear guns, Ivanova's Starfury was rocked by a plasma burst a lot closer than she found comfortable. But she returned the fire, and one of her shots made a direct hit, blowing away a rear cargo section and one of the transport's thrusters.

Seeing that, the rest of the raiders seemed to figure that their hijacked cargo was lost and it was time to save themselves. The leading pair of raider ships accelerated ahead, through the jump gate, passing into hyperspace with sudden successive flares of light. *Damn!* Ivanova cursed to herself, but they were beyond her reach now.

Now panic started to spread through the surviving raiders. They broke off the fight, racing each other for the gate, followed at a rapidly increasing distance by the abandoned, limping transport. "Damn!" Ivanova swore again in frustration as one more passed through and escaped her, then another.

There was still the transport, crippled and outgunned, with Alpha Wing closing in. Ivanova opened the channel again to call for its surrender. But before the cargo ship could respond, two of the last raiders, both diving for the jump gate at the same time, collided, both fighters obliterated in a single explosive fireball. A third was unable to veer away in time to avoid the blast wave, which slammed it into one of the jump gate's extended arms.

"Pull up!" Ivanova ordered her ships urgently, and they broke off the pursuit, evading the massive energy surge that flashed out from the damaged gate's power node.

Ivanova's scan readout broke into static as the energy

level went off the scale. She watched in a kind of horrified awe to see the disabled transport, out of control and unable to change course, slide inexorably into the intensely charged field. There was a blue-white flash that struck at her eyes even through her polarized viewscreen, and then the ship was gone.

She let out a breath. "This is Alpha Leader, all ships return to formation. Let's check out the damages."

Mokena in Alpha Two had reported somberly, "We've found the *Cassini,* Commander. The crew's dead. They gutted the ship, tore the cargo section open to get at it."

Now Ivanova was seeing the devastation for herself, the ruined, lifeless ship, the gaping hole in the cargo hold. Her fighter drifted almost motionless past the wreckage, close enough that she could see the carbon-scoring from the raider's blasts along its hull, the ruin of the flight cabin's interior, the empty hold. What had it been carrying, what was worth so much destruction, so many lives?

There were sometimes moments, like seeing the raider transport drift helplessly to its destruction, when Ivanova would start to feel doubt, to wonder if the killing could be justified. Sights like this one made the doubts disappear. Some things had to be fought, had to be put down.

The other ships had already taken the *Cassini* crew's remains onboard, salvaged the ship's records, its log, the black box. Once they got back to Babylon 5, they might reveal something.

Ivanova activated her command channel. "This is Alpha Leader. Form up. Nothing more we can do here. Let's go home."

CHAPTER 3

They started out looking for a fugitive. Not such an easy job, not with Babylon 5's population crowding a quarter million sentient beings. Eliminate the methane-breathers, narrow it down even further to humans, and the scale of the problem still was a lot to contend with. The alien sectors of the station still had to be included in the search, just in case this Ortega fellow might be hiding in there, maybe inside an environment suit.

But this was part of Michael Garibaldi's job description, and there was no one who knew the ins and outs of Babylon 5 better than he did. He wouldn't deserve to be chief of security if there was, would he?

The job meant just about everything to Garibaldi. He figured it was his last chance, and he'd given up most everything he had left to come here and take it. Given up Lise and any chance of working things out with her—and now he'd never know whether they might have made it together. She was married now, and he supposed he wished her well.

But he'd been on the long slide down for a long time, ever since the mess on Europa. Came close to hitting the bottom more than once. And then Jeff Sinclair had pulled him off the slide, given him this job, this chance —Chief of Security on one of Earth Alliance's most sensitive outposts. Only now things had changed again. Jeff Sinclair wasn't commander of Babylon 5 anymore. He was ambassador to the Minbari, and Captain John Sheridan had the commander's desk now, and Sheridan had seen Garibaldi's file, had to know the kind of man who was holding this job—almost certainly not the kind of man he would have chosen himself.

So here was the bottom line: Garibaldi knew he couldn't afford to screw up. This Ortega case was a big one—Priority One fugitive alert. Earth Central wanted this guy real bad. Garibaldi called in his entire security staff on it.

"All right, listen up. This is our man. J. D. Ortega. You all have a copy of his file, right? Study it carefully. You can see that he's wanted for terrorism and conspiracy on Mars. Probably related to last year's uprising, Free Mars, the separatist movement.

"Now, somehow, he got onto Babylon 5 without triggering our scanners, and that brings up the possibility that he may have some kind of forged identicard. Also possibly confederates here on the station. You'd better believe we're going to be looking into *that*. But right for the moment, our job is to find J. D. Ortega and take him into custody. That means we search this station until we've crawled through every ventilation duct and unbolted every wall panel, if that's what it takes. All right, you all have your assignments. Are there any questions?"

There weren't any, to Garibaldi's relief. Because of the nature of the charges, because of Commander Ivanova's involvement, there were aspects of the case he didn't want to discuss with his whole staff. Just as there were parts of the file he hadn't distributed to all of them —a matter of security clearances. Earth Central wanted this one kept shut tight.

They were looking for a fugitive, and so when Command and Control called in on his link that someone had reported a body in one of the fighter maintenance bays, Garibaldi deputed one of his subordinates, Ensign Torres, to check into the matter.

A few minutes later, Torres called back. "Chief, it's him. The body—it's him!"

"Him? You mean Ortega? He's dead? You mean he was killed?"

"That's what it looks like, Chief."

Garibaldi's first thought was that this didn't really solve anything. So they'd found Ortega; now they had to look for his killer. And what about Ivanova? When she found out her old friend was dead?

But he reacted according to the book. "All right, Torres, I hope you have the area sealed off. Good. Keep it that way. No one in or out, nobody says anything to anyone until I get there. You've got whoever reported the body? Good. I want you to hold them for questioning. Whoever's seen the body, whoever knows it's there. Got that? I'm on my way. Remember, nobody into that area except me and Dr. Franklin from Medlab. I'm calling him right now."

Garibaldi's priority call got him through to the head of medical services on Babylon 5. "Doc, this is Garibaldi, I've got a dead body here, and I need you to examine it right away."

"Look, Garibaldi, I've got an experiment in progress here. I'll send—"

"No, I need you, personally. This is a security matter. Something Earth Central wants kept quiet. You've got the highest security clearance on the medical staff."

"A homicide?"

"Could be. Most likely it is. But that's one of the things I want you to find out."

A sigh of resignation. "All right, Garibaldi, I'll be right there. Where did you say you put this body?"

"Fighter maintenance bay one." Which, he suddenly realized, was Alpha Wing's maintenance bay.

* * *

They gathered around the equipment locker: Garibaldi, Franklin, and Garibaldi's best evidence technician, Popovic. Franklin and Popovic were busy with the corpse, running scanners up and down the length of the body, taking samples from the locker and the floor around it. Garibaldi took a few steps away, leaving them to their macabre work. He'd seen the dead man's face for a moment, long enough that he was mortally certain it was J. D. Ortega. That was as much as he needed.

So. They'd been looking for a fugitive, but they'd found a corpse. And a mystery. No, Garibaldi didn't think this was going to simplify the case.

He opened his link to C&C. "This is Garibaldi. I'm calling off the search for J. D. Ortega. We've found him."

Then he turned to the other end of the bay, where Torres was holding a small unhappy group from leaving. There was the maintenance foreman, the technician, who'd actually found the body, and an unfortunate fighter pilot who'd shown up to check on the progress of the repairs to her ship just as the discovery of the body was made.

Or was it really luck? Maybe the pilot was involved in some way, maybe she was planning to move the body and the ship was just an excuse? Garibaldi didn't mean to leave any questions unasked.

He started with the mechanic, who was not at all unwilling to talk.

"I came in a little early, to get to work on this ship. Got to rebuild the upper starboard engine."

Garibaldi glanced briefly at the impatient pilot. So she was with Alpha Wing, Ivanova's group. Stuck here with a crippled ship while the rest of them were out chasing raiders. He wondered if that had any significance for the investigation.

The mechanic was saying, "So I get my brazing arc,

and somebody else's been using it, got the feed line all clogged. I hate that, people using my tools! So I go to the locker to look for a new feed line. And there he is.''

"The body?"

"Yeah. All stiff and staring at me. So I call Brunetti to come see, he calls security, and then you guys all show up."

The foreman nodded, silently confirming this account of the events.

"No one else?" Garibaldi asked.

"Only her." The mechanic looked at the pilot, who said, "Look, I just came in here to check on my ship, all right? I came in, these guys were looking at something in the locker, I came over to see, and there was this naked dead guy. But I just came in to check on my ship!"

"All right, one at a time. Now, do any of you recognize this man? Any of you ever seen him before on the station? Or anywhere else?"

Three heads shook vigorously in the negative.

"You're sure? Never seen him before? A long time ago, maybe? During the war? On Earth, Mars?"

They were sure.

"All right, so he was a total stranger." Back to the mechanic now. "He was like that when you found him? No clothes?"

"Not a stitch."

"And you didn't see his clothes around on the floor or anywhere? In another locker?"

"Nope."

"All right, what time do you usually come on duty? Were you late this morning or maybe a little bit early? Who was the first one into the bay?"

He wasn't halfway through with the questioning when Franklin came over to him. "I've done everything I can here. For the rest, I'll have to take him to Medlab. I've ordered a cart to come pick him up."

"Sure, Doc, that's fine. You and Popovic have everything you need?"

"Yes, we're finished. There's no need to keep the site secured. This isn't where he was killed."

The fighter pilot was on her feet. "That means we can go, right?"

"Not quite yet," Garibaldi stopped her. "I still have a few more questions."

The next time he saw J. D. Ortega's body, it looked much different. The corpse in the locker had been stiff, contorted into a grotesque position to fit it inside the confined space, teeth bared in a rictus, eyes staring. Now it lay covered as if the dead man were asleep, and Garibaldi didn't turn away when Franklin pulled off the cover to expose it to view.

"He looks better already," Garibaldi said dryly.

"I used a compound to reduce rigor," Franklin explained. "Makes it a lot easier to conduct the autopsy. So here's what we've got. These bruises and abrasions are posthumous. They were probably made when the body was being forced into the locker. Now, *these* marks are not. There was a struggle. He tried to fight them off."

"Then it was a homicide."

"Oh, yes." Franklin flashed a pointer at a small livid spot in the crook of Ortega's arm. "This is where they injected the poison."

"Ah. So what was it?"

"Chloro-quasi-dianimidine. Injected directly into the bloodstream."

Garibaldi frowned. "I thought that couldn't be detected, that it broke down within a few minutes after death. Or am I thinking of something else with a longer name?"

"No. That's the general belief. As it happens, recent

research has come up with a more sensitive test. It's not widely known.''

''Maybe a good thing that it's not.''

''True. Now, as to time of death, I put it at around 20:00 hours yesterday.''

Garibaldi frowned, remembering what Ivanova had told him. ''How sure are you about that time?''

''Give or take an hour either way. No more than that. The breakdown of the drug is a good guide, besides the usual signs, rigor and all that. No way to pin it down much more closely, though.''

''And you're sure they killed him someplace else, then brought him into the maintenance bay to hide the corpse? Any idea how long ago that was?''

''I'd say within a couple of hours after he was killed. No longer than that.''

''And obviously, they took off his clothes before that. To search him, I suppose.'' Garibaldi wondered, *What were the killers looking for?*

Franklin echoed his question aloud. ''I wonder if they found whatever they were looking for. I suppose it was something fairly small, easily concealed.''

''Like a data crystal,'' Garibaldi said, speculating. He had a sudden thought. ''It couldn't still be . . . inside there?''

Franklin shook his head. ''I scanned him. Not a thing.''

''And I suppose the killers could have scanned him, too.''

''It's not hard to get that equipment,'' Franklin said, covering up the body again. ''Well, what do we do with him now?''

''Wait. Until I contact Earth Central. They may have specific instructions. I don't know what they're going to think about this. Orders said they wanted him taken alive and shipped to Earth.''

"All right, then. I'll try to keep him fresh for them."

"Um, before you put him away . . ."

Franklin paused.

"I think there's someone else who ought to see him. Someone who can give us a definite ID. After she gets back."

Franklin was just leaving the autopsy room when she saw Talia . . .

CHAPTER 4

Ivanova was just leaving the briefing room when she saw Garibaldi waiting outside. "Garibaldi. What is it?"

"Commander, I know you're just back from a tough mission, but I think there's something you should see."

Ivanova shut her eyes wearily. All through the long debriefing, she'd been anticipating the moment when she could fall into her bed. Or maybe into a stiff drink first and then to bed. But her eyes flew open again when she heard Garibaldi say, "We've found your friend Ortega."

"Ortega? J. D.? You have him in custody?"

He shook his head. "I think you'd better see for yourself."

Garibaldi looked at Captain Sheridan, standing in the doorway behind her. "Maybe you want to see him, too, sir."

Sheridan sighed. "Maybe I should."

Ivanova was numb with exhaustion and shock as the small group headed toward Medlab, and she didn't react when they showed her the covered form on the treatment table. Dr. Franklin's grave expression would have prepared her for the sight, even if nothing else had. "Go ahead."

They were all stiff, standing almost to attention as the doctor pulled aside the cover and exposed the dead face. "Commander, can you identify this man?"

She blinked. It was strange. At her first, brief glance, the face on the table was almost the face of the J. D. she'd known ten years ago, not the man who'd sent her the message to meet her last night. The harsh lines of strain were softened. They looked like laugh lines again. She could almost imagine his eyes opening, his mouth breaking into one of those smiles.

But in the next moment the signs of death were all too obvious—the discoloration of the skin, the slackness of the flesh. She turned away abruptly, glad the eyes had been closed. "Yes, that's J. D. Ortega. What happened? How did he die?"

"Murdered," said Franklin, frowning as he covered the body again. But the head of Medlab took all death seriously. It was his enemy, as the raiders were hers.

"Murdered how?" Her voice had recovered its usual crisp tone.

"An injection. Poison. The death itself was probably painless. But he tried to fight off his attackers beforehand.

"I see." It wasn't all. She knew from the way they were all looking at her that it wasn't all.

It was Garibaldi who told her. "We found him in an equipment locker out in fighter maintenance bay one. He'd been moved there after he was killed."

Ivanova knew what he was saying. "That's our maintenance bay. It's just one level down from the Alpha ready room. Where he was going to meet me."

Garibaldi nodded. There was more. "The doc here estimates the time of death at around 20:00 hours, yesterday."

"20:00 hours. Yesterday?" Ivanova shivered suddenly. At the exact moment she'd been in the ready room, waiting for Ortega, wondering why he was late, someone had been stabbing a lethal poison into his bloodstream. She'd been waiting for a dead man all that time.

"At least now we know why he never showed up," Garibaldi said. "They got to him before he could get to you."

Captain Sheridan interjected, "Commander, you say you have no idea why this man wanted to meet with you?"

"No, sir. I assumed, from his message, that he needed my help, that he might have enemies on the station."

"Which obviously he did," Garibaldi interjected.

"You didn't know he was a wanted fugitive, then?"

"No, sir. Ortega was an old friend, from after the war. I didn't know he was on the station until I got his message. When he didn't make the meeting, I queried the computer. That was when I found out about the alert and contacted Mr. Garibaldi."

"I see." The captain looked distinctly unhappy about this situation that had fallen into his lap. "Well, according to Mr. Garibaldi, it looks like he might have had friends on Babylon 5 as well as enemies. I hope you can help us find both of them."

"Of course." Ivanova's already-straight back went slightly stiffer, her shoulders squared. "Anything I can do."

Sheridan nodded in approval. "But I suppose it's a matter for security right now. Why don't you get some sleep, Commander? Unless there's anything else?" he asked Garibaldi.

"No, sir," said Garibaldi. "Not yet. We're still investigating. Questioning the witnesses who found the body."

Ivanova turned to him. "Let me know if you find anything."

"Of course."

After she'd left the lab Sheridan said, "Mr. Garibaldi."

A muscle in the side of Garibaldi's face twitched. "Yes, sir."

"Tell me I'm wrong, tell me these latest developments

aren't going to make this case more complicated than it was before."

"Sorry, sir, can't do it. Before, all we had to do was nail Ortega, turn him over to EA, and be done with him. And maybe find out how he got onto the station. Now, it looks to me we've got to find whoever killed him and whatever they were looking for when they did it."

"Whatever they were looking for?"

"The body was stripped. To me, that means searched —real thoroughly. Yeah, I think they were looking for something."

Sheridan sighed. "Garibaldi, I've gone over the files on this case since you first reported it to me. Earth Central seems to consider it highly sensitive stuff. I have every confidence that you'll give it your highest priority. Have you sent them a report about finding the body?"

"Not yet, sir. I thought I'd wait until Commander Ivanova got a look at him. Positive ID."

"Well, now she has."

"I'll get on it right away."

"And you'll keep me informed."

"Absolutely, sir. As soon as I find anything, you'll know about it."

"Good." Sheridan started to leave the lab, then paused. "I can't help wondering—why did he come here? Why did he want to see Ivanova?"

"Maybe we'll learn that when we find out who killed him."

"I hope so. I really do."

On his way back to the maintenance bay, Garibaldi encountered one of the people he wanted to see, Ms. Talia Winters, registered telepath, the station's only representative of the Psi Corps. While she wasn't a member of his security department, her duties included assisting in difficult investigations. And in this one Garibaldi was using all the resources he had available.

"Ah, Ms. Winters! So you're finished with the witnesses? Did they all agree to be scanned?"

She nodded gravely, slightly stiff in her long, unattractive skirt and jacket. She smoothed down the skirt with gloved hands. It was something Garibaldi often noticed about her, that contact with other minds didn't seem to make the telepath very happy. It was like she carried around some secret cloud of grief.

The Psi Corps made Garibaldi just a little nervous. It made most people he knew a little nervous. Someone knowing what was going on inside your head . . .

But Talia's tone was dry, businesslike. "They all agreed, yes. They seemed to feel a scan was the quickest way of putting an end to the questions."

"Well, I'm glad they cooperated. So, what did you find out?"

"Nothing. I'm sorry, I mean none of the witnesses know any more than they've told you already."

"The truth."

"Yes, the truth," she agreed. "The fighter pilot just came into the bay to check on her ship—she very much resents your trying to link her to your investigation, by the way."

"That's just too bad for her," Garibaldi replied, unrepentant.

"The mechanic who found the body and his foreman have told you everything they know, too. I'm sorry, but there just isn't anything more."

"Well, thanks anyway, Ms. Winters. Every bit of information helps, even if it isn't what we wanted to hear." She turned to go, still stiff, untouchable. "Um, Ms. Winters?"

"Yes? Mr. Garibaldi?"

"I was just wondering. Just . . . hypothetically.

There wouldn't be any way of doing a telepathic scan after a person's dead, would there be?"

She recoiled visibly. "No! And even if there were, I would certainly never want to attempt such a thing. I can't imagine anything more . . ."

He shrugged, a wry grin on his face. "Oh, well. It was just a thought. Thanks again, Ms. Winters."

The door to the maintenance bay closed behind her. "Damn," said Garibaldi.

CHAPTER 5

There were raider ships everywhere. She kept firing, firing, but the raiders kept coming at her. From above, behind. She had to protect her wingman. He was in trouble. She could hear him calling her: "Commander Ivanova!"

Strange, it was Garibaldi's voice, not Mokena's. Garibaldi wasn't her wingman? Was he?

"Commander Ivanova!"

Groaning, she struggled to open her eyes. C&C? No, they couldn't be calling her already, she was just back from a mission, she wasn't supposed to be on duty yet, she had to sleep.

"Commander Ivanova!"

"Uh . . . Ivanova here," she mumbled, still too much asleep to speak clearly.

"Commander, this is Garibaldi. Are you awake?"

"No," she said, letting her face fall back onto the pillow.

"Ivanova, sorry to wake you, but there's something I'd like you to see."

"Garibaldi, in case you didn't know, I was just out tangling with about a hundred raiders. I just got to sleep, it's the middle of the night—"

"Actually, it's 10:30 hours."

"Um . . ." Ivanova shook her head and opened her eyes. Was it really? "So, what is it?"

"We found another piece of evidence in the Ortega case. I think it involves you."

"I'll be right there."

A life in the military had taught Ivanova how to get

herself quickly into uniform while still asleep, but this time Garibaldi's news had galvanized her awake. What was this new evidence? How could it involve her?

"That was quick," said Garibaldi approvingly as she came into the briefing room. Ivanova was taken slightly aback to see that Captain Sheridan was there as well. The security chief took an evidence packet from his pocket and removed a small slip of paper, security sealed.

Ivanova handled it cautiously. The paper had been tightly folded at one time, then opened and smoothed out. She could easily read through the clear seal: *S I – hardwır*. She shook her head slightly, not understanding.

"You've never seen this before? You don't know what it means?" Garibaldi asked.

"*S I:* I suppose that could mean Susan Ivanova. But I don't know what the rest of it means. I never saw this before. Where'd you find it?"

"In the ready room. Where you were waiting for Ortega. We put it through some pretty fine scans and managed to pick up enough to make it certain. This was Ortega's. He'd handled the paper, at least, even if he didn't write the note."

"In the ready room?" There was disbelief in Ivanova's voice. "He left me a note?"

"On the floor. Near the door to the rest room."

"But I never saw . . . You mean, it was there while I was waiting for him? All that time?"

"You probably wouldn't have noticed it. My team was going over the place a centimeter at a time. It was under a counter. And you know how pilots are—they don't always toss their stuff into the recycler. There was other trash on the floor."

She remembered slowly that it was true, the newspapers thrown here and there when people were done with them, wrappers on the floor.

Garibaldi rubbed his forehead, right where the hair was receding. "Tell me, Commander, were you on time for that meeting with Ortega? Or maybe five, ten minutes late?"

She closed her eyes to recall it. "All right, I got there, the room was empty, Ortega wasn't there. No, there was this guy—"

"What guy?" Garibaldi demanded eagerly.

"I don't know. No one I knew. Just this guy. Just when I came in the door, he was coming out of the rest room. He looked like he was in a hurry, he left."

"Do you think you could identify him?"

"I don't know. I didn't really look at him, once I was sure it wasn't Ortega."

"All right, we'll check on that later. What about the time?"

"I checked the time. I remember. Right after I came in and saw the room was empty. It was . . . I can't remember exactly. I was maybe four or five minutes late, I think. No more than that. I queried the computer, it'd be in the log, wouldn't it?"

"You first queried the time from that location at 20:04 hours," Garibaldi confirmed.

"Then that was right after I came in. I remember, when he didn't show up, I kept checking the time."

Sheridan interjected, "Commander, that note—do you know what it means?"

She read it again: *S I hardw r*. Shook her head. "No, I don't."

"No idea at all?" Garibaldi asked.

"Well, I assume it means 'hardware.' Maybe, military hardware, weapons? That kind of thing?"

Garibaldi took it, peered at the handwriting. "Or 'hardwar' maybe? Whatever that would mean?"

He passed it on to Sheridan, who had held out his hand to see it. "Looks more like an 'i' there. Like it was supposed to be 'hardwire'?"

Garibaldi took the paper, examined it again. "Yeah, it does, now that you mention it. Hardwire. So what does that mean? Computer?"

The voice responded: "Hardwired: Primary reference: obsolete, primitive electronic computing machines: instructions permanently embedded in physical structure of computing device.

"Secondary references: instinctive behaviors, genetically encoded behaviors.

"Tertiary references: late-twentieth-century futuristic fiction. Derivative references: wetware, cyberware.

"Do you wish expanded information on any of these references?"

The others looked at her. Ivanova shrugged. "Sorry."

"Maybe he didn't have time to finish what he was going to write. He heard someone coming," Garibaldi suggested. "But if he wrote it to you, it ought to mean *something* to you."

"I'm sorry, it doesn't," Ivanova said again with a touch of irritation in her voice. Hadn't she already said so? "Is that it? Is there anything else?"

"Not yet," Garibaldi answered her. "Nothing definite. We're still trying to find just where Ortega was killed. Checking out the ready room first, though it isn't very likely, not if you were there at 20:04 hours. Of course, I'll let you know if anything else turns up."

"Thanks."

Sheridan stood. "Well, I tell you what, Commander, now that you're up, how about I treat you to breakfast before you have to go on duty? I think I have some news you'll be a little happier to hear."

"That's a very good idea, sir. I accept."

* * *

Breakfast turned out to include a rare and much-appreciated treat: real coffee, imported from Earth. Eyes closed, Ivanova held the cup to her face and inhaled the fragrance, deeply, then rolled a single sip around in her mouth before swallowing it. "Oh, that's good! The real thing. I don't know if I'd have decided to go into space if they'd told me how hard it was to find real coffee. I don't know how Earthforce expects people to wake up in the morning and function on that synthetic stuff."

"It was a gift from my father. Shipped out here for my last birthday. Two pounds of it, direct from Earth. I thought I remembered how much you liked it. It was even harder to get back when we were stationed off Io, right after the war."

"I remember."

"Anyway," said Sheridan, putting down his empty cup, "I've got the information you asked about, on the *Cassini.*"

"Ah! The cargo!" She'd simply been too tired to check the records after debriefing—and the trip to Medlab to view J. D.'s body.

"Their cargo. What was so valuable it cost all those lives. It was morbidium ingots. Shipped from Marsport."

"Morbidium. That's a strategic metal. Trade restricted."

Sheridan nodded. Morbidium was vital in the production of phased plasma weapons, an essential element in the alloy that made up their central coils. Difficult and expensive to manufacture. Earth Alliance restricted trade in all the strategic metals, setting prices and prohibiting sale to all unapproved buyers. The predictable result was a strong interest on the black market, where weapons and components were among the most heavily traded commodities. The temptation for pirates was obvious. The profits would be enormous.

"You think there was a leak," Sheridan said. "Somebody slipped them the routing information."

"You remember, Captain, it's what the *Cassini*'s pilot said: 'It's a setup.' They were waiting for that transport, they knew where and when and what it was carrying. They even brought their own transport along to haul off the cargo. Now, that takes advance planning."

Sheridan agreed. "I know. No matter what you do to tighten security, as long as raiders are willing to pay for the data, it gets out. Tell a routing clerk she can earn five thousand credits for just one bit of information. You'll get it. And the more they steal, the more they can afford to pay to bribe someone else."

"Raider activity seems to go in cycles. We hurt them last year, cut off their source of heavy weapons. Now it's starting to look like they're back again. Too many incidents the last few months. There's got to be something behind it. A new bunch of raiders on the scene. A new supplier of information. Something. If we can just find out what it is . . ."

"You want to look into it?"

"Just to see if there's something I can pick up. With the jump gate in 13 down for repairs, there'll have to be some wholesale rerouting. Maybe a pattern will show up. Of course, what we should have are regular Earthforce patrols of all the jump points and shipping routes."

"With the current political climate on Earth, we'll be lucky if they don't cut back funding. Space isn't exactly the most popular budget item on the new administration's agenda. I wouldn't hold my breath and count on the ships for more patrols."

"I know," Ivanova said glumly. "Even though you'd think they'd want to protect strategic metals shipments, at least. Maybe if there are more losses, or the shipping companies start to complain, something will be done."

"Well, good luck with it, Commander. I'll look forward to seeing your report if you find anything significant.''

"Thank you, sir. And thanks for the coffee." Ivanova started to stand up. It was just about time to go back on duty, already.

"Ah, Commander? This other business? This murdered terrorist suspect. I know it's rough, when it's someone you haven't seen in a long time. The way people can change."

She sighed, sat back down. "I still have a hard time believing it. That J. D. Ortega could be mixed up in something like that. You know, I kept thinking, before they found his body: when we find him, when we investigate, we'll find out it was all a mistake. Mistaken identity, or . . . something. But now—I just don't know. He was *murdered* . . ."

"Well, I hope it's all cleared up as soon as possible. When Garibaldi finds who killed him."

"So do I."

Things were already busy in the Observation Dome when Ivanova arrived. A lot of outgoing traffic had to be rerouted away from the Red 13 transfer point until the damaged gate could be repaired, and that meant schedule changes all the way down the line—absolutely necessary if you didn't want to have two ships occupying the same space at the same time in some sector three jumps away.

Ivanova noticed several curious looks aimed in her direction as she came into the dome. It made her wonder, what were they thinking about? Her engagement with the raiders or Ortega's murder? Of course, no one was supposed to know about the murder, and she didn't really want to talk about it. She was glad the technicians were professional military personnel, who knew better than to ask personal questions while on duty.

Lieutenant Nomura did offer a brief "Glad to see you

back in one piece, Commander," as she relieved him at the control console, but no more than that. No congratulations on her victory over the raiders. They were both professional enough to realize that Ivanova hadn't won a real victory, and no congratulations were in order when even now arrangements were being made for the disposal of the bodies of the *Cassini*'s crew.

"I'm glad we all made it back," was her response.

After that, it was all business as Nomura briefed her on the ongoing operations. It wasn't a pretty picture. "Every pilot or shipowner who's been delayed by even five minutes is demanding to talk to 'someone in higher authority.' To Captain Sheridan, to Earth Central . . ."

"I'll try to handle them," Ivanova said dryly.

"Good luck." Nomura turned over the console and left the problems in her lap. He'd coped with them long enough. Ivanova very quickly realized there was going to be no spare time today to check out her speculations about the recent raider activity. Not with all the questions, complaints, and demands the rerouting was generating. Nomura hadn't exaggerated. Schedules, deadlines, perishable goods, guaranteed-on-time clauses in delivery contracts: everyone was convinced the rerouting was a conspiracy designed to affect their business alone, and that their own case deserved priority over all others.

Ivanova was soon heartily weary of the words: "Don't you understand? I have a *schedule* to meet!"

It wasn't long before she had to restrain herself from shouting back: "Don't *you* understand? Someone may have already sold your schedule to the raiders! This delay may just save your precious cargo." But of course her actual reply was more on the order of: "I appreciate your scheduling difficulties, pilot, and I personally promise to make sure your departure is given the highest possible priority, consistent with station regulations."

Which was simply another way of saying that they could take the schedule she gave them.

But worse by far than the commercial interests were the diplomats and their staffs. Like the pilot of the Minbari courier ship—arrogant, warrior class down to the bone—who all but suggested the war would break out again if Babylon 5 delayed the delivery of his dispatches by as much as an hour. If he weren't given clearance *immediately*, he might even call in a war cruiser more than capable of opening a jump point on its own power. Ivanova crisply suggested that he go ahead and do just that, since it would solve quite a few of her scheduling problems.

Or the Narn captain who expressed doubt that there even was a breakdown of the jump gate. "This could be some kind of trick, a plot on the part of our enemies to delay us at this station! I *demand* clearance! Now!"

At which Ivanova took a deep breath. "Captain Ka'Hosh, I was there when the damage was done. I can personally attest to the fact. Now, if you don't want your flight to be rerouted around that point, then you're going to have to wait until the repairs are completed. We estimate the jump gate will be back on-line within thirty-eight Earth hours. At that time, you'll be given all the proper priority, I guarantee it. And in the meantime, if your enemies are here on this station, they're not going anywhere through that gate, either."

Which seemed to satisfy the Narn, for the moment.

Ivanova checked the time, suppressed an urge to groan. It'd only been two and a half hours since she came on duty.

It looked like it was going to be a very long day.

CHAPTER 6

Later—much, much later—Ivanova sat at the computer screen in her own quarters. "Computer, I want the records of all raider attacks on cargo vessels in Earth Alliance space within the last year. Graphic display mode."

"Accessing."

"Display by type of cargo. How many attacks on ships carrying strategic metals?"

The information appeared on her data screen. Strategic metals—yes, there they were." Ivanova closed her eyes for a moment. They were tired. She was tired. It had been a perfectly harrowing day, coping with the mess caused by the damaged jump gate. At least, after tomorrow, it ought to be fixed. But then who knew what new crisis would erupt?

Now that she was finally off duty, she ought to be able to relax, but the matter of the raiders had been nagging at the back of her mind all day. She knew it would chase her through her dreams if she didn't get some kind of answer first.

She opened her eyes again. "Compare hijacking of strategic metals with previous years, back, oh, ten years. By total tonnage stolen and by number of attacks." When the display changed, she nodded. Yes. Both figures were up, starting a little over a year ago. But was the increase in all strategic metals, or just certain ones? The *Cassini,* she recalled, had been carrying morbidium.

"Break the figures on strategic metals down by type of commodity."

And there on her data screen, the answer leaped out at

her. Total tonnage of morbidium hijacked had gone up dramatically beginning about sixteen months ago. An increase of 184 percent during one year alone. That was hard to believe.

Maybe there was simply more of the metal being shipped. But when the computer displayed the figures, it was clear that although there was an increase of tonnage shipped, this by no means could account for the amount being hijacked. And no one at Earth Central had noticed? With a strategic commodity?

To Ivanova, morbidium meant armaments. Specifically, the power coils of phased plasma weapons. And unfortunately, these days, trade in armaments was at an all-time high since the Earth-Minbari war.

Ivanova rubbed the sides of her forehead with her fingertips. "Computer, can you give me a breakdown of the price of strategic metals on the black market over the past two years?"

But at this point, the computer was unhelpful. "Those data are not available," the voice said primly.

"Damn," Ivanova muttered. But she supposed the black market didn't issue regular financial reports. Not, at least, into the Earthforce databanks. She supposed Garibaldi might be able to find out something. He seemed to have contacts with certain underworld types. She made a note to herself to ask him, later, maybe tomorrow.

Maybe another approach. Like, where were the raiders getting their information? Was there some common factor? What kinds of persons had access to the data?

"Computer, display all raider attacks on strategic metals shipments during the last year. Break down the data by transport company."

She stared at the screen. No pattern seemed apparent. "Highlight shipments of morbidium." She shook her head. Still no pattern. Then she was frustrated by the fact that the station's databanks didn't contain the information on ownership or the insurance company covering the cargo on all transports, only those logged through Babylon 5. Finally, "Display the data by point of origin of cargo."

And there it was! A distinct, sharp increase in total hijacked cargoes originating from Marsport, beginning sixteen months ago, at just about the same time as the increase in hijacked morbidium shipments. The *Cassini* had shipped out of Marsport. Just to be sure, "Highlight attacks on cargoes of morbidium originating from Marsport."

Yes, that was it. She had the answer. Marsport shipped a load of the strategic metal every two to three days. In the last sixteen months, twenty percent of those cargoes had been the object of raider attacks, most of them successful.

There was her leak. No doubt about it. Someone in Marsport was leaking transport routing data to the raiders, and the commodity they were targeting was morbidium.

Incredible that no one had picked up on this so far. Or —maybe "incredible" wasn't the right word. Maybe "suspicious" was.

She leaned back from the desk, stretched stiff muscles. Well, it was a beginning, at least. And it was good to remember there was more than one way to hit at the raiders besides plasma fire. Without information, they were blind. "Just plug that leak," she said aloud.

The computer, always literal-minded, replied, "No leak detected at this time."

Ivanova shut her eyes. "No more input," she told it. "I'm finished for tonight. I'm going to bed. Hold any calls."

* * *

The mess hall at breakfast—dozens of uniformed figures hurrying with full trays to their tables, getting ready for the morning duty shift. Ivanova spotted Garibaldi heading for the empty seat next to her. He sat down with a heavily loaded tray.

"Planning to skip lunch?" she asked, raising her eyebrows at the sight of his meal. "And dinner?"

Swallowing a generous mouthful, he said, "You know, I've noticed that about women. You never like to see a man enjoy a good hearty meal."

Her eyebrows went up again. "You call that hearty? A few more meals like that, you won't have a functioning heart left."

He put down his fork. "See what I mean?"

"By the way," she asked him, "any more news on your investigation?"

He slapped his forehead. "Oh! I forgot I meant to tell you. You were off-line last night. Well, we found out where Ortega was killed. In the head."

She drew back in dismay. "You mean, the head right off the ready room? He was killed right there? Then he must have been in there all that time! Are you sure?"

He nodded. "We found traces of the poison on the floor. And slight traces of Ortega's blood."

Ivanova shivered. "Then . . . that man, the one who brushed past me. He must have been—"

"The killer. Right."

"And he was probably just outside the room all that time, just waiting for me to leave."

"Or for someone else to show up," Garibaldi agreed. "That guy must have been sweating blood, wondering what else was going to go wrong. Here he'd planned a nice, peaceful private murder, and you walk in on it."

"I just wish I could have been a couple of minutes earlier," she said regretfully.

"I don't. Or we might have had two corpses down in

the equipment bay. That guy was a pro. That particular poison isn't something amateurs can get ahold of.

"Anyway, it looks like you're the only witness who can identify him. Sometime soon I want you to come into my office, try again to identify this guy."

"Of course." She shuddered again, her appetite gone.

"If you want me to put some security on you, just to be safe—"

"No, I don't think it's necessary, is it? Nobody else knows about this, do they?"

"Nope, this is strictly need-to-know stuff. Ultraclassified, though I'm not quite sure I know why." Garibaldi gave an interested look at her tray. "Say, by the way, the captain says you're doing a little investigating of your own?"

"Just running down some data through the computer. I was wondering where the raiders are getting their information. Now I know."

"And?"

"Marsport. Someone in a shipping office in Marsport is selling transport routing data."

Now he was the one to raise his eyebrows. "That was easy."

"Easy? I was up half the night!" She shook her head. "No, you're right. Once you look at the figures the right way, it's obvious. And the station's computer doesn't even have all the data available. Someone on Earth or Mars should have spotted this months ago. Maybe even as much as a year ago. Someone, for whatever reason, hasn't been doing their job.

"Anyway, I'm putting a report together to send on to Earth Central later today."

Garibaldi prodded a piece of fruit with his fork. "Are you sure that's such a good idea?"

"What do you mean?"

"I mean stirring around in someone else's anthill.

Suggesting that people in other departments might be negligent—or worse.''

She stared at him in indignant disbelief. "Garibaldi! I don't believe you! Raiders are hitting ships out there, crews are being killed!''

"Yeah, I guess you're right. Just be careful, all right? I've seen these things turn ugly. It could be you'll be stepping on some toes a lot higher up than yours.'' He took another look at her tray. "Say, aren't you going to finish that?''

He was starting to reach toward the tray when his link sounded. "Garibaldi here.''

"This is Captain Sheridan, Mr. Garibaldi. Something's come up. Could you meet me in the briefing room?''

"I'm on my way.'' He looked up to see Ivanova carrying her half-finished breakfast tray away and sighed in regret.

Garibaldi came briskly into the briefing room. Sheridan looked up at him. "Mr. Garibaldi, I've been reading your latest report on the Ortega case. Good work. I have to say, you've been very thorough in investigating this. So I don't want you to think that this is because I have any reservations with the way you're handling the job.''

What is? Garibaldi wondered silently, thinking that this didn't sound good at all.

"But I have to order you to terminate your investigation.''

"What? Close the case? A murder investigation?'' He couldn't believe what he was hearing. "Sir?''

Sheridan looked slightly uncomfortable. "Like I say, this doesn't reflect on you. And it wasn't my decision. I have orders directly from Earth Central. They're sending a special team of investigators to take over the case. Apparently, with the connection to the Free Mars movement, they consider it too sensitive for the regular Babylon 5 security staff to handle.''

Garibaldi started to open his mouth to say something which probably would have sounded like ''Horsehockey,'' but he closed it in time.

Sheridan went on, ''So, as of now, you're ordered to pull all your staff off the case, seal all your files and records, and be ready to hand them over to the special investigators when they arrive on the station.''

''Which will be when?''

''They're already in transit onboard the *Asimov*.''

''They didn't lose any time, did they?''

Sheridan looked up at him, started to say something, then decided against it. ''If you have no more questions, that will be all. Thank you, Mr. Garibaldi.''

CHAPTER 7

"Oh-oh," Garibaldi said to himself. He was checking the monitors from Security Central as the passengers from the *Asimov* started toward customs, and he was getting his first glance at the special investigation team from Earth Central. "Bad news."

It was impossible to mistake them—stiff and ultramilitary in their Earthforce blues. Three officers, two men and a woman, but they all had flinty, hard eyes that said, *We know you're guilty of something, and we'll find out what it is, no matter how long it takes.* One look, and the security guard at the customs gate jumped to attention like she'd just touched a hot wire. Even through the monitor, Garibaldi could almost see her sweat as she followed the prescribed routine: take the identicard, check the face on the card against the holder, run it through the scanner, confirm the data, welcome the passenger to Babylon 5 if and only if the check is positive.

Once past the checkpoint, the three of them passed out of sight of the monitor, heading for the lift tubes. Heading, Garibaldi realized, for him.

So he was ready when they came into the security office like a three-man assault team—one on point, one securing the door at the rear, and the main force, flashing the insignia of a commander's rank, heading straight for the primary objective: the computer console.

Garibaldi moved to put himself in the way. "This office is a restricted area," he announced firmly. "Do you have authorization?"

The Earthforce commander, a wiry man of around forty with short-cropped blond hair and sharp, thin features, took another step forward, with a scowl built on order to intimidate. "Are you Garibaldi?"

"I'm Michael Garibaldi, Babylon 5 Chief of Security."

"You're required to turn over all your records and files on the Ortega case. I'll need your passwords," he snapped, a lot like a short-haired terrier or one of those other kinds of small dogs that bite.

Garibaldi stood his ground, which happened to rest on Earthforce regulations. "I have to see your ID and authorization first."

The commander's lips thinned to a straight line, but he produced the documents, slapped them into Garibaldi's hand. Garibaldi scanned through them, nodded. Identicard in the name of Commander Ian Wallace. The authorization, of course, was all in order, security clearance up to ultraviolet and maybe beyond. "Commander," he acknowledged crisply, handing them back, but also adding, "I'll need their ID, too."

"You've seen my orders, *Mister* Garibaldi. You know I have full authority here."

"Not quite, Commander," Garibaldi insisted firmly. "You have full authority over the Ortega case, but this is the Babylon 5 security office, and my files hold references to other classified matters that aren't related to that case in any way, so I have to make sure anyone who's going to have access has got the proper clearance."

Angrily, Wallace gestured for his aides to come forward, and they handed their ID cards to Garibaldi, who noted that they were Lieutenants Miyoshi and Khatib. Miyoshi was a full-bodied woman who looked like she was wearing a stiff corset under her uniform. To Garibaldi she seemed rather old for her rank. Khatib—Khatib was one of the coldest-looking men he had ever seen. Black eyes, a sharply beaked nose, a lipless mouth like a snake's. Garibaldi almost expected to see a forked tongue flicker out. *Very bad news.*

But his ID was in order, and his security clearance. Garibaldi took a step back from the computer terminal. "Clearances are all in order. I'll get you the passwords." As he handed them to Wallace, he grinned insincerely. "Welcome to Babylon 5, Commander. I hope you enjoy your stay."

"Damn, I hate those stupid games," Garibaldi said, jamming his hands into his pants pockets.

"What games?" Ivanova asked, with half her attention on the command console.

"Power games, status games. Like a couple of dockyard dogs snarling at each other over a bone."

Ivanova was dubious. "But you were right. Following procedure. Are you sure you're not just talking about one of those male things? Chest-thumping, testosterone?"

Garibaldi shook his head. "No, it's more than just that. I know this kind of bastard. First time you meet him, it's got to be a test. I *know* I was right. That's the whole point. He doesn't like me now, but I tell you, if I'd given in, it would have been worse."

He paused to look out through the Observation Dome at the bright, distant flare of the jump gate as a ship passed through into the vortex. Ivanova's attention was still on her console. "Anyway," he continued, "I'm off this case. But you're still an important witness. You're probably going to have to talk to these guys sometime soon. Be careful, all right? These guys are serious trouble."

"Garibaldi, you worry too much. Remember, I've survived ten years in the military. I know the type you're talking about. I don't think I'll have too much trouble with them."

"Well, sometimes there's reason to worry. All I know

is, someone up in the brass-hat department is really interested in this case.''

Now she turned away from the screen to face him. *''That's* what really bothers me, if you want to know the truth. We have raiders out here, we have ships being attacked, crews killed, and what do they do about it? They cut our budget. They won't send out more patrols. They ignore reports of corruption and inefficiency in the bureaucracy.

''But push the right buttons, when they hear words like 'terrorism'—when it threatens them politically— then they send up a team of investigators on the next ship, don't spare the trouble, to hell with the expense.''

''Ah, I take it you haven't heard back about your report on the leak of the transport routes to the raiders?''

She shook her head, then turned back to the console. ''Of course, I only sent it out the day before yesterday. These things take time.''

''Well, just be careful, that's all. If you do get into trouble I don't know how much I'll be able to help you. These guys are setting up their own little private kingdom on the station, outside Security Central. Wallace says he doesn't want interruptions or interference. I've got to assign a team of security agents to him—they follow his orders, nobody else's. He's got his own command center in briefing room B, he's brought in his own computer system—ours isn't secure enough for him— and he's even setting up his own lockup facilities.'' Garibaldi scowled. ''I don't like it.''

Ivanova had seen that look before. ''So what are you going to do?''

''Do? Nothing. Those are orders.''

''Well, you be careful, too,'' Ivanova said. She knew Garibaldi.

* * *

There was a part of Babylon 5 that they called Down
Below, down in Brown Sector, although officially there
was no such place, but officially didn't much matter in
Down Below. It was a place where you had to crawl
through maintenance hatches to get where you were going, where power and water came from illicit taps on the
station's lines, where people slept in empty cargo drums
and lived in corners behind a screen made out of rags.

With a population the size of Babylon 5's, there were
always people who would slip through the cracks, who
existed in the marginal habitat along the edge of legality.
Some slipped over that margin, and they were Garibaldi's business. The rest of them—it was a case of live
and let live.

You could buy almost anything in Down Below; the
commerce covered the spectrum from off-white to black.
People sold their bodies—that was a given. There were
regular business establishments and there were furtive
characters in the hallways with hidden pockets in their
coats. Information, like any other commodity, was for
sale here, too, which was one reason Garibaldi tolerated
the place. This was his ear on the black market, on the
coming and going of persons and goods who might not
belong on the station.

But all the business, no matter how technically legal,
tended to pause when Garibaldi entered the area. Goods
were quickly put away, people found that they had business elsewhere, urgent transactions were no longer so
urgent. The station's chief of security was not a popular
customer in Down Below.

Wherever Garibaldi looked, people acted even more
furtive than usual. His usual informers had evaporated.

But there was more than one way to hunt for information. Garibaldi decided to capitalize on the effect of his
presence. He wandered. He lingered. He examined, one
by one, the counterfeit jewels on the tray of a very reluc-

tant vendor. He asked to see the entertainment licenses of a trio of corridor musicians and the customs certificates of a rack of imported skink-skin boots which the proprietor of a makeshift shop had tried to hide under an equally dubious rug. He was very bad for business, and he showed no inclination to leave.

Finally a sallow-faced figure came up to where he sat at his ease, sipping mineral water at a table in the Happy Daze Bar, an establishment not licensed to sell intoxicating beverages, where he was presently the only customer. "What you wants, Garibaldi?"

It was Mort the Ear, purveyor of information, finder of things, and current owner of the bar.

"Want? Oh, I don't want anything in particular, Mort. I just thought I'd do a little shopping, see the sights, visit a few old friends."

"How comes you gots lot time on you hands now, Garibaldi? Two, three day ago, big investigating, big case. Now . . ." Mort paused, grinned crookedly.

Garibaldi wondered how long it would take the news about Wallace and his investigative team to get out. If it wasn't already all over the station. Wallace hadn't exactly been an inconspicuous arrival on Babylon 5. He grinned back with a show of teeth. "Well, I just thought I'd take some time off to come down here and look up an old friend of mine. Louie. Yeah, Louie's an old buddy, haven't seen him in years. He moved to Mars a few years ago, worked around here and there. Now, what do I hear but my old friend Louie's right here on Babylon 5!

"So I say to myself: Mike, you've got to go look up your old friend Louie, you used to be so thick together. So I go to look him up, and—guess what? The station registry doesn't have any record of Louie coming onto the station! None of the checkpoints recorded old Louie coming through! Now, isn't that crazy?

"Because, you know, it's real nice when people come

in customs the right way and we put their identicard through the scanner and their name in the registry. See, then we know who's on the station. We know where to find them when we're looking for them. So I say to myself, Mike, why don't you just go hang around the station for a while, look around, and maybe you'll run into old Louie. We can have a few laughs, talk about old times, and then maybe I can find out what happened with his ID when he came onto the station, so it won't happen again. Then I can look up old Louie anytime I feel like it, and I won't have to come down here, looking for him.''

"You not makes sense, Garibaldi."

"Then let me make it more clear, Mort. Somebody's been coming onto this station through the back door. Maybe with fake ID. I don't like that. I want to know what kind of a counterfeit identicard can fake out our scanners. I want to see it for myself."

"You wants fake ID?"

"You got it, Mort."

"I gots lot fake ID, you want it." He started to reach into a pocket somewhere in the interior of the layers of clothing that didn't conceal his scrawny frame, but Garibaldi stopped him.

"Huh-uh, Mort. Not that junk you peddle to the tourists. The real thing."

Sullenly, "Maybe I asks around."

"That's good to hear. And maybe I might come down here and do some more shopping in a day or two. After all, I have all this time on my hands now, like you say."

He strolled off. It was a fishing expedition, but something might come of it, you never knew.

He hesitated before taking the next step, because it was treading awfully close to Wallace's investigation, but, dammit, people sneaking onto Babylon 5 cut right to the heart of station security. And if there were forged identicards floating around, he needed to find them.

Up in a more respectable section of brown deck, a woman named Hardesty ran an establishment called the Wet Rock, a place where station workers came after their shifts to have a beer or two or three. The beer was as cheap as beer can be on a space station off in the middle of nowhere, and the food she served with it was a little bit heavy on the starch and the grease. Garibaldi liked it.

"Hardesty, how you doing?"

"Doing all right," she said, in a tone that meant: Is this call business or pleasure, Garibaldi?

"You haven't seen Meyers around lately?"

"Think he left the station. Went out on an ice hauler a couple, few days ago. Maybe."

"How about Nick?"

"Nick Patinos?"

"The one."

"Think he works the swing shift now. Awfully hard to get hold of him."

"He still come in here sometimes?"

"After work, yeah. Mostly he's at that stupid game parlor, though. Or the gym."

Garibaldi knew where the game parlor was. Nick was one of about a dozen participants seated at tables where immaterial ground cars raced each other around a virtual track and ghostly holographic figures sparred in gladiatorial contests. Garibaldi joined the spectators for a while until one of the figures fell to its knees and expired, after which a new challenger sat down to contend with the winner.

"You're getting better with that broadsword, Nick," Garibaldi remarked.

The man looked up from a beer. He was a dockworker with dark eyes and hair turning gray on the edges. "Hey, Mike. Yeah, I can go ten minutes sometimes with Cass these days."

"Maybe we can play a round sometime. Or go over to

the gym, spar a round or two in the lo-grav. Like we used to, on Mars.''

"Yeah, maybe." He paused, gave Garibaldi a look. "But you didn't come down here today to play holo games, did you, Mike?"

His silence admitted it.

"What I heard was, you're looking into things." Nick looked back down into his beer. "Maybe the kind of thing that's going to cause a lot of trouble."

Good news sure spreads fast, Garibaldi thought sourly. "You heard that, did you?"

Nick made an offhand gesture. "Here and there."

"Well, there was a fugitive alert a couple days ago. A suspected terrorist—"

But Nick slammed his beer down angrily on the table. "Terrorists! You know what, ever since the uprising last year, you Earthforce types have got nothing on your brains but goddamn terrorists! I'm sick of it! You show your ID card, and every time it's 'Oh, you're from Mars, we've got to check your stuff, check you out just in case you've got explosives in with your dirty socks.' I'm tired of it, Mike!"

"Hey! Look, Nick, you know me. I'm not just 'Earthforce,' all right? Maybe somebody's probing into the terrorist thing, but it's not me. Not now. Hey, you can believe me, can't you? We knew each other on Mars for, what, three years?"

"Yeah, but things are different now. You've been out of touch."

Garibaldi was, for an instant, bitterly reminded of Lise. She wouldn't come with him to Babylon 5, he wouldn't stay with her on Mars. Yeah, he'd been out of touch too long, 'til it was too late.

"All right," he said, forcibly putting her out of his mind, "we're not on Mars now, we're on Babylon 5: a space station, a closed environment. I have the safety of this place on my hands. All I want to know is: how does a guy get onto the station without going through customs? Does he get smuggled in with the cargo or use a fake identicard, or what? Nick, think about it. Forget politics for a minute, Earth and Free Mars and all the rest of it. Nobody wants a crazy getting onto the station, running around with explosives, biohazards, whatever! Come on! Help me out here!''

''I'll think about it, Mike. I'll ask around. But this really isn't a good time right now. Things . . .'' He shook his head. ''I'll see.''

''If you know anything—''

''I don't know about any threats to the station. I can tell you that right now.''

''Or illegal entries? Or counterfeit identicards?''

Nick shook his head, put down the empty glass of beer, stood up to leave. ''I'll ask around. But it really isn't a good time.''

You could say that again, thought Garibaldi. It was a lousy time. And he had a feeling it was going to be getting a lot worse, real soon now.

CHAPTER 8

The interview did not start out on a cordial note.

Lieutenant Miyoshi barely looked up when Ivanova came into the briefing room.

Ivanova waited a moment, then, "Lieutenant, judging from the number of messages you sent while I was on duty today, I assumed you had some questions to ask me. But if you're busy, I can certainly come back later."

When Miyoshi did look up, her expression reminded Ivanova, too late, of Garibaldi's warning this morning. "Not at all, Commander. I'm glad you can finally spare the time to help with this investigation."

Ivanova sat down opposite her, uninvited. "I'm sure you can appreciate, Lieutenant, that my duties on this station can't always be dropped at a moment's notice. I am the executive officer. We've had a transit point jump gate out of commission recently, and a number of other urgent matters that I had to deal with."

"Yes, I understand you were involved in that . . . accident. However, in the interim, I've had time to review your file—in particular, your correspondence with the fugitive terrorist J. D. Ortega."

Correspondence? Ivanova frowned. She didn't like this. "Don't you mean 'alleged terrorist'?"

"If you insist. So, how long have you known this 'alleged terrorist,' Commander?"

"About ten years. Since shortly after the war. He was my flight instructor when I was in training."

"You were close?"

"No closer than cadets and instructors usually are."

Miyoshi raised a dubious brow. "And after the war, you maintained a correspondence."

"Not really, not after he went back to Mars, no."

"Indeed? What would you say if I told you we had records, notes signed by you, in your handwriting?"

Tightly, "If you want to call a couple of holiday greeting cards a 'correspondence,' then I suppose we did, for a year or two."

"And can you produce any of the notes he sent to you?"

"I'm an Earthforce career officer, Lieutenant. I've been posted a half-dozen different times in those years. I don't save holiday cards from all my old buddies."

"So, since the time of your last known meeting with the suspected terrorist, you've disposed of all written records of your correspondence."

Furious now, Ivanova got to her feet. "I don't have to sit here and take this—"

But it was as if Miyoshi had been waiting for her outburst. A smile spread across her broad face. "Commander, yes, you do. Let me remind you, we have full authority here to conduct this investigation. *Full* authority, Commander. I could, at this moment, have you arrested until you agree to answer my questions."

Glowering, Ivanova sat back down.

"Now, to continue." But having made her point, Miyoshi kept the rest of her questions closer to the facts. "You claim that when Ortega contacted you, you had no idea he was a terrorist suspect or a fugitive."

"That's right."

"But there was a priority alert sent out by Earth Central."

"That alert was sent out to all Earth Alliance installations. To their security offices. There was no particular indication that he might be here on Babylon 5."

"But Mr. Garibaldi recognized the name."

"Mr. Garibaldi is head of security on the station. That's his job. Not mine."

"And when you became aware that he was the subject of a fugitive alert, you immediately contacted security, is that right?"

"That's right. I called Mr. Garibaldi."

"But why the delay? Why wait until Ortega had already been dead for almost two hours?"

"What do you mean?"

"I mean that we have a certain number of facts here. Ortega was supposed to meet you in ready room one at 20:00 hours. According to Dr. Franklin, whose credentials are more than adequate, he was killed at approximately that time, probably in the adjacent rest room. The log of the station's computer places you on the scene intermittently from 20:04 to 22:06. And by your own admission, you were near the body for over two hours."

"That's correct."

"Approximately twenty-three hours after the murder, Ortega's body was found in an equipment locker in an aircraft maintenance area just one level from where he was killed. His body was stripped, and his clothing and personal effects have not yet been recovered."

"That's right. So just what are you implying?"

"I'm stating the facts, Commander. These facts are consistent with a number of different interpretations. Let's look at some more facts. From the time of Ortega's death to your meeting with Mr. Garibaldi over two hours later, you have no witnesses to your presence in the ready room. No one saw you there—except for one man you claim to have seen leaving just after you came in. But you haven't been able to identify this man, am I correct? You'd never seen him before, you haven't seen him since. In *fact,* there's no reason to suppose the existence of this mysterious figure, is there? Except for your testimony."

Ivanova was too stunned to reply.

"Now, we have one other piece of evidence, Commander. A note, addressed to 'S.I.' We all suppose we know who S.I. is, don't we? Susan Ivanova. This note, addressed to you, Commander Ivanova, says, 'hardwir.' You claim, don't you, that you have no idea what this might mean. 'Hardwir.' "

Miyoshi leaned forward a little in her chair, closer to Ivanova. Her hair was black, pulled back away from her face, and shone with what seemed to be some kind of perfumed oil. "This note is one of our very few tangible pieces of evidence, Commander. It's been positively linked to Ortega—our own forensics tests confirm this as well as the scan performed by your station security office. And I don't think there's any argument, is there, as to the identity of S.I.?"

She leaned even closer. "He wrote this to you, Commander Ivanova. He meant for you to understand it. Do you still claim you don't know what it means?"

Ivanova couldn't think of the words to say, she was so furious and confused. Finally, stiffly, "You already have my testimony."

"Yes, we do." Miyoshi sat straight again, spent a few moments glancing back at the data screen in front of her. Then, "It would be a very good thing, Commander, if you could manage to recall the significance of this note. A very good thing for you and for all of us.

"That will be all, for the moment."

Ivanova stood, still too shaken to speak, and stalked out of the briefing room. She was alternately flashing hot and cold—anger, disbelief, and a trace of real fear battling for control of her reactions.

What was happening? What was going on? Reality seemed to be shifting beneath her feet.

Could they really do this to her?

Garibaldi. He warned me. He tried to warn me.

He said that it was something they did deliberately—
try to make you so angry you'd make a mistake, say
something you hadn't planned to. But why? Could they
really think she'd murdered Ortega? Been involved in his
murder? But only a few minutes ago Miyoshi was almost
outright accusing her of conspiring with him, carrying
on an illicit correspondence! It just didn't make sense!
So why were they doing this to her? What did they want?
What side did they think she was on?

CHAPTER 9

Something was going on.

Michael Garibaldi had been in the security business for a long time. Over the years, he'd developed the instincts. Sometimes you could see it out in the open, the way it had been last year when the dockworkers were working up to go on strike. Trouble coming on and nobody trying to hide it. But this was something else. It was in the way people wouldn't look at you straight—down at the floor, out into the distance, anything to avoid meeting your eyes. They knew—but they wished they didn't.

The only problem was, he was dead certain it was connected to the Ortega thing, and that meant terrorism, separatist politics, the Free Mars movement—stuff way up out of his league. Sheridan had told him straight out, "Earth Central is taking over the Ortega case. It belongs to Wallace now. Stay out of it."

Good advice. Maybe he should take it.

But, hell, since when had he been any good at taking advice?

Take Nick Patinos, now. A good guy. Life-support systems engineer. Worked on all the big domes on Mars in his day. Been on Babylon 5 since the construction phase. Garibaldi had met him originally in Gerry's Lo-G Gym in Marsport, where they'd worked out together some. He'd developed into a good, reliable source. Garibaldi could always count on Nick to put him straight. Not that he was an informer, no. You had to be clear on that. Guys like Nick didn't turn in their own. But: Hey, Nick, I hear there's a lot of skimming going on out of the warehouse in Syrtis. You suppose organized crime's got a hand in it? Or: Nick, there's a rumor that Biggie Wiszniewski is back on the docks, starting up his old operation—you hear anything about that? And Nick would set him straight. A good contact.

But now Nick wasn't talking—Nick was *afraid* to talk, and that meant something was seriously not right.

Back at his office in Security Central, Garibaldi called up Nick's file from the computer, just to see if he could stir up a hunch, reading through it. What he didn't expect was the prim computer voice saying: "That file is not available."

Garibaldi sat up straight at his console. "That's the file on Patinos, Nick. P-a-t-i-n-o-s."

"That file is not available. The information is restricted."

"What?"

"The security file on Nick Patinos, spelled P-a-t-i-n-o-s, is restricted. No access is permitted."

"This is Chief of Security Michael Garibaldi. My security clearance is ultraviolet-alpha, the current passwords are Ginseng, Rabbit, Arawak. Acknowledge? Or do I have to key it in?"

"Clearance and passwords acknowledged. The information you have requested is restricted. No access permitted."

"Restricted to whom, dammit?"

"That information is restricted."

"It's Wallace, isn't it! That bastard has locked up my files!"

"That information is restricted."

He thought for a moment. "Give me a list of the unrestricted files on all station personnel—No, that'd be too long. Give me a list of the unrestricted files on all persons known to have worked on the Mars Colony."

It was a very short list. His own name was on it. Two others—security personnel. That was all.

Garibaldi stared at the data screen. "The bastard—he's locked up my files!"

Captain Sheridan had placed himself between Wallace and Garibaldi, which was probably a good thing, unless his Chief of Security tried to go through him to throttle the Earthforce investigator.

Garibaldi was livid. "He has all my official passwords! He has access to all Babylon 5 security records! He's gone into the station database and put a lock on the files! Not just Ortega's—he's locked up every damn file of all station personnel who've ever worked on Mars! I can't access any of them! He's crippled the security operations on the whole damn station!"

Wallace only gave him a cold, narrow look and directed his reply to Sheridan. "How does he know? How does he know Ortega's file is restricted if he hasn't tried to access it? Or the files on these other suspects? This simply proves my precautions were necessary. There are *very* sensitive aspects to this case, which neither Mr. Garibaldi nor anyone else on this station have a need to know. I don't want every file clerk and security grunt accessing the records of my investigation. And, quite frankly, I have serious doubts about some of the personnel on Babylon 5."

"If something affects the security of this station I damn well right have the need to know what it is!" Garibaldi snapped back.

But Sheridan interrupted with a sharp chop of his hand through the space separating them. "All right! Let's get this sorted out! Commander Wallace, you admit you've restricted access to these records? You've restricted access to Babylon 5 security files from Babylon 5's own security chief?"

"My authorization—"

"Commander, your authorization does *not* give you full control over Babylon 5! That happens to be *my* position. You're here to investigate the Ortega case, not take over the security functions of this station and hamper its officers in the performance of their normal duties."

"Let me correct you, Captain. My authorization covers more than the case of one mining engineer's death. We're here to investigate a serious terrorist conspiracy, a threat both to this station and to the established government on Mars Colony."

"That may be the case, Commander, but I can't let the security requirements of Babylon 5 be compromised. You've exceeded your authority here, and I'm ordering you, as the commander of this station, to restore access to those records."

Wallace replied tightly, "I have to insist that the files on the Ortega case itself remain sealed. Even from Mr. Garibaldi. I have my reasons."

"All right, but *only* those files directly concerning Ortega. The rest are to be restored immediately. And I don't want to see you pulling this again, Commander. Is that clear?"

"Captain," Wallace acknowledged with stiff formality.

"And as for you, Mr. Garibaldi," Sheridan went on, "you will, as ordered, *not* involve yourself in Commander Wallace's investigation."

"Yeah, but how far does that go? If there are people sneaking onto this station, I need to find out about it, I need to be able to plug up the holes before more rats crawl onboard. And what if we've got guys with counterfeit identicards? That affects security on the whole station. I'm not supposed to investigate it? Some of my best contacts happen to come from Mars. I'm not supposed to meet with them? Just because it might happen to interfere with *his* investigation?''

Sheridan shook his head. ''I have to agree with the Commander on this one, Mr. Garibaldi. Probing into the way Ortega got onto the station could well interfere with the investigation of this case. Now, if you find other evidence that somebody on Babylon 5 is churning out counterfeit identicards, then that's your business. But not if it involves Ortega. Let it go.''

How can I find evidence if I can't investigate? Garibaldi thought but didn't ask aloud. At least he was getting his records back. That was the main thing.

But Wallace wasn't finished. ''There's one more thing, Captain. A serious matter. One reason, in fact, why I saw fit to restrict access to these sensitive records. In my opinion, the security of this station is compromised. Seriously compromised. You have an officer on your command staff who is gravely implicated in this case. I have to insist—''

Garibaldi was the first to catch on to whom he meant. ''Now you just wait one damned minute—''

Wallace ignored him. ''I have to insist, Captain, that this officer be placed under arrest pending the completion of our investigation.''

Sheridan's eyes widened. ''If you mean—''

''Confined to quarters, or, at the very least, suspended from her duties.''

''—Commander Ivanova—''

''You've got to be crazy!'' Garibaldi exploded.

Wallace was impervious. ''You've ordered me to restore access to highly sensitive files, on the grounds of maintaining Babylon 5's security. This means that Commander Ivanova, as a member of your command staff, would have access to them. Commander Ivanova, let me make it plain, is a suspect in this case. She has maintained a correspondence with a suspected terrorist. She arranged a clandestine meeting with this terrorist and was present at or about the time he was killed, under extremely suspicious circumstances. A note addressed to her by this terrorist was found near the scene of his death. It's obviously in some code, but Commander Ivanova has refused to reveal what it means. The commander was hostile when questioned by my investigator. She only agreed to answer questions under threat of arrest. She claims to have seen a suspect in the murder, but there are no other witnesses to identify this man. In fact, there are no witnesses to support her version of events.''

Garibaldi furiously interrupted, ''You haven't got a scrap of evidence—''

Ignoring him, Wallace continued. ''Most important, we also have reason to believe that when the suspected terrorist J. D. Ortega came onto this station, he brought with him some information: vital information concerning a matter I am not authorized to reveal. When his body was discovered, there was no sign of this information. His clothing and personal effects have not yet been located, which gives us reason to believe that this information was taken from him and is now in the possession of some other party. He may have passed it on to a contact before his death—or it may have been taken from him, either by his killer, or someone who discovered the body after the killer left. We think it is quite possible that Commander Ivanova may be one or another of these persons. Given the circumstances and the extremely sensitive nature of the information in question, I think it imperative that the Commander be placed in custody. Certainly, it's unthinkable that she be allowed to remain in her current position, with access to sensitive records.''

Garibaldi was staring at him as if he'd grown scales and a tail, but Sheridan looked disturbed. ''You have these charges in your report?''

''They aren't charges, Captain. Not yet, at least. But,

yes, all our findings to date are in our report. Read it, Captain. Ignore your previous ties to the commander and read it with an objective mind."

Garibaldi burst out, "Captain, you can't let him—"

But Sheridan cut him off. "That'll do, Mr. Garibaldi. And you, too, Commander. I'll give the matter my consideration and let you know what I decide. That will be all."

Sheridan was alone. Alone with Wallace's report on his desk.

A lot of hard things he'd had to do in the course of his career. Writing those letters to the families of the men killed under his command—that was the worst, hands down. But this wasn't much far behind.

He'd read the report. Read it, as Wallace intended him to, the way Earth Central would certainly read it when it showed up on their desks. It twisted the facts. Twisted them until they bent backward in both directions, sometimes. But—the facts were there. Indisputable. Ivanova was—compromised.

His link chimed softly. "Captain? This is Ivanova. You wanted to see me?"

Sheridan forced himself to meet her eyes when she came into the command office. The anxious look on her face—she knew what this was about.

"Sit down, Commander. I won't keep you hanging. I'm not happy about it, but Commander Wallace's report really leaves me no choice. Until further notice, you're suspended from all duties as a member of the command staff of Babylon 5."

It hurt her. He could see it. Her face went white and she remained on her feet, eyes front, almost at attention. No matter how much she thought she was prepared, it hit her hard.

"Do you have anything you want to say?"

"Only . . ." She swallowed. "Do *you* believe the charges, Captain?"

He shook his head. Emphatic. "No. I don't. But what I believe isn't the point. Commander Wallace's position is . . . probable. The way he puts it. And, unfortunately, he's right—it's just your word that things didn't happen the way he insinuates."

"My word . . . as an Earthforce officer . . ."

"Is enough for me. Absolutely," Sheridan said firmly. "But the position of executive officer, in a command like this one, has got to be above all suspicion. And—you are compromised. Until we find evidence to the contrary. I'm sorry, Susan," he added gently.

But Ivanova stiffened to full attention. "If the Captain would excuse me now?"

"Of course."

"Damn," he said aloud once she'd gone. Why did a thing like this have to happen to an officer like Ivanova? He knew her kind. All these years with a perfect record. The military was her life. Her career was everything to her. She'd been on the track to flag rank—up until now.

Now—face it. No matter whether Wallace filed formal charges or not, the suspension was on her record. The suspicion. Every promotion board that looked at it from now on would see it, would pass her by. She would never have a command of her own.

Her career was effectively over.

What a damn shame.

CHAPTER 10

Garibaldi stood in the corridor outside the closed door. "Ivanova. C'mon, I know you're in there. It's me, it's Mike Garibaldi. Let me in, all right?"

Silence. He cursed under his breath. "Look, Ivanova, this isn't going to help."

No response.

"I'm not going to go away, you know. I'll just wait out here and clutter up the corridor—"

From inside came a muffled, "All *right*! Come in, if you're not going to go away."

The door slid open. Garibaldi stepped cautiously inside. Ivanova's quarters were dimly lit. She stood up from the couch to face him. She was wearing, he could see, a plain collarless shirt, rather rumpled, and nondescript civilian pants. Her shoulders were slumped, and Garibaldi could just make out the redness in her eyes.

"So," she said dully, "now you're inside, cluttering up my quarters. Is it an improvement?"

"Look, Ivanova, you can't just sit in here in the dark like this. Come on. You have to face this thing. You can't let it lick you."

"I'm already done for, Garibaldi. I've been suspended. My security clearance has been revoked. I'm compromised. It's on my record. No matter what happens now, it'll stay on my record. Every time I have to go through a security clearance, they'll see the red flag there. Did you know that, up to now, I had a perfect record?"

She turned away. "I just don't see how the captain could go along with it. I mean, he *knows* me. I served under him on Io, he knows what kind of officer I am. If it were some other commander—''

''Listen to me,'' Garibaldi intervened in Sheridan's defense. ''I was there. In the Command Office. I heard what Wallace said. He wanted you put under arrest at first. Confined to quarters. He would have gone to Earth Central on this, I'll just bet on it. Him and his authorization. Is that what you would have wanted? Sheridan was trying to protect you from that. What else was he going to do?''

She shrugged. ''He says he believes me, of course. He says he trusts my word.'' She looked away—up at the ceiling, over at the corner. ''I hear that I'm going to be assigned to some other duty—something 'less sensitive.' Not as part of the command staff. I could be a shuttle pilot, maybe. Or sit a tech post in C&C. I'm qualified for that, anyway. I guess when they ship me back to Earth, I can find some kind of job . . .''

''Now, come on! I can't believe this! Are you going to let the bastards get away with this? Let Wallace beat you without fighting back?''

Suddenly the pent-up emotion flooded into her voice. ''But *why*? That's what I want to know. Why are they doing this to me? Do they really believe these crazy charges? Do you know what they're saying? It doesn't even make sense! One minute they say I've been conspiring with Ortega; the next minute they decide I'm the one who killed him. What's going on, Garibaldi? Why . . .''

But at that point she choked up, and Garibaldi found himself holding her, feeling her body shake as she fought down the sobs. After a moment, he was disturbingly conscious of her body heat, the softness of a female form pressed against his own. Out of uniform, with her hair down . . . he found himself wanting to stroke her hair to comfort her.

But that—no, that would be the wrong—very, very wrong thing to do. Not Ivanova. No.

Awkwardly, he made himself pat her shoulder. She pulled back, straightened, wiped her eyes. "Sorry."

He let her take the time to pull herself back together, wondering why it was somehow all right for women to cry—or maybe why men had to find it so hard. There'd been enough times in the last few years when he'd wanted to cry, when he'd even almost wished there was someone to hold him like that while he did it. And maybe that was the worst part—there wasn't, and he was starting to think maybe there wouldn't ever be anyone like that in his life again.

But that was another train of thought he didn't want to get onto right now.

They both sat down. Garibaldi gathered his words. "Look, Ivanova, I know what it's like to be framed, all right? I've seen it done. This—looks like a frame job."

"But *why*?"

"Well, I hate to say it, but if they were looking for a suspect, you're the obvious one. I mean, who else are they going to pick? No one else on this station seems to have any connection to Ortega. So say they're trying to cover up for someone. Say they don't want it getting out who really killed Ortega. Best way is to pin it on someone else. You're available, they can make the evidence fit. So the case is closed.

"Now, I know you might not want to hear this, but if you could *prove* you were telling the truth—"

"No." She stood, agitated. "No, we've been through this before. I won't submit myself to that. Someone probing around in my mind. Even if Psi Corps was allowed to scan defendants in these kinds of investigations, and they're not."

He sighed. He knew all about Ivanova's aversion to the Psi Corps, which she held responsible for her mother's death. She often had to make an effort even to be polite to a telepath. "All right. Then there's just the other alternative."

"You mean—find out who really killed Ortega?"

He nodded. "Which of course *shouldn't* be a problem. That's my job, after all. Only now . . ."

"You've been ordered off the case."

"Not just off it. I'm not supposed to go anywhere near it. Sheridan handed me a direct order. Stay away from Wallace's investigation. Don't interfere. Did you know— the bastard had locked up half the station's security files? Not just Ortega's. The records on just about everyone who ever worked on Mars were restricted. They *really* don't want anyone to know what's going on with this case. Damn! I wish I could get into those files!"

"I thought they were restored."

"All but Ortega's. That one's still restricted. Anyway, I'll bet if I so much as sneeze in the direction of that file, it'll set off alarms so loud they'd hear them at Earth Central. *And* I'll bet Wallace is just sitting there waiting for me to try it, the bastard."

She sat beside him. "Do you think they were trying to frame Ortega, too? I still do have trouble believing he could be involved in something like terrorism."

He shrugged. "Who knows? Unless we can find out why he was here in the first place."

Ivanova went thoughtful. "You know, Miyoshi said . . ."

"Said what?" Garibaldi asked.

"She said they had reason to believe Ortega had smuggled information onto the station. And passed it on to someone."

"Such as you."

"That's what she seems to think." Ivanova was starting to look worried. "You know, Garibaldi, I think I can almost make sense of it. Listen: Ortega sends me a mes-

sage. I meet him at 20:00 hours, as arranged. He gives
me the information. As soon as I have it, I kill him, drag
his body into the head, wait two hours, querying the
computer about the time, to make it look like he never
showed up—"

"And then run straight to me and report him missing,
to establish an alibi . . ."

"Whose side are you on, anyway, Garibaldi?"

He was glad to see she was recovered enough to joke
about it. "No, but really. You needed those two hours. To
search him, to strip off his clothes—"

"For what? If I already had the information?"

"All right. So maybe you didn't. Maybe he refused to
give it to you, and that's why you killed him. Then you
searched him, found the information, dragged the body
off to hide it—"

"Did I have time to do that? In the two hours?"

"I think you did. According to Doc Franklin, the body
was moved into that locker when it was still fairly recently dead. Afterward, you were with me, you didn't
have time."

She shivered. "This is starting to scare me. Do you
think they really believe this? Do they think I have that
information, whatever it is, and they're trying to force it
out of me?"

He patted her shoulder again, a safe, brotherly gesture.
"Don't know. I do wish . . ."

"What?"

"I wish you could figure out what Ortega meant in
that note. 'Hardwir.' He must have thought it would
mean something to you."

"Maybe he never finished what he was going to write.
Maybe he didn't have time? He was worried. I've been
over it again and again in my mind. He was worried.
Someone was after him. Suppose he thought they knew
about the meeting place. He couldn't contact me, but he

wanted to be sure I got the information. So he came early, started to write the note, to leave it where I'd find it. But whoever killed him got there first, before he could finish writing it."

"And didn't see the note?"

"I didn't. Nobody else did, 'til your security team swept the room. It was on the floor, crumpled up. He knew it was too late and he didn't *want* them to find it."

"Could be," said Garibaldi glumly. "But so far, whatever happened, that note seems to be the key to this whole mess. If you could just remember—"

She pressed her hands to the sides of her head. "I just can't! Don't you think I've tried?"

"Well, I'm going to find out."

"What do you mean?"

"I mean getting to the bottom of the whole thing. From the beginning."

"But you can't do that!"

"Why not?"

"Sheridan gave you a direct order."

He snorted. "Hell, do you think I'm going to let something like a stupid order stand in my way, when it's your career at stake? Maybe even more?"

Maybe even more. The words stopped her automatic protest. But . . . "What about your career?"

"Hey, let me worry about that."

"No! Garibaldi, I can't let you—"

"Look, I'm already involved in this thing. Wallace has got me on his hate list. So the only way to make sure both of our careers are safe is to find out what's going on."

"I suppose," she said dubiously.

"I *know,*" Garibaldi insisted.

"So what are you going to do?"

"Ask around. Wallace may have the records, but I have something he doesn't—contacts. Although," he added, "it's not going to be easy getting anything out of them. People are worried. Scared."

"Of what?"

"If I knew that . . ."

"And what do I do?"

"Think. Try to remember. Everything about Ortega you can. Write it all down for me. And listen. *Don't* trust the computer. Not even your own personal log. I don't know what kind of access level Wallace has, but he has all my passwords and maybe some we don't even know about.

"The bastard," he added.

CHAPTER 11

First you set out the bait. Then you go around and check your trapline, see what picked it up.

Garibaldi liked the trapper image, which he'd picked up from an old book. There were times in the security business when you had a lot of time on your hands to sit and read. Not, however, since he'd come to Babylon 5.

The station was like the old Earth frontier, though, when he thought about it. Out on the edge of the new. Full of risks and hazards, yes, and some of them unknown. But that was how he preferred it. Without too much time on his hands to sit and brood about the past.

And so, thinking of traps and bait and what he might catch, he strolled down into the Down Below section, to see what had been stirred up by his recent conversation with Mort the Ear. At first he didn't notice anything much out of the ordinary, just the usual sullen and hostile looks directed at him by the usual sullen and hostile denizens, upset at having their business interrupted by the intrusion of station law. But after a while he began to notice—things weren't quite the same today. He looked around at the sign that advertised the Happy Daze bar. Someone had finally fixed the flickering D.

Frowning, he slipped inside the hatch and made his way through the smoke and haze that passed for an atmosphere in the place, up to the bar. Instead of Mort, there was a new bartender, one of the Drazi who seemed to be opening up a lot of new businesses in this section. "Say, friend, have you seen my buddy Mort—Mort the Ear? Owns this place? I was hoping to run into him down here today."

"Mort gone."

Garibaldi frowned. "What you mean—gone? Gone where?"

The Drazi made a sweeping gesture. "Gone. From station. Took transport yesterday. Sold business. Took big loss," he announced with a smug expression.

"What?"

The Drazi made a gesture of confirmation-of-improbable-circumstance. "Mort say, too much trouble here now. Sell bar. Move to Euphrates Sector for peace and quiet."

Garibaldi swore. This was one thing he hadn't expected—to find his trap empty. Things must be worse than he'd thought. Maybe a lot worse.

But just as he was wondering how, a call came in through his link. "Mr. Garibaldi."

"Garibaldi here."

The call was direct from Security Central. Immediately he was alert. "What is it?"

"We may have had another murder."

"I'll be right there."

There were no cemeteries on Babylon 5. But people did die, and when they did, their mortal remains had to be disposed of in various ways, according to the customs and beliefs of several dozen races, with more than a hundred major religions among them. Sometimes their bodies were shipped home for the proper rites, sometimes they were shot into the heart of the nearby sun. In certain rare cases, they were ritually consumed by the friends and relations of the deceased, a practice tolerated by the station authorities, tolerance being policy on Babylon 5.

But it was a general rule that the remains of sentient beings were never dispatched to the inevitable destination of all other organic waste on the station: the recycling system.

And yet—Garibaldi, the recycling tech, her supervisor, and the two security agents who'd first responded to the report had all examined the object. All concurred in their judgment: it was a humanoid foot, cleanly severed at the ankle joint. Best bet, a human foot.

"Got the evidence pouch?" Garibaldi asked.

"Here, Chief." One security agent held it out. Garibaldi, using a set of tongs provided for the purpose by the recycling supervisor, inserted the evidence into the container, sealed it. "Get that to Medlab, give it to Doc Franklin for analysis. He's already expecting it."

The agent hurried away with obvious relief to be out of the noxious atmosphere. Garibaldi looked at the recycling supervisor, a man about his own age, named Ryerson. "Is that it?"

"As far as we can tell."

"Then maybe we can get out of this place?"

They went back across the catwalk above a huge vat, Ryerson leading the way, then the remaining security officer, the petite young ensign named Torres. Garibaldi followed them down a narrow flight of stairs, crossing the network of color-coded pipes, each greater in diameter than a man's body, that led to it. It was a place as impressive in its own way as the fusion power plant. And larger, in order to serve a population of a quarter-million in a closed environment.

"Does this kind of thing happen often?" Garibaldi asked, taking a breath of the cool air on the other side of the door. It certainly hadn't happened here on Babylon 5 before now.

"More often than you might think," Ryerson said, nodding. "People don't like to think how the recycling system really works. Stuff goes in *here* and comes out the other end *there*. All automatic, untouched by human hands, unseen by human eyes. Nice and clean, nice and sanitary.

"And that's so, just as long as people follow the recycling regs like they're told. But they don't, see. They never do. Blockages happen all the time. We got to know where the problem is, where to shut the system down. And nine times out of ten, it's people not following the rules, throwing stuff in where it doesn't belong, throwing in stuff that has no business in the system. You wouldn't *believe* some of what we've dragged out of those pipes. Out of the alien sectors, especially. Sometimes I wonder, I really do."

"Like a human body? Blocking the pipes?"

"No, a body isn't going to make that much trouble. Not if you cut it up right so it fits. Human body's one hundred percent organic matter, system ought to handle it just fine. No, what made that stoppage was about sixty pounds of silicon solar sheets that some dipwit stuffed into the organic disposal system and *didn't* put through the shredder, like the regs say. Happens all the time, though. You can't teach some people. *Then* we gotta go in there, open up the lines, clear it out. Your foot here just got caught up in it."

"But don't you have scanners? Wouldn't they spot something like body parts in the system?"

"Hell, yes, there's scanners! But they're mostly used to check for trouble, for blockage. Or, say, somebody flushes a data crystal with all the station's defense codes in it—we could scan for it. But do you know how many kilometers of line we've got in this whole system? You know what it would take to scan and monitor every piece of waste that comes through, every second of every day? Oh, sure, it could be done, but you know what it would cost? You imagine Earth Central springing for the cost?"

"All right! So you're saying you can stuff a human

body down the recycler and the monitors won't pick it up?''

"Toss it down whole and they will, sure they will. Whole body'll block up a pipe somewheres. But you chop it up into small enough pieces, it'll go through. System's *designed* so stuff will go through, if people just follow the regs. Now, I do remember one time, on Luna Colony, woman killed her husband and his girlfriend, caught them together, you know? Chopped them up with the kitchen knives and stuffed them into the system. Husband's head, though, got stuck in the line, and they pulled it out, traced it to her. But that must have been a small line. Or the guy had a big head—''

Ryerson stopped as his link went off. "Yeah?"

"Boss, how soon can we get that line moving again? We're getting backup in the shunt from section Brown 62.''

Ryerson turned to Garibaldi. "Well?"

"You're sure you've checked? There are no more body parts in there?''

"Not in the main line. Not upstream of that stoppage. Downstream, now, things get a little harder to sort out. Past the digestion vat there. If your foot had made it past that junction—''

"I get the picture," Garibaldi said quickly. "So I guess there's nothing more we can do here.''

His assistant, Torres, looked vastly relieved to hear him say that. Together, they left the recycling facility. Garibaldi rubbed his forehead, where his hairline had lately retreated. "Just when you think you know everything, seen it all, something like this comes along.''

"It makes you wonder, doesn't it, how many more bodies get tossed in there and never recovered," Torres remarked.

"Yeah, it does," Garibaldi said thoughtfully.

They went up the lift tube to Medlab, where Dr.

Franklin told them to wait, he was just finishing up his analysis of the remains. "If this keeps up," Franklin said, finally coming into the office, "security's going to have to hire its own forensic pathologist. Not that this consulting sideline isn't interesting, of course, but I do have my own research, and a patient or two . . ."

"All right," said Garibaldi, "just tell me what you found."

"It's human, that's the first thing. Human and male. And I got a reasonably decent plantar print, considering the condition of the specimen."

"DNA?"

"Still analyzing."

"Cause of death?"

"Unknown."

"What about time of death, that kind of thing?"

Franklin shook his head. "Not with this one, Garibaldi. Cell structure shows that the tissue was frozen first before it went into the system. No telling for how long. Maybe as much as a year."

"Anything else?"

Franklin nodded. "They used a laser to sever the foot. You can see clearly where the tissue was seared."

"So. First freeze the body, then cut it up. Not bad, not much mess that way. You can keep the pieces on ice as long as you want, dispose of them one by one through the recycling system, one piece here, another piece there . . . This is just great!"

"It could be a serial killer!" Torres exclaimed with some enthusiasm.

"Just what we need around here," said Garibaldi with less. "A serial killer, a professional assassin—civilian or military, alien or human, just take your pick."

Franklin gave them a quizzical look. "Isn't that a lot to assume, just from one body?"

The computer interrupted. "DNA analysis of the specimen is complete."

Garibaldi asked quickly, "Computer, can you identify the specimen?"

"Accessing." Everyone in the room waited.

Simultaneously: *"What?"*

Obediently, the computer responded: "DNA pattern is identified as belonging to Fengshi Yang. Arrived on Babylon 5 on 04/18/59, departed 04/20/59."

Torres was the one who asked the obvious question: "He left without his *foot*?"

CHAPTER 12

Garibaldi retreated to his own console in Security Central to continue to probe the mystery of Fengshi Yang. Unless there were two Yangs (an identical twin?) or the man, as Torres suggested, had left the station with only one foot, then something was seriously wrong.

It turned out to be easy enough to find out, when Garibaldi checked the passenger lists of the ships arriving and departing the station on the dates in question. Yang had in fact arrived on Babylon 5 five days ago, on the eighteenth. The very day, as Garibaldi wasn't likely to forget, when J. D. Ortega was killed. But although the station registry had him leaving on the *Asimov* two days later, there was no Fengshi Yang listed in the *Asimov*'s own passenger list when it departed on the twentieth. At the very least, there was a discrepancy in the records.

Now, the head of Babylon 5's security section didn't like discrepancies in his records on general principles. He didn't like the idea of people being on the station when they weren't supposed to be, when they weren't in the registry at all or when the registry said they'd left three days ago. And he most especially didn't like it when the subject of the discrepancy was chopped up in little bits and tossed into the station's recycling system. Such circumstances tended to make him suspicious. By the time Yang was officially leaving Babylon 5, Garibaldi was willing to bet, he was probably already dead, frozen, and on his way to being reduced down to his basic chemical elements.

But none of that was what had captured Garibaldi's

attention. What had jumped out at him from the passenger list was Yang's port of departure: Mars.

Garibaldi believed in coincidence about as much as he believed in the tooth fairy. Two men murdered, both of them from Mars. Except that according to Yang's file, he wasn't from Mars. He was an import-export rep for a clothing firm on Earth. All right, but at least he'd been on Mars, right before he came to Babylon 5.

Two murdered men, both from Mars, both with discrepancies in their files in the station registry.

Coincidence? Garibaldi snorted.

All right, first assumption: they were both killed by the same agency. But maybe not. Disposition of the bodies was different. Ortega's was hidden almost in the open. Unless, Garibaldi wondered, the killers hadn't meant to leave it there. Did they mean to come back for the body later? To freeze it and send it down the recycling system the way they'd done Yang's?

Maybe that was assuming too much. What else?

He thought a moment, then tapped his link. "Doc? This is Garibaldi. I've got one more question for you on this murder business. Yang."

"Yes?"

"When you said you couldn't determine the cause of death, did you try that test you told me about before—for that poison, chloro-quasi-dia-whatever?"

"Dianimidine. I tried it, yes, but with the condition of the tissue, I couldn't get a reading."

"So it could have been that same stuff as you found . . . in another case we had on the station once." He was deliberately not referring to Ortega's murder and hoped Franklin would pick up the hint.

"That's right, it could have been. But there's just no way to tell, one way or the other. Not unless you find some other part of him that's better preserved."

"Not much chance of that, according to Ryerson. Thanks, Doc."

"Anything else?"

"No. Not right now."

Garibaldi thought for a moment, then called in Ensign Torres. She was young, bright, very enthusiastic, although her enthusiasm did have its limits when it came to the recycling system. Certainly she was ready for more independent responsibility.

"Chief?"

"Torres, it looks like the records on our Mr. Yang have gotten mixed up."

"That's for sure. You know, actually, I was wondering if this case might be related to that other one—the other murder? You know, neither of them in the station registry correctly?"

Maybe even too bright, Garibaldi thought. Very deliberately, he said, "I really don't think there's any grounds for supposing any similarity between the two cases, Torres. After all, if there were, it might involve matters we're not authorized to investigate."

Her expression sobered. "Yes, Chief, you're quite right. Now that I think about it, I don't see any similarity between the two cases at all."

"Well then, since that's so, how would you like to do some digging into the Yang case?"

Now her face brightened again. "Yes, Chief!"

"Good. Now, here's Yang's file. As you can see, there's not too much to go on. But he was in the clothing business, so that might be a good place to start. Check out the merchants on the station, find out who he might have been dealing with, who his associates were, if he had any enemies. Was he carrying valuables? You know what kind of questions to ask."

"I'll get on it right away. And thanks, Chief!"

"Fine. I'll be looking forward to your report."

Torres left the security office, full of proud enthusiasm. Garibaldi told himself he ought to be ashamed of himself, pulling a trick like that on a nice bright kid like Torres. But the experience in investigation certainly wouldn't hurt her, and, who knows, she might even turn up something useful.

And while she was looking into that—Garibaldi turned back to his own screen where Yang's official file was displayed, next to the passenger list from the *Asimov*. One entry, one word that could be the key to it all: Mars.

This time he wasn't just fishing . . . or baiting traps or whatever. This time he meant business. He had questions and he by damn wanted answers.

He found Nick Patinos in the Lo-G Gym, doing tae kwon do exercises with a tall dark alien woman who danced and drifted with slow-motion grace as she parried and returned the strikes of Nick's wooden staff. Their steps and leaps in the low gravity were deliberately slow, controlled. Every movement seemed elongated. Nick was having a hard time keeping up with his opponent, but Garibaldi, watching, knew enough about martial arts to be able to see that his old friend had gotten a lot better since the last time the two of them had sparred. He doubted that he could beat Nick now and regretted that a thousand things—pressures of the job—had kept him from staying in shape the way he knew he should have. Not, of course, that he'd call himself *out* of shape, not exactly . . .

The match ended, and Nick bowed to his partner, then propelled himself with a long, slow roll in Garibaldi's direction, landing about two meters in front of him. "Mike." He held out the staff. "Ready to try a round or two?"

Garibaldi shook his head. "Not this time. I'm here on business, Nick."

Nick turned away as abruptly as possible in the low gravity. "Look, Mike, I thought I made myself clear, before. I'm not talking. Not now. Not about this."

"Not about *what*?" Garibaldi struggled to lower his voice as he saw people in the gym turning their heads in their direction. "Dammit, what's going on around here that nobody will talk about?"

Nick led him away, into the locker room where the sound of showers and blowers would cover their voices. "I'll tell you, Mike, I don't know what's going on. All I know is—I don't want to know. It's safer that way. What I don't know, no one can pry out of me."

"What are you talking about? I'm the Chief of Security on this station!"

"Yeah, but those guys from Earth Central aren't working for you on this, are they? They're working for somebody a whole lot higher up. They've been all over the station, dragging people in for questioning—people who've done *nothing*. They don't say why, they don't say what they're looking for. I don't want these guys picking me up and reaming out my brain for something I don't know anything about."

"What are you talking about? Reaming out your brain?"

Nick looked uncertain. "That's what I've heard."

"You mean they've got a telepath working for them? But there's only one telepath on this station." He hesitated. Was he sure about that?

"Look, Mike, I don't care how many telepaths they've got." He paused, looked around, but the locker room was empty at the moment. "You want to know what's going on? All right, I'll tell you what it's like. You weren't on Mars last year, were you? During the uprising? You were safe on this station."

"So were you."

"Yeah, but I've got a brother and sister at home. What they told me—it was bad there, Mike. Troops all over the place, making arrests everywhere, not asking questions before they did, either. My sister's two kids were in school—Olympus University. There were demonstrations. Troops moved in, closed the place down, detained everyone they saw. They held my sister's kids for three months. No charges, they didn't have anything against them, only they were in the wrong place when trouble broke out. But that was enough to make them 'suspected terrorists.'

"Now do you hear what I'm saying? I know those kids, I halfway raised them, after their own dad died in the mining accident. So they might have joined a peaceful demonstration, but there's no way they would have joined Spear of Ares, or any of those Free Mars groups. But did that matter to Earthforce? No, they held them for three months.

"And now you've got these guys on this station, hauling people in for interrogation for no other reason except they come from Mars, talking about 'suspected terrorists.' You want to know what's going on, that's what's going on, and, yeah, it's got people scared.

"And I'll tell you something else, too. Some of the people they've talked to—haven't come back."

"What are you saying?"

"Just that. A friend of mine had a date for dinner last night—she's a clerk in one of the survey offices. She told him she wasn't sure if she could make it, she was supposed to go see this Earthforce officer to answer some questions, she didn't know about what. Well, she never showed up for dinner, never answered his calls. He checks, she's been shipped back to Earth. Shipped back this morning. No reason."

Garibaldi was appalled. Not that it was going on—he

was no innocent. It was Wallace, of course it was. But why didn't he know about this? Why hadn't anyone told him?

Of course, he'd been trying to help Ivanova, and then this Yang murder coming up. Still . . .

"Nick, I swear, I didn't know! I'll look into this for you, I promise. Your friend, what's his name?"

"Nope."

"*Dammit!* Nick!"

"Hey, I don't turn in my friends, Mike. I never have. I've maybe set you straight on a couple things before, but that's it."

"So your friend might be involved in this?"

"I didn't say that. I don't know. All I know is, he doesn't want his name mentioned to anyone from Earthforce Security."

"All right," Garibaldi sighed, "let's start over. Look, the guy I'm looking for now has no connection to . . . this other thing. Like you said, I'm off that case. This is a completely separate investigation." At least, officially it was.

Nick frowned, waited. Garibaldi took out a projector and clicked on the holographic image of Fengshi Yang as taken from his official file. It hovered in the space between them like a ghost. "Do you know this guy? Have you ever seen him?"

Nick shook his head. "Seen him where?"

"Here on the station. Or maybe on Mars."

"Sorry. Can't say I have. Why? Who is he?"

"Who was he, is more like it. His body turned up early today."

"You mean he was killed?"

"Looks like it, yeah. We're trying to trace down his movements, who he might have seen, you know."

"Well, why come to me?"

"He might have come from Mars. At least, his last port of departure was Mars."

Nick exploded. "You're telling me this doesn't have anything to do with that other thing? You expect me to believe that? 'A completely separate investigation'? C'mon, Mike! A guy gets killed, and the only lead you've got is that he might have come from Mars? What, was he a suspected terrorist, too? Who's next?"

"I don't know! Why do you think I'm trying to find out? If the killings are connected, I want to know, too. But I've got nothing to go on! I don't even know if his name's really Yang. Somebody's messed with his file in the station registry. Only thing I've found out so far is that he came here from Mars. So I go with what I've got. And if this case turns out to be connected to the first one, and this Earthforce guy Wallace finds out, the guy who's been hauling in all your friends for questioning, then he takes over and leaves me nowhere."

Nick shook his head. "Sorry. I really can't help." He turned to leave.

Garibaldi tried once again. "Um, I don't suppose this friend of yours, this guy you were talking about, might know who Yang was?"

"I'll ask him, all right? I'll ask around. That's as much as I can do, Mike. Even for you."

"Thanks," Garibaldi said. Nick pushed his way through the door and was gone. A couple of men came into the showers, gave Garibaldi a questioning look. He put away the projector with Yang's holo image.

He didn't like what he was starting to hear. And Nick —was he still holding something back?

If he was, though, maybe he had a good reason.

And that reason was Commander Ian Wallace.

CHAPTER 13

Reaming out my mind.

Garibaldi sometimes wondered what it would feel like. People were afraid of telepaths—most of them were, anyway. Having all your weaknesses exposed, all your worst secrets, the things about yourself you never wanted anyone to know. He certainly had enough secrets like that. And even with all the Psi Corps regulations and restrictions, he still sometimes had the uncomfortable suspicion that Talia Winters could tell what he was thinking.

The lift tube door opened, and there she was. Coincidence again? She glanced at him, then shut her eyes. She looked drawn-out, exhausted, pale. But from what?

Garibaldi had a good idea. Officially, at least, Ms. Winters was the only telepath currently on Babylon 5. So if anyone was reaming minds, she had to be the one doing it. Only, that didn't fit what he knew of Talia Winters. She just wasn't the mind-reaming kind. Not that they didn't exist. Garibaldi had met at least one Psi Cop who'd burn out your brain as soon as blink at you. But Talia, as much as she might like to present a cool, impervious exterior, was a sensitive. To have to probe into a cruel or deviant mind was actually a painful experience for her. But—it was her job. If it needed to be done, it was her duty. The Psi Corps took care of its own, but that was the cost.

And tonight it looked like the cost had been high.

Garibaldi had left his interview with Nick in a mood to bite off heads. Wallace's by preference, but he could think of a lot of other heads that would do. People being arrested all over his station and he didn't know about it?

But suddenly another source of information had presented itself. "Um, Ms. Winters? Talia?"

She opened her eyes wearily. "Mr. Garibaldi?"

"You look tired. Would you maybe like a drink?"

"I don't know—"

"There's something I'd like to ask you."

She sighed. "I could use a drink, actually. It's been a long day."

In the restaurant, she sank down into a chair and brushed back her blond hair away from her paler face with a gloved hand while Garibaldi went to get both their drinks, her wine and his water. "Thanks," she said, taking the glass.

"A hard day, huh?" Garibaldi asked. "I don't suppose it involved monitoring interrogations for Commander Wallace?"

She straightened, managed to look stern. "Mr. Garibaldi, you know I can't talk to you about that. If that's what you had in mind."

"Look, Ms. Winters, I'm not asking for a transcript of the questioning, I'm not trying to interfere with his investigation . . ." A slight pause, while he recalled that she could tell if he was lying—if he was thinking about her knowing he was lying . . .

"Look, I've talked to some people, and they're scared. People are being arrested, pulled in for questioning. Someone mentioned telepaths, 'reaming out your mind.' So, if it's not you . . ."

"I see." She sighed again. "All right, Commander Wallace has asked me to assist in his investigation. But nobody's reaming out anyone's mind. I simply report if the witnesses are telling the truth. Just as I would in any investigation of this kind."

"And they've all agreed to this? The witnesses? They aren't being coerced?"

"Mr. Garibaldi, I can't say—"

"But they are scared, aren't they?"

"It's perfectly natural for a person being questioned by the authorities to be apprehensive. You ought to know that."

"But the findings of a telepath aren't admissible in court."

"I don't believe . . . that a court of law is the question here," she admitted reluctantly.

"Have you heard anything about certain witnesses being shipped back to Earth for more questioning?"

"No, I don't know anything about that."

"And what about Commander Wallace? Is he telling the truth?"

"Mr. Garibaldi!"

"All right!" He admitted defeat with poor grace.

"I don't even know why you're asking me all these questions. After all, a man's been killed, there's a serious terrorist threat—"

"Is there? Really?"

"I don't know what you mean."

"Don't you?" He was genuinely curious.

"I've *told* you, it's against Psi Corps rules to intrude on a person's thoughts."

"All right, so you don't know what I mean. Tell me, do you think Commander Ivanova could really be involved with the Free Mars movement? With terrorists? That she had anything to do with Ortega's death?"

"I can't really say—"

"But Wallace wanted her suspended from her command. Do you know why? Does *he* believe it?"

She shook her head, turning away from him. "You *know* I can't talk about that! Why do you keep asking me?"

"Because I want to help Ivanova. And find out the truth about what's going on around here. That's why."

Winters found her wine on the table, took a drink of it. "I'm not even sure if she'd want my help," she said slowly. "I'm not exactly Commander Ivanova's favorite person."

"You know, it's not personal," Garibaldi said.

"Oh, I do know. And I understand her reasons. I know how she feels about her mother and what the Psi Corps did to her. She looks at me, and all she sees is Psi Corps. I know that. But it doesn't make it any easier to deal with her. I've tried."

"You'd want to help her, though?"

"If I could. But I can't. Not if she doesn't agree. You do understand? I'd *like* to help her . . ."

"I understand."

"There are rules."

"I know."

Winters twisted her fingers together, looked at her half-empty glass of wine. "You're that sure she isn't involved in . . . any of this?"

"As sure as if I'd read her mind," Garibaldi said firmly. "She's being set up. Framed. Wallace is doing it. I don't know the reason, but I'm sure."

"I see," Winters whispered, looking down into her wine. "I think I see."

It was early in the morning, but Captain Sheridan was already in the Command Office. So much to do. Babylon 5 was different than any command he'd ever held, diplomatic at least as much as military, and with so many civilians coming and going it was almost like commanding a city. At least he'd had an experienced executive officer—up to now.

He missed Ivanova's support. There were other junior officers on the station, of course, but there was no one, really, to take her place, no one with the experience that she had of running this place. Without her, there seemed to be ten times as many calls, ten times as many emergencies he couldn't delegate to anyone else, had to handle himself, even when he recognized that he didn't really have all the necessary experience yet, either.

If only Ivanova hadn't gotten herself mixed up in this damned Ortega affair. *That* was something he wished would get cleared up and over with as soon as possible. He had enough problems right now, new to this command, without a terrorist threat hanging over the place.

Garibaldi had been in late last night, breathing fire, complaining that Wallace was establishing a police state on Babylon 5. That there were rumors spreading all over the station about people being arrested for no other reason than being from Mars. Rumors about forced telepathic probes, even torture, drugs.

But were the rumors true? Sheridan had asked. Were they even substantiated?

"I'm not sure yet how much they're substantiated," Garibaldi had said. "They're not groundless, I do know that. But even if they are just rumors, this points to substantial unrest on the station. The workers, the people we count on to run this place, are scared. They're scared and they're angry. In my opinion as Chief of Security, these rumors constitute a serious threat to order and safety.

"And another thing," he'd gone on, as if that much wasn't enough, "I understand that Commander Wallace has ordered the members of the security staff assigned to him *not* to take orders from me, not to report to me any details on what he's doing on the station. All these arrests going on—my own men were ordered to keep them from me. Hell, half the station knew about it before I did!"

So that was another problem Sheridan knew he was

going to have to deal with sometime today—Garibaldi and Wallace fighting over jurisdiction again. He sighed.

"Captain Sheridan?"

Sheridan swore to himself, then took a breath. He might as well give up. Once it started, it wouldn't stop. "Yes? What is it?"

"Captain, Ms. Winters would like to meet with you. Are you available?"

Resigned, he said, "Yes, have her come in. Are there any other calls?"

"Not yet, Captain."

The telepath entered the office. She looked anxious, nervous about something. He smiled to put her at ease. "Ms. Winters. Come in, sit down. Is there a problem I can help you with?"

"Well, Captain . . . ." She sat straight and forward in the chair. "I'm sure you must know, Commander Wallace has asked me to help him question witnesses in the Ortega case. I know that it's part of my duty to assist the authorities in this kind of thing, but I really . . . Captain, can he require me to do this?"

Sheridan frowned, remembering what Garibaldi had said last night. "Why? Is there something wrong?"

"I don't know. Some of these people don't seem to have consented freely to being probed. Commander Wallace calls them witnesses to Ortega's murder, but most of them don't know anything about it. He talks about terrorism, but it seems to me that he's the one doing the terrorizing. I'm just not happy being involved in all this."

"I see. Well, Ms. Winters, if you mean can Commander Wallace order you to cooperate with him, the answer, strictly speaking, is no, he can't. You're not under military orders. On the other hand, as you know, your license as a telepath does require you to cooperate with the legally constituted authorities. You can refuse, but then Commander Wallace would have the right to complain to Psi Corps and possibly request the assistance of another telepath. You probably know better than I do how Psi Corps would react in that case.''

Winters looked unhappy. ''Well, yes, I'm aware of that. What I suppose I was wondering . . . I mean, you outrank him, you're in charge of Babylon 5, can't you order Commander Wallace to conduct his investigation some other way? Besides dragging in all these innocent people?''

''I see,'' Sheridan said, more slowly this time. ''There, we have a problem. I am in command of this station, but in the matter of this investigation, Commander Wallace's orders come directly from Earth Central. They give him full authority in the matter. So if you're asking exactly where my authority ends and his begins, that's kind of a gray area. What neither of us wants in this situation is to have to appeal to Earth Central.''

''I understand.''

''I can talk to the commander, of course. I can express your concerns.''

''Thank you, Captain.''

''I'm sorry I can't be any more help, Ms. Winters, but I'm afraid that if the commander insists on your cooperation, in the end, this will be between you and Psi Corps.''

She stood. ''I'm glad you could take the time to hear me.''

Sheridan watched her leave, glad he wasn't a telepath. Psi Corps had its own discipline, different from the military. Secretive. The strongest telepaths assigned as cops to control the others. He supposed that was the way it had to be, but there was something sinister about it, definitely something sinister about the Psi Cops in their black uniforms.

He hoped Ms. Winters would be all right, but he'd

only told her the truth: he couldn't really intervene to help her. Not, at any rate, without challenging Wallace.

But maybe Wallace would agree to see reason. He hoped so.

He toggled his link. "This is Captain Sheridan. Commander Wallace, I'd like to speak with you at the earliest possible opportunity today."

There was no reply. Sheridan ordered C&C: "Contact Commander Wallace for me, please. Have him call me. Make it a priority request."

But a moment later there was a reply. "Captain, there is no response from Commander Wallace."

Sheridan's expression hardened. "Contact him again. Keep trying until you do. I'm ordering him to report to my office. Now."

Wallace didn't show up in the next minute, or in the next ten minutes, but two hours later he was at the door to the Command Office. Sheridan could see the cold anger at being summoned. He didn't care.

"Commander, I called you some time ago. You didn't respond."

"I was interrogating a witness. I ordered all communications held."

"Commander, I'm starting to have some questions about your use of your authority on this station. You're adding to them right now. As commanding officer of Babylon 5, I'd appreciate a response when I try to contact you. Or do you consider yourself exempt from the requirement to observe normal Earthforce regulations and procedures?"

Wallace said stiffly, "No, I do not."

"In that case, I'll expect that in the future you'll make yourself available for emergency communications. Now, as I've said, there are starting to be some questions about the way you're conducting your investigation. There are rumors that you've been using unauthorized methods of obtaining information, and they're causing unrest on the station, to the point where it raises concerns about security. And the station's registered telepath has expressed reservations of her own."

But Wallace's expression was implacable. "Captain, I am not answerable to you about my conduct of this investigation. If your station has security problems, then Mr. Garibaldi will have to deal with them. That's his job, as he repeatedly insists.

"And if you want to question my authority, Captain, I suggest you contact Earth Central."

"I'll do that, then, Commander."

"Is there anything else, Captain?"

"No. You can go. But . . . stay in touch. That *is* an order."

CHAPTER 14

Somehow, it seemed a lot easier to breathe in the Command Office with Wallace gone. But Sheridan had an uneasy feeling he might have made a mistake. No doubt that he'd lost his temper, which was an effect Commander Wallace seemed to have on people. But now he was going to have to ask Earth Central to clarify just where the lines of authority lay, and there was no guarantee at all that he was going to like the answer when he got it.

But maybe it had been inevitable all along, ever since the first moment Wallace stepped foot onto Babylon 5. Garibaldi had seen it coming, tried to warn him.

Well, if it was inevitable . . .

"I'd like a Gold channel opened for a transmission to Earth."

He might as well get it over with.

Talia Winters paused before she opened the door of the interview room. Interrogation room was how she thought of it, part of Commander Wallace's private interrogation system, what he called his command post.

There was a man seated in a chair in the center of the room, and at her desk Lieutenant Miyoshi, who looked up with her flat black eyes. "You're late."

"I had other business. And an appointment with the captain."

"Every minute you're late delays this investigation." Miyoshi glared at her. "From now on, you *don't* have other business. You're the only registered telepath on this station. Our investigation requires your services. We were assured that you'd be available."

"Now, just wait a minute!"

"No, I've already been waiting! More than a minute! I have four more witnesses to examine today. They're all probably lying." Miyoshi turned back to her desk, unlocked a drawer, and took something from it. "I want you to look at this, Ms. Winters. Commander Wallace told me you've been questioning our authority."

Talia took the object reluctantly. It was a viewer card, and at the touch of her gloved hand, the PSI symbol took holographic form and rose, glowing, from the card. Simultaneously, the message forced itself into her mind: *Obey. No questions. Obey.*

Talia recoiled with a soft sound, and the card returned to its flat, featureless state. Miyoshi, watching her, had a faint smile on her lips. "Now do you question my authority, Ms. Winters?"

She shuddered. "No," she said faintly.

"Good," Miyoshi snapped. "Now, let's get to work. I've already wasted too much time, and I've got a lot of questions to ask."

"Commander Ivanova reporting as ordered, Captain."

Sheridan sighed inwardly. Reporting on time, correct, in uniform. Her salute could have been put into a textbook. Only her eyes were different, a different look in them, like defeat. He tried to pretend he didn't notice it.

"Commander. Please sit down. You know that I've been thinking about a temporary assignment for you, until things get straightened out. Now, I've been reading your report."

He paused, seeing her expression turn puzzled. "Your report on the current situation with the raiders," he explained. "How they're targeting strategic metals shipments. Very good analysis there. And some excellent suggestions.''

"Then, have you . . . heard back from Earth Central about it?''

"Ah, no. Not yet. There was no reply except that they'd be studying the matter further.''

"Oh.''

"Well, as I said, there are some excellent suggestions here. I especially agree that if your analysis is correct it ought to be easy to identify the transports at highest risk for attack and supply them with an escort. I know—your report stressed the fact—that our resources are too thin to provide escorts to every freighter who comes through into Grid Epsilon. But if we do as you suggest, identify the transports coming out of Marsport with these cargoes of morbidium and other strategic metals, I think we'll see results that more than justify the effort.'' He paused. Ivanova looked suddenly stunned. ''Commander?''

"Uh, yes, sir. Transports coming out of Marsport. Shipments of morbidium. That's right.''

"Yes. Now, what I want you to do is take command of Alpha Wing and pursue this strategy as vigorously as possible. Once the vulnerable shipments are identified, the routing and scheduling information plotted, you'll be able to intercept the transports and escort them in.

"Do you have any questions?''

"No, sir. I appreciate your giving me this assignment, very much.''

"I want to see results, remember.''

Her smile was slightly crooked. ''Well, I always did say I wanted to see more flight time, didn't I? Thank you, sir.''

The first thing she did was turn on her link to contact Garibaldi. ''This is Ivanova. I think . . . I know what it is!''

"What what is?"

"The . . . connection. The real reason they're trying to frame me! It's Mars!"

Garibaldi had a sudden paranoid image of Wallace, listening in through some patch in the station's communications system. "I think we'd better talk about this—face-to-face," he warned Ivanova.

A moment of puzzled silence from the other side of the link. Then, "I'm just outside C&C."

They met there, decided to talk in Ivanova's quarters. Before he would let her say a word, he deactivated her computer and swept the rooms for bugs. "All right," he said finally, "what's this about Mars? You mean Ortega, that he was part of the Free Mars movement?"

"No! You remember, that report I did—the raiders, the hijacked transports. What you warned me about. Well, those transports all shipped out of Marsport!"

"You mean the . . ."

"Morbidium shipments. Morbidium shipments from Mars! *That's* the connection, I'll bet on it!"

Garibaldi's eyed widened. "I think you just might have hit on it. Why did Wallace and his crew pick on you when we all know there's no real connection between you and Ortega. When you're not from Mars, you've never been on Mars, there was *nothing* to link you to Mars, just a couple of holiday cards.

"Until you went and figured out that somebody on Mars is leaking shipping information to the raiders."

"Not just that," Ivanova explained. "Or they would have figured it out a year ago. Somebody in charge is sitting on the information. Keeping it quiet. Whoever's involved in this is someone high up in Earth Alliance."

"All right," said Garibaldi enthusiastically, "so where's the link to the terrorists? Where does the Free Mars movement come in? And your friend Ortega? How does it all fit together—morbidium . . . raiders . . . terrorists."

"Weapons," said Ivanova. "Terrorists need guns, and morbidium is essential in the production of plasma weapons. And the sale is restricted."

"Except on the black market," Garibaldi added. "Where terrorists would buy. Terrorists with a link to the raiders. Somehow they get the transport information, pass it to the raiders, who hijack the morbidium, sell it on the black market, and Free Mars takes their pay in the finished product."

"So maybe I stumbled onto something bigger than I thought." Ivanova shook her head. "But if this is true, you know what it means!"

Garibaldi nodded slowly. "Wallace. He might be a part of it. If Earthforce officials are involved, even just in covering this up, then the first thing he's going to do is try to get rid of the person who uncovered it."

Ivanova raised a hand. "But wait a minute. That can't be it. Earth Central sent Wallace here to investigate even before I sent that report. They couldn't have known about it."

Garibaldi frowned in thought. "All right. They didn't know at first. They just sent Wallace to investigate Ortega's death. Then they get your report. They don't know how much you know, but you're a loose cannon. Too dangerous to be allowed to go around probing into things they don't want to get out.

"But that's another thing!" Ivanova said eagerly. "If Wallace is part of the cover-up of the link between the terrorists and the raiders, then why go to so much trouble to track down Ortega? It has to mean that J. D. wasn't involved with the terrorists at all!"

"Maybe . . ." Garibaldi shook his head in confusion. "It turns everything around backward. All right, let's think it through. Say that Ortega's a good guy, like you say. He's found out something. About this link between the terrorists and the raiders. He contacts the authorities, but they're involved, too. They try to shut him up. He runs. They put out a fugitive alert on him. He comes here to Babylon 5, tries to contact you, you're the only honest Earthforce officer he knows. But he gets killed before he can pass you the information. Only, the bad guys don't know that. They think you know what it is."

"That makes sense," said Ivanova slowly, "except—who was the murderer? It can't be Wallace or either of his aides, they were on Earth. And . . . if they killed him, then wouldn't they *know* I didn't have the information? So why all this?"

"Yeah, what are they still looking for?" Garibaldi asked himself. "And why did they kill the other guy?"

"What other guy?"

"Oh, I forgot, you don't know—now we've got two murders."

"By the same murderers?"

Garibaldi's voice betrayed his frustration. "I wish I knew! I'm not any closer to knowing who killed Ortega since the day we pulled his body out of that locker. And I won't be, if Wallace has his way.

"And as for this other guy, Yang, I don't know anything for sure about him except that part of him's missing. His name might not even be Yang. But I *think* he came here from Mars."

"He was killed after Ortega was?"

"We don't even know that. They had him frozen. Who knows for how long?

"I hate this, you know. Here I am, head of security on this station, and I'm groping around in the dark, blind and deaf. I can't try to connect Yang's murder to the Ortega case, because if I do, Wallace will come down out of the sky like a harpy and snatch it away."

Ivanova couldn't resist. "I thought harpies were supposed to be women."

"You know what I mean."

"So what can we do?"

"You? Be careful, that's what. Watch your back. I'm going to be watching it, too."

"And you?"

Garibaldi took a breath. "So far, I've kept the Yang thing quiet." He bit his lip. "I mean, I've kept it out of the computer files."

"Because of Wallace?"

He nodded. "Once he finds out, once he makes the connection, then it's all over. I won't have anything to go on. So it's a race. I've got to find out who killed Yang before Wallace does. I've got to dig so deep I might just end up in the fusion core, but that's the only way."

Ivanova frowned. "You could get in trouble. Your job—"

"Never mind my job. I'll take care of that. Remember, I've been in this business a long time, and I'm still around. I've learned a few tricks. Trust me on this, all right?"

Ivanova still looked dubious, but she was interrupted by the sound of his link. "Mr. Garibaldi, would you report to the captain in the Command Office."

"I'll be right there." And to Ivanova as he left, "Just trust me."

Alone in the lift tube, on the way to see Sheridan, Garibaldi wondered how much he should say about Wallace. What he and Ivanova had cooked up between them was raw speculation, nothing but. He didn't want to go to Sheridan with no proof, no evidence, nothing but a crazy conspiracy theory. The captain would probably kick him out of the Command Office, and rightly so.

No, this was something he was going to have to handle

on his own, his own way. For Ivanova's sake. She was young, she still had everything ahead of her—a brilliant career if he could just prove those charges were part of a frame-up. As for himself, he knew the risks. But Mike Garibaldi had had his chances and, mostly, blown them. What he had to look forward to—didn't really look all that inviting, the closer he got to it.

If he could have made it up with Lise . . . but that was over.

For Ivanova's sake, then.

He paused in front of the door to the Command Office, making sure he knew his own mind.

"Captain Sheridan, you wanted to see me."

The captain turned slowly in his chair. "Mr. Garibaldi. Have you ever seen a Code Ultraviolet message?"

"Not too often, sir."

"Well, take a look." He keyed a code into the computer console. The ultraviolet security logo appeared on the screen, and a familiar face.

"That's . . ."

"Captain Sheridan, this is Admiral Wilson of the Office of the Joint Chiefs. Commander Ian Wallace has been sent by this office in order to conduct an investigation of the utmost importance to the security of Earth Alliance. As commander of Babylon 5, you and your staff are to afford him every degree of cooperation. His authority in all matters pertaining to this investigation is not to be questioned.

"I trust this clarifies the concerns you expressed."

The image blanked on the screen, leaving Garibaldi stunned. "Direct from the Joint Chiefs?"

"You saw it for yourself. The personnel of this station are ordered to cooperate with Commander Wallace in the conduct of his investigation. That's a clear order. Isn't it, Mr. Garibaldi?"

"Yes, sir. Very clear."

CHAPTER 15

There was trouble in the casino, a fight had broken out, and it was still going on when Garibaldi arrived on the scene, despite the security agents already pulling the combatants apart and threatening them with shock sticks. The security chief himself waded into the middle of it, hurt his knuckles on some alien's bone-armored gut, and after a few more minutes, order was restored to the point where he could try to find out what the hell was going on.

"All right, what is it? What's the problem here?"

Accusations from all sides: "He started it."

"No, he did!"

"She cheated!"

"I cheated? I? You cheated! You're the one!"

"You were reading my mind! That's cheating! That's against the law! She oughta be under arrest!"

Garibaldi didn't have anything against aliens, not really. But there was something about poker—plain, old-fashioned Earth poker—that in his opinion made it a human game. Human mind against human mind. You got aliens playing poker, especially with humans, and this kind of thing always seemed to happen. This time, the argument was between a human and an alien tourist, a Hyach. The Hyach was a female, backed by a larger version in male who seemed to be her mate. The female had claws. Her human antagonist's face had bleeding scratches, which he was wiping with the sleeve of his shirt.

From the senior security guard on the scene, Garibaldi learned that the fight had spread to the spectators and other casino patrons, basically along racial lines—human against alien. This factor increased the potential for further violence and made a quick, fair, open solution imperative—now.

"He was cheating!" the Hyach kept insisting. "He was making marks on cards!"

"You see any marks on those cards? Huh? You see any?" the human yelled back with considerable heat, playing to the spectators. "She's the one who cheated! Crawling around inside my mind, spying on me, reading my hand! Sneaking, cheating telepath!"

As the crowd pressed in, muttering in hostile tones, Garibaldi noted the number of credit chips spilled over the table—and more on the floor. He made a *look out* gesture to the nearest security guard, who nodded and stepped over to keep the space clear, shock stick held openly across his chest.

As for Garibaldi, he didn't need to be a telepath to know that the human gambler had been cheating, and how. On one of his fingers there was almost certainly an E-Z MarkR implant, favorite device of amateur cardsharps. A matching implant behind his eye would pick up the faint electromagnetic trace left as the player marked the cards. More sophisticated gambling establishments on Earth scanned the players as they came through the door, and anyone caught with a MarkR implant was usually taken out to the back of the casino for a short, painful discussion on gambling etiquette.

But this was Babylon 5, and Garibaldi had his own views on dealing with gambling etiquette. He grabbed the protesting gambler by the wrist and dragged him a short way across the floor of the casino to the manager's office. "I think we've got a MarkR implant here, do you have a scanner?"

The scanner was duly produced, and when Garibaldi

switched it on, the flashing light and loud alarm as much as branded the gambler on the hand: CHEAT.

Immediately a small group of people began loudly demanding their money back, as Garibaldi turned the squirming gambler over to one of the security staff. *Dumb amateurs, they never learn. The only people who ever make any money with those implants are the cheats who sell them.*

But there were still a number of voices loudly declaring, "Hey, what about her? What about the telepath? Yeah, I'm not going to gamble with any telepaths around."

Followed by the manager, Garibaldi intercepted the Hyach as she was starting to gather credit chips from the card table. "Wait just a minute." Her mate behind her glared. Garibaldi glared back for an instant before he turned to the female. "Lady, are you aware that house rules in this casino prohibit telepaths from taking part in games of chance?"

"What you mean? You prove it yourself. He was cheating, he was the one. Not I. Not I."

She reached again for the chips, and again Garibaldi stopped her. "But are you a telepath? Because if you are, I'm afraid your winnings will have to be forfeited."

"What is this *four-feet*? What do you mean? He was the one who cheat!"

"Just because he was cheating, doesn't mean he was the only one." Garibaldi tapped on his link. "Ms. Winters, this is the chief of security. We have a situation here that may involve a telepath. Can you come to the casino, please?" He glanced up at the surly crowd, clearly unwilling to disperse before the issue was settled. "Yes, I'd say it was a sort of an emergency. All right, yes, definitely an emergency."

While they waited, the Hyach continued to protest, shrilly demanding to see her ambassador, the commander of the station, a lawyer. On Garibaldi's other side, the casino manager made nervous noises. He kept sending urgent mental messages to Talia Winters: *Hurry up, will you? Before this situation gets out of hand? Before she ruptures my eardrums?*

On Earth, of course, or in any territory under Earth Alliance law, this situation would have been unusual. The Psi Corps ruled its members with a firm hand, and activities like poker were strictly forbidden. No one wanted to gamble with a telepath.

But this was Babylon 5, where the rules were different. Earth law wasn't the only system that counted here, and the Psi Corps had no authority over an alien telepath. But the house rules of the casino applied to everyone, even to members of alien races who considered telepathic powers perfectly normal and placed no restrictions on their use.

Finally Ms. Winters arrived, looking fragile and weary. Garibaldi realized she'd probably been asleep when he called her. But as the surly crowd parted to let her through, her expression grew serious.

"Sorry to bother you, but I was afraid this situation might get out of hand. I don't want to have to put down a riot," he apologized. "This lady just won a lot of money at poker, and she denies that she's a telepath."

Talia turned to the Hyach, met her eyes, held them a moment. Then the alien furiously turned her head away.

"She's a telepath," Talia said flatly.

Garibaldi nodded. He'd had a hunch it was so. "Sorry, lady, but I'm afraid you can't take that money. Using telepathic powers is considered cheating here. You're forbidden to enter the casino again as long as you remain on Babylon 5." He gestured for a couple of guards to remove her from the room, screaming and protesting all the way to the door, her surly mate following in silence.

The crowd, mollified and under the eyes of the rest of the guards, began to subside.

"Thanks, Ms. Winters," Garibaldi told her, sincerely grateful. "I wanted to settle this thing down without using weapons. We don't need more human-alien tension around this station." He paused. "It's a good thing they were both cheating."

"You're sure she was cheating?"

Garibaldi's eyebrows went up. "She wasn't?"

Talia rolled her eyes back. "Oh, of course! Why else would a telepath ever want to play cards? What other amusements do we have, besides prying into other people's minds?" She sounded bitter.

"Hey, sorry. But I was fairly sure she was cheating some way or other, even before I knew she was a telepath," Garibaldi said cautiously.

Talia pressed her hands to her eyes. "I'm sorry, I'm a bit on edge lately. But, no, I don't know for sure if she was cheating. We don't probe—not even each other. Not without permission."

"I know. You've told me that. I guess I just thought . . . I don't know."

"I could feel her shielding, and her anger, and that's all I needed to know—that she was a telepath. That was all you needed to know, wasn't it?"

"You're right. And I am sorry. Look, if you want to get back to your quarters, I'll walk you there—or at least to the lift tube. Unless you'd like a drink?"

She shook her head. "No, I do need some sleep."

He walked with her through the crowd, now mostly returned to their own various devices. As they reached the lift, he said, "If there's anything I can do, any way I can help . . ."

"No. It's an internal matter of the Psi Corps. Thank you, though, for asking."

The lift door opened, and she stepped inside. As it

closed, Garibaldi wondered: why was she so exhausted? It was Wallace, he was sure, but what was the bastard doing with her? What kind of secrets was he fishing out of people's minds?

With order restored, Garibaldi decided to stroll down to the lockup and check out his newest prisoner. If the guy didn't have a prior record for gambling offenses, he'd just as soon simply kick him off the station as haul him in front of the Ombunds for formal sentencing. And he didn't really think this particular cardsharp had a prior record. He just wasn't good enough at it.

But Garibaldi also wanted to make sure that whoever sold him the stupid implant wasn't operating here on Babylon 5. That was one more kind of trouble he didn't need.

A call-up of the guy's record revealed no priors for gambling offenses, several arrests for brawling, and one conviction for taking indecent liberties. He was an asteroid miner named Welch, his ship was stopped-over here on Babylon 5 for a crew R&R, he came from the Mars Colony, he had no war record. A more-or-less typical spacer. But—he came from Mars Colony. It was a long shot, but maybe he knew something.

Welch, when Garibaldi got another look at him in the interview room, did not look happy. He tried to conceal his hand behind his back when the security chief remarked, "E-Z MarkR implant, huh? I'll bet you saw their ad: *Make Colossal Credits playing cards with your friends! They'll never know your secret!* Is that so?"

Welch squirmed.

"Look, friend," Garibaldi said, deciding to teach this fellow a few of the basics, "do you know how lucky you are that you didn't try to use that thing in some high-powered casino on Earth or Mars? The enforcers in those places aren't nice guys, like I am. First . . ." He grabbed hold of Welch's hand, forced it down flat onto the table. "First they'd whack this thing off. Then they'd feed it to you. One finger at a time. Whether you were hungry or not. Next . . ." He pressed a thumb up next to Welch's eye where the visual implant was. "They'd pop this right out. And feed it to you for dessert. And after that, if you were lucky, they might leave one or two working parts. Do you get my drift, Mr. Welch?"

He nodded quickly.

"That's good. But, like I said, I'm a nice guy. And you're a lucky guy, because I've looked at your record, and I don't find any prior convictions for gambling offenses, which means you just got this thing or you haven't been caught yet." He lifted Welch's hand by the wrist, rotated it to get a clearer view. "No fresh scar. I guess that means you haven't been caught yet. So you've been lucky. Let's see how lucky you're going to be now. We can handle this two ways, Welch. One, you're in trouble. Two, you're in a hell of a lot of trouble. And that depends on how you answer my questions. So which will it be?"

Welch squirmed again, trying unsuccessfully to pull his hand from Garibaldi's grip. "I din't know. Din't think it was against the law."

Garibaldi shook his head. "Fraud: Obtaining goods, services, or other items of value by deceptive or misleading means." He tapped the gambler's hand against the table. "This is a deceptive means. A damned cheap one, too. Now, where'd you get the implant?"

"This guy. He has a clinic, out in the Belt. I owed him some money I couldn't pay back. And he told me—that's all right, 'cause he could help me. He'd sell me this implant, and I could win money playing cards with the guys on the ship, pay him back the next time I was in port."

Garibaldi sighed. Why didn't they ever have a different story? Something interesting for a change? "How'd you lose the money in the first place? Gambling?"

Welch nodded miserably. "So I did what he said. Except when I went to pay him back, he said I still owed him for the implant, it was real high-tech stuff. But the guys on the ship, they weren't playing with me anymore, and so I figured it was time to get out of the Belt. I signed on with this out-system operation. And ended up here."

This guy has a vacuum for brains, Garibaldi thought. "And I suppose you ended up in the Belt after you got in trouble on Mars? Except it really wasn't your fault?"

"Something like that, maybe."

"All right, I tell you what you're going to do now. You're going to our Medlab, where a nice technician is going to remove that implant and throw it away like the piece of trash it is. Then you're going to sit in our lockup until your ship pulls out, and then you're never going to set foot on Babylon 5 again as long as you know what's good for you.

"Oh," he added, "and there'll be a charge for removing the implant. Our medics don't work for free."

"A charge?"

Garibaldi sighed again. "Don't tell me you don't have the money?"

"Well, I mean, I did, but it was all on the poker table, before that snake-eyed, telepath, alien bitch—"

"Never mind that. So you don't have the money. I'll contact your ship, then, and they can take the cost out of your pay. Unless you'd rather tell it to the Ombunds?"

"Aw, sheesh, look, can't you give me a break? I never woulda done it if I had the money. . . ."

"If you want a break, you've got to earn it. Now, let's start with the name of this guy out in the Belt?"

Welch didn't want to say, he squirmed a lot more, he whined, he was going to get in trouble. But Garibaldi was persuasive. When he had the information on the source in the Belt, he went on, "Now, how would you like to talk about Mars?"

"I don't know no names on Mars. I mean, it's been five, six years since I was there. Who can remember?"

"Try," Garibaldi urged him. "For example, what do you remember about a guy named Yang? Fengshi Yang?"

"I dunno. Never heard of him." But Welch's eyes were evasive.

"Let me jog your memory a little." Garibaldi pulled his viewer. "Here. This is what he looks like. Remember him now?"

"Maybe."

Yes! Garibaldi exulted inwardly. *Finally!* But he kept his expression blank as he pressed for more information. "Maybe what? Maybe you saw him on the Mars Colony once? Or twice? Maybe he worked for Earth Alliance?"

"Maybe I did. Back when I was working the deep mines I mighta seen him. Back before I got into space."

"Yang was a miner?"

"Nah." Welch was starting to squirm again. "But he worked around the mines. Maybe for one of the companies, I don't know. Metallicorp, maybe. Or AreTech. I think . . . people said he was like an enforcer. If, say, you owed money to somebody. Or somebody didn't much like you."

"I see. So this Yang would have been the kind of guy to have a lot of enemies?"

"Yeah, I guess so. I wouldn't want to mess with him, though. Not from what I heard."

"I see. And do you think any of these enemies might have been political?"

"I don't know what you mean."

"Sure you do. Was Yang involved in the Free Mars

movement? Do you think he could have been involved in any of the terrorist activity?''

Vehement head-shaking. "I dunno. I don't. That was after my time. I took off from Mars Colony six, seven years ago. Never was involved in any of that stuff. Far as I know, Yang worked around the mines, that's all. I didn't try to cross his path, you know what I mean?''

"I know what you mean." Garibaldi took a moment to decide. It was a direct order. All the way from the Joint Chiefs. Then he asked the question: "What about a guy named Ortega? J. D. Ortega. Did you ever see him when you were on Mars Colony? Working in the mines?''

"Nope. No, I don't think so. Name doesn't mean anything.''

And that, for all that Garibaldi kept pressing him, was about all the information he could get out of Welch. But at least it was something. At least the guy had heard of Yang, and placed him on Mars.

Garibaldi made a decision. "So," he said, "I tell you what. I'm going to give you that break I talked about. 'Cause it sounds to me like you might have reason not to want to run into this Yang character. Right?''

Welch's eyes got very wide and the pitch of his voice went up. "Here? On B5? You mean he's *here*?''

"That's what I thought. So I'm going to do you a favor and let you go back to your ship now. You stay there 'til you pull out of the docking bay and you don't set foot on this station again. Got it?''

Vigorous nod of the head.

"I'll make sure no one knows you were ever here. And you'll do the same, right? You'll never mention to anyone that we had this little talk.''

"Yeah, right.''

Garibaldi called a guard to come and escort Welch to Medlab and then back to his ship. He hoped the guy had enough sense to keep his mouth shut. Because if Wallace ever found out he'd been asking questions about J. D. Ortega and the Free Mars movement, he was going to be in deeper trouble than Welch could ever imagine.

CHAPTER 16

Ivanova ran through the preflight check like a litany, secure in the familiar space of the Starfury's cockpit, suited up for space, hands on the controls. It felt good. It felt right.

"Escort Wing, ready for launch."

Sheridan had given her back what she needed. A command, if not the command they had taken away from her. And more than that: flight.

"Escort Wing launching. On my mark. Drop!"

The ship fell away from the station through the open door of the bay. As soon as she was clear, Ivanova hit the ignition, and the thrusters roared into life. She could feel their power, the force of acceleration trying to press her back into her seat. The rest of the escort formed themselves up behind and around her, and the six ships headed as one into the jump gate's infinite vortex.

Six Starfuries. Not the whole of Alpha Wing, but they were still going out in force, expecting a fight. Hoping, at least in Ivanova's case, for one. Hoping to splash some raiders, hit them where it hurt. And if she had a mental image of Commander Ian Wallace as the target when the plasma hit, well, so much the better.

The gate flung them out of hyperspace with Ivanova coolly ordering, "Hold your formation, Escort Wing." Their rendezvous was two and a half hours away, across Blue Sector, with the heavy hauler *Kobold* as it came through the transfer point carrying raw ingots of iridium, titanium, nickel, and morbidium from the mines of Mars.

No problem getting a ship like that to show up on the mass detector, Ivanova thought. Almost as heavy as a small planet, with the inertia to match. Flying it would be about as exciting as a tug pushing a barge up a slow stream.

Her hands hovered over the fighter's controls, just to feel the temptation, just for a second, to cut loose with the afterburners. Yes, it was good to be back.

"2:20 hours 'til estimated time of rendezvous," she said, because she had no orders to give now that they were through the gate and still so far from their destination. The fighters were all in formation, all on course. You couldn't have aimless chatter in the cockpit when the ships were out on patrol, but sometimes on the long stretches space could seem like an awfully big, dark silent place and a friendly voice was good to hear.

"Copy that, Alpha Leader," Mokena replied from Alpha Two.

By the time the jump gate showed up on the long-range scan, Ivanova was ready for the confrontation she expected and hoped would happen. "Weapons systems on. Keep on the alert for raiders," she ordered, but the fighter pilots had all been briefed on the nature of this patrol. They knew what was likely to show up, and they were ready for it.

Then there was a sudden massive energy surge showing up on her instruments, a blaze of blue light from the jump gate, and the transport came through from hyperspace at the maximum acceleration for a ship of her class.

Ivanova made immediate contact. "This is Earthforce Commander Susan Ivanova, commanding Escort Wing Alpha. Are you the *Kobold*?"

"Affirmative, Commander. Earth Alliance transport *Kobold,* out of Marsport. We're glad to see you out here."

"Glad to be here, *Kobold,* We've come out to give you

an escort as far as Babylon 5. We've heard raiders might be taking an interest in your cargo."

"Thanks, Commander. I've got to say, it's about time, and then some."

"Take escort formation," Ivanova ordered her command, and they fell into place around the transport, matching velocities, heading back in the direction of Babylon 5.

It was too easy. Ivanova found herself almost wishing the raiders would show up. Once they were all on course, the transport's pilot came on-line through Ivanova's comm channel. "Commander, can I ask—you said you heard raiders might be taking an interest in our cargo?"

"That's right."

"Well, could I ask—where you heard this? Your source?"

"Meet me once we're on Babylon 5," Ivanova told him, "and we can talk about it there."

"It's a date, Commander."

Alpha Two broke in: "I'm picking up something on scan. Bearing 80 by 44 by 122."

"I've got it, too," reported one of the other fighters.

Ivanova checked the screen. A trio of tiny points, at the limit of scan range, but closing in fast. Raiders, she thought at once, and the computer confirmed the probability: small, fast ships—certainly fighters of some kind, and in this sector, that meant raiders. "Heat up your weapons," she ordered. "Keep alert. Any more of them out there?"

"Negative, Commander. Just those three."

"Well," the *Kobold*'s pilot said, "it looks like your information was correct, Commander."

But where are the rest of them? Ivanova wondered. The raider ships were small and usually operated in packs.

"Are we going to take them on?" Alpha Three asked

as the three ships closed the distance while remaining well out of the Starfuries' range.

"They're trying to draw us away," Ivanova declared. "Three and Six: take off after them, get them if you can, but don't let yourselves get separated or drawn into a chase. Our job is escorting this transport."

At her order, the two fighters spun about with a burst of their thrusters and headed after the raider ships, which suddenly fled, leading them away. "Diversion," Ivanova said, mostly to herself. It was easy to follow the chase on her tactical display, as the pair of Starfuries bore down on the smaller, boomerang-shaped ships. Silently, she was cheering them on, her hand poised above the button of a phantom plasma torpedo, aching to fire. *Go! Get them!*

The raider pilots had judged the distance and their opposition well. As soon as Alpha Three and Six started to come within firing range, the three ships split up, attempting to divide the pursuit. "Don't do it!" Ivanova was about to order, but Alpha Three read the situation the same way she did.

"Stick with me!" he told his wingman. "We're going after the one heading off at ten o'clock!"

Together they pinned down their target. Alpha Three got off one good shot that singed the raider's tail and left him vulnerable to the next burst of plasma from Six, which finished the job.

In the meantime, the other two raiders had fled out of range. "Alpha Leader, should we continue pursuit?" Three asked Ivanova.

"Negative, Alpha Three, break it off and return to escort formation. Good shooting, you guys."

"Commander, do you think they'll try it again?" the transport pilot asked, but the question was answered before Ivanova could, as one of the other fighters reported, "I've got more of them on scan. Four this time."

"Hold escort formation," Ivanova reminded her command. "They're trying to draw us away. Remember, it's the transport they want."

But this time the raiders kept a more respectful distance. "They're looking for their friends," Ivanova conjectured. But of the first raiders, one was splashed and the other two turned tail, and eventually these newcomers retreated out of scan range, giving up on their anticipated prey. Ivanova watched their images disappear from her display. There was a sharp stab of regret for the opportunity lost, the chance to take off after them, weapons hot and ready. But, as she knew full well, the transport was her primary responsibility.

"It looks like clear sailing back to Babylon 5," she announced to the *Kobold*. "Just sit back and enjoy the ride."

"Commander, you have no idea just how good that sounds," the pilot said in a very sincere tone.

When Garibaldi started to add up the facts he had so far, one minute it seemed almost conclusive, the next minute it had all vanished to a handful of threads so thin you couldn't hang a feather from them. It felt strange to be working without the computer, but ever since Wallace had wiped his files, he wasn't sure what kind of bug the Earthforce investigator might have placed in the system. Generally, he considered himself sharp enough when it came to computer security, but he had to figure that Wallace had come from Earth Central with passwords and override codes to override anything he might have.

But before they had computers, they had paper and pens, and so did Garibaldi.

So, adding it all up, so far he had Mars Colony, with Free Mars terrorists, with morbidium mines, with the raw material for plasma weapons. Out here in Grid Epsilon, he had raiders, hijacking the cargoes of morbidium.

Linking them together, he had J. D. Ortega, maybe part of the Free Mars movement and maybe not, turning up dead on Babylon 5 with some mysterious, now-missing piece of information. He had Susan Ivanova, investigating the hijackings, sent a message by Ortega that might or might not have referred to that mysterious information. And now: Fengshi Yang, again from Mars, again showing up dead on Babylon 5. Yang, whose records were not what they should be: an "enforcer," somehow connected with "the mines."

Was he an agent of the Free Mars movement? A terrorist? Welch didn't seem to think so, but Garibaldi didn't think much of relying on Welch's mental powers. An agent of the raiders, maybe? The agent who passed on the shipping data? Had he come to Babylon 5 to meet Ortega? To work out a deal? Pass on a warning?

To kill him?

Garibaldi pushed squares of paper around on his desktop, arranging them in different configurations. Which arrangement made it all make sense? A square of paper marked X for whoever had killed Ortega. Another X for whoever had killed Yang. But was X one person, or two? Maybe one X had killed another X. Then there'd be only one X left. What side was X on? Or should that be what sides?

His data screen stared at him blankly. Damn! It would be so easy just to access the computer and ask it to search the records for anyone on the station with a previous involvement in mining on Mars. Yeah. And how much do you want to bet that won't bring Wallace down on your head, Garibaldi?

Well, there was more than one way to search. This sure as hell wasn't getting him anywhere. He flashed the squares of paper. He had all that stuff in his head, anyway. What he needed now was to have another talk with someone.

* * *

It hadn't been easy to set this up. Garibaldi still didn't know the guy's name. Just that he was Nick's friend, whose lady friend had worked in the survey office, been interrogated by Wallace, and shipped back to—presumably—Earth. Mineral surveys, assays. Did that have anything to do with mines? With morbidium shipments? Terrorists? Fengshi Yang?

Nick's friend was a nervous-looking guy. Claimed he didn't know anything, he wasn't involved, didn't want to be involved. But he had, Nick had grudgingly admitted it, been involved with mining. Or at least with mining machinery, a company that built the big loaders.

The meeting place was down in the machine shops, one of the dozens of different divisions of the Engineering Department on Babylon 5. The man—he still wouldn't give his name—had his fists clenched inside grease-stained coveralls and wouldn't take them out. Garibaldi got the feeling there was something in his background behind it, maybe something in his record he didn't want to come out, some incident in his past that had made him generally hostile to the kind of authority Garibaldi represented, to Earthforce.

"I only agreed to this because Nick asked me to. And mostly because he said maybe you could do something about Sonia. Find out . . . something. Where they took her. What they did with her. Why."

"I can try. I'll do what I can. But I've got to tell you up front, whatever happened to your friend is out of my control."

A frown. "You're Earthforce, you're security, aren't you? Nick said you were the head guy."

"I'm head of Babylon 5 security, yes. But there's an independent investigation going on that I'm not directly involved in. Nick should have told you that. I'm not mixed up with what this Commander Wallace is doing on the station. But I'll try. And if I do find out what I'm looking for, it could help your friend.''

"So what is it you're looking for?"

Garibaldi handed him the viewer. "This man. Whatever you know about him. We think his name is Fengshi Yang. He might have called himself something else, though."

A frown. "You think Sonia might have been involved with this guy?"

"I don't know. I don't know what Sonia was involved in. If you told me, you know, that might help."

But he abruptly gave back the viewer. "No. No, never saw him before."

Garibaldi thought he had the sudden intuition of what it must be like to be a telepath and simply *know* when someone was lying. "What I've heard," he said, "is that he worked as a kind of enforcer on Mars. Around the mines."

Quickly, "I wouldn't know. I wasn't a miner. Look, I've got to go. I don't have anything to say."

Garibaldi tried to stop him, but the look in the guy's eyes—he was scared. He dropped his arm, let him go. Damn, there was another lead that went nowhere. More time wasted. Everyone was scared, no one would talk. A dozen interviews so far, and only Welch had talked, and Welch had dead space for brains.

Now what? There were other workers in the machine shop area. A few of them gave him a curious glance. Garibaldi wondered if he ought to go over, show them Yang's holo, ask if any of them had ever worked in the mines on Mars. But he already knew what they'd say: No, sorry, never saw him before, never heard of him. No, I wasn't a miner. I don't know anything.

Would they rather have Wallace asking the questions? he wondered, leaving the shop area. Would they rather have a telepath probing around in their minds, digging out the truth?

Garibaldi knew he was looking at a dead end. If he didn't find any leads soon, he was going to be the one facing the real trouble—failing to file proper reports, concealing the truth about his investigation. As soon as Wallace found out.

Well, maybe Torres had uncovered a lead. He could hope. He was supposed to meet her now, anyway.

Preoccupied, he didn't notice the guy who came up behind him, the other one from his side, didn't notice the shock sticks they pulled, didn't see—

Then pain radiated through his entire nervous system, short-circuiting all thought processes, all other functions. His muscles spasmed out of control, and he didn't even feel it when his head connected with the deck.

CHAPTER 17

He came to slowly, conscious only vaguely of pain, a general, body-wide hurting. It was dark. He tried to reach out, to grope for a surface, but he couldn't move his arms. He tried again, realized they were tied somehow, fastened behind him. And—yes—his legs, too, tied together at the ankles, bent up against his chest. His back was pressed up against some hard, unyielding surface, his arms trapped between them, cramped, circulation cut off. He tried to shift to a different position, to ease the discomfort, but there was no room to move. His back was against one wall, his shoulder against another, and if he leaned over to the other side, he hit a third wall. And his feet and knees were pressed up against the fourth. He was crammed into this dark place that was almost too small to hold him, tied up—why?

Fear made his heartbeat race. It was hard to breathe in here. The air felt hot and stale, as if there wasn't much oxygen. And that thought instantly triggered the sensation that he was stifling, choking— No, wait. In his mouth, a gag.

So where was he? A dark, small, enclosed place. A locker?

A locker . . .

Ortega! Now real panic hit him, making him kick out and strain against his bonds. This was how they'd found J. D. Ortega's body, crammed into a locker just like this! Garibaldi couldn't help remembering the sight of the corpse, stiff with rigor mortis, knees bent up against the chest to fit it inside. Was this why he was tied up in here?

Was he supposed to die in here the same way, in this dark, airless place?

No! He kicked out with both feet together, as much in protest as a serious attempt to break out of his confinement. He could just manage it, just draw his feet back far enough to make an impact.

He kicked out again. *No!* they weren't going to get away with this. *No!* he wasn't going to let them. *No!* not like Ortega. *No!* he wasn't going to die in here. *No! No! No!*

He paused, falling back, aching, sweating, gasping for breath that wouldn't come through the gag in his mouth. His head throbbed and his ears were ringing from the din of the repeated kicks against the locker walls. It was too much.

Get ahold of yourself, Mike! All right, calm down. Think.

He remembered then that J. D. Ortega hadn't suffocated in the locker, that he'd been poisoned and shoved inside after he was dead. Didn't mean, of course, that he couldn't die in here, but at least it wasn't the same, not quite the same. And if they'd meant him to die, they would have killed him already. Wouldn't they? Unless they thought he was dead before they put him in here.

All right, all right. It didn't help to dwell on any of that, did it? After all, he was alive, and that's what mattered. And staying that way.

If he could reach his link, he could call for help. Shouldn't be too hard, his wrists were tied together. He groped for the link, found his wrist, the back of his hand —but no link. It was gone. Damn!

Now what?

All right. Let's think this through, Mike. Problem: My link is gone, I'm tied up and shut into this locker. Assuming it is a locker. So let's assume it is. Then it should have a door. Four sides, one of them should be the door.

Can't tell which one, it's too dark. Can I kick it open? Well, the lockers on the station aren't all that strong. I should be able to. But I was just kicking the hell out of it, and it's still shut tight. So maybe that side isn't the door.

To say that Garibaldi couldn't move at all was to exaggerate the facts by just a bit. He had freedom enough to move his bound legs enough to kick. And, he now discovered, he could manage to twist and rotate his entire body a centimeter at a time until he was facing another one of the locker's walls, which he hoped would prove to be the door.

It was a slow, exhausting process that again left him breathing hard, as if he were running out of air. The locker must be airtight, then, he thought. Or maybe it wasn't really a locker at all, maybe it was something a whole lot harder to break out of.

Desperately, he kicked out. The locker's sides rang with the impact, hurt his ears again. Loud.

Someone ought to be able to hear that. He paused. Again, his ears were ringing. It was like his whole skull was vibrating with the sound. Made it hard to think.

No, have to think. All right. If I'm making so much noise, why doesn't anyone hear it? Maybe there's no one around. Or maybe they're making so much noise themselves they can't hear me.

But the way his ears were ringing, he couldn't tell. It didn't matter, though. He had to keep trying. Someone might come by and hear him. Or he could finally manage to kick the door down. Only if he kept trying, though.

So he kept trying.

On the main communications display in the Observation Dome Commander Ivanova was saying, "No, I don't expect another attack. The first one was just a feint, to see if they could draw us off. The second time they didn't even come into range. No, we've scared them off.''

''Good work,'' Sheridan said enthusiastically. ''I think we'll be able to show Earth Central that this approach can work. Results, Commander. That's what counts.''

''Yes, sir. We'll be bringing the transport in. ETA in 3:50 hours.''

''Good work,'' Sheridan said again, pleased for her, pleased for the safety of the transport and the success of this approach to fighter escort patrols. A good officer, Ivanova. Innovation, initiative, just the right degree of aggression. Good qualities.

''Captain Sheridan?''

He turned to see another officer standing slightly behind him, an ensign, security insignia on her uniform. Short, red-haired. Seemed to be upset about something, but controlling it. ''Ensign Torres?'' he recalled her name.

''Yes, sir. Could I speak with you, sir?''

''Of course.''

She glanced around the busy center of the Observation Dome. ''In private?''

''Of course.'' Once behind the closed door of the briefing room, he asked, ''So what's the trouble, Ensign?''

''Sir, it's Mr. Garibaldi. I'm afraid he's missing. I can't locate him.''

Sheridan reached for his link, but Torres shook her head. ''He doesn't answer his link. And C&C can't trace it. I've already tried. And . . . I have reason to believe he may be in danger.''

''Better tell me about it, Ensign.''

''We've been investigating a murder—''

''Not the Ortega case?''

''No, sir. A different murder. A man was found . . .

that is, part of him was found in the recycling system. We were able to ID him through his DNA code. His name was listed as Fengshi Yang, but there's a mix-up with his file in the station registry, inconsistencies. We've been trying to trace him, determine his true identity.''

Sheridan frowned. "I don't think I was informed about this, Ensign. Why not?"

Torres's small white teeth bit down on her lower lip. "I don't know, sir. But Mr. Garibaldi wanted this case kept quiet, in case information got out to the wrong parties, I suppose. I think I was the only one working directly on it with him. But . . . I didn't know you hadn't been informed."

The captain's frown deepened. Torres was having trouble keeping her eyes straightforward. There was something she wasn't saying, at least. "Go on," he said impatiently.

"Yes, sir. He was supposed to meet me more than three hours ago. To discuss our results. When he didn't show up, I tried to reach him on his link. I supposed at first that there might be some reason why he might have gone off-line. But he never does that. And then when I asked C&C to check on him, they reported no trace to his link at all. Sir, I'm worried, but because this could be a sensitive case, I didn't know if I should issue a stationwide search alert."

"What do you mean, a sensitive case?"

Torres looked away for just an instant. "Well, sir, we weren't sure . . . I mean, there was no evidence, and Mr. Garibaldi told me not to mention anything, but it's possible there could be a connection between this murder and the Ortega case. And I think that may have been what he was investigating."

"You think?"

"Sir, he didn't tell me. He *said* there wasn't a connection, but I think . . . he thought there might have been. And he didn't want anyone else involved. I wasn't sure what to do—"

"I see," said Sheridan shortly. "Do you have any idea where he might have gone, where he might be?"

"No, sir. If I had, I'd have checked myself. But he didn't tell me. I don't think he told anyone what he was doing."

Sheridan nodded. Time enough to get to the bottom of the mystery later, time enough to get the true story out of Garibaldi—once they found him. "This is Captain Sheridan, I'm calling a general stationwide alert. Mr. Garibaldi is missing."

"Come on, Ensign Torres. I haven't been on this station very long, but after we get through taking it apart, I may know every square meter of it. We're going to find Garibaldi."

How long had it been? Wearily, Garibaldi kicked again at the side of the locker. Was it starting to give? If it was, he sure couldn't tell. Why'd they have to make the lockers on this station so damn strong, anyway? His hips ached, his back. His shoulders were agony, with his arms twisted back behind him. His head throbbed with pain.

He twisted himself around again until his back was pressed up against a new surface. Got to keep trying. He kicked out. Was this the door?

Got to keep trying.

No, wait. What was that? A sound? A voice?

He tried to call out through the gag, choked, then kicked the side of the locker again—I'm here!

Did they hear him?

Yes! Relief flowed through him. Oh, yes! Someone calling his name! *Garibaldi?*

He kicked twice. *Once for no and twice for yes. Where did I hear that?*

"Garibaldi? Is that you? Where are you?"

Here! he wanted to yell, but the gag prevented it. Two kicks again. Not so hard this time, not so loud. Just so they could find the locker he was in.

"Garibaldi? Are you in here?"

The captain's voice. Sheridan. *Thank you, Captain. Thank you.*

"He's in here! In this locker! Get it open, now!"

There was a grating, wrenching noise. "Dammit, then try the next one! I know he's in here!"

He kicked out again, to be helpful, but suddenly there was another loud ripping sound of metal tearing, and the wall on his left side gave way and he was falling, couldn't catch himself.

Blinding light. Hands grabbing hold of him, easing him down to the floor.

"Get him untied! Garibaldi, are you all right?"

The gag was pulled from his mouth. He gasped, tried to swallow, managed to croak an inarticulate response. Swallowed again. "Fine. Just fine."

Even managed a grin. "Real . . . happy to see you . . . Captain."

They took him to Medlab. Garibaldi didn't really want to go to Medlab, but they didn't ask his opinion in the matter, and the captain ordered it, and so it was done.

Dr. Franklin examined him, gave him something that made his aches and pains fade away, peered into his eyes with an instrument and said he was lucky he had a hard head, but one of these days he was going to hit it too many times.

"Concussion?" the captain asked.

The doc shook his head. "No, I don't think so. It was a glancing blow, like he struck it when he fell. Now, *this* is a shock-stick burn.'' He pointed to a place on the side of Garibaldi's neck.

Funny, he couldn't remember that place hurting before, in the locker. But it was coming back to him now. A shock stick. Yeah. That's what it must have been. Not the first time he'd been shocked. It wasn't the kind of experience you forgot. Yeah, first the shock. Then coming to in the dark. He remembered it now.

Experimentally, he shook his head. It almost didn't hurt. He sat up, to Doc's protesting ''Hey, take it easy.''

''I feel all right. I'm just sitting up.'' He turned to face Sheridan. And there was Torres, behind him. Torres? ''Thanks for pulling me out of there, Captain.''

''You had us a little bit worried there for a while.''

And Torres, apologetic, said, ''I'm sorry, Chief. I wasn't sure what you wanted me to do, but after I couldn't raise you on your link, I told the captain. I hope—''

''I think that was a good decision,'' Garibaldi said sincerely. ''Thanks, Torres.''

Sheridan was looking at him. ''You want to tell me about it now?''

Franklin started to protest that his patient had just been hit on the head, but Garibaldi sat up straight. His head felt clearer now, though he knew that was probably the drugs.

''I don't know how much there is to tell, Captain. I was interviewing a possible witness, who didn't have very much to say. I left him, I was heading back to the lift tube, to meet with Torres, and then—zap!''

''I understand you're investigating a murder. A man named Yang? Is there a connection? Do you think it was Yang's killer who zapped you? Someone who didn't want your witness to talk?''

Garibaldi closed his eyes a moment. Maybe he wasn't really ready for this. But it was too late now.

Sheridan's expression was starting to take on a more severe look. "According to Ensign Torres here, there might be a connection between Yang's death and the Ortega case. But there's nothing to that effect in the file on Yang's case. In fact, there's almost nothing in that file."

Torres, still behind the captain, looked pained and guilty.

Garibaldi shook his head, winced. "It was only a hunch. No facts. No evidence. Nothing to put into a file. All I really know is that Yang departed for Babylon 5 from Marsport on date 04/18 and died sometime within the next five days."

Sheridan looked dubious. "That's your hunch?"

"One more thing. According to the station registry, he left Babylon 5 on 04/20. Passenger manifest says he didn't. Fact that we found his body three days later says he didn't. So somebody must have tampered with his file in the station registry. That's my hunch. That's it."

Garibaldi was earnestly glad there wasn't a telepath in the room at the moment. He was thinking of Welch, and the information that Welch had given him, tying Yang to Mars and the mines there. But Welch was safely back on his ship, with nothing in his record to suggest he was anything but a gambler thrown off the station for cheating at cards.

Sheridan started to say something, then turned his head. There was noise out in the corridor, someone shouting. Franklin looked furious, strode to the door. "Keep it down! What's all this about? I'm not having my patients disturbed!"

But Garibaldi shut his eyes. Suddenly his headache was coming back. He recognized the furious voice demanding that someone get out of his way and stop obstructing his investigation if she didn't want to face "very serious charges, Technician."

Just what he needed right now. His favorite head-hunter, Commander Ian Wallace, had come to visit him.

CHAPTER 18

Wallace burst into the treatment room followed by his aide Khatib and a seething Franklin. "All right, Garibaldi, this is it—"

But he was stopped short by the sight of Sheridan standing at Garibaldi's bedside, a Sheridan who did not look like part of a welcoming committee. "I *hope,* Commander, that you have some reasonable explanation for barging into Medlab like this, disturbing the patients?"

Wallace drew himself up straight. "Captain, I have reason to believe that your chief of security has been interfering in my investigation, in defiance of both my orders and yours. And I believe you understand *now* how important my findings are to Earth Central."

But if this last remark was intended to intimidate Sheridan, it had the opposite effect. Babylon 5's commander did not like being reminded of Wallace's knowledge of his personal, restricted message from the Earthforce Joint Chiefs. "What I understand at the moment, Commander," he said tightly, "is that you have one minute to either justify your presence here or leave Medlab."

"Very well, Captain. We can continue this discussion in your office. Where I intend to demand that you relieve Mr. Garibaldi of his duties as head of Babylon 5 security and hold him under arrest. He was ordered explicitly and repeatedly not to get involved in the Ortega case. Now I discover that he's been questioning *my* witnesses! Getting himself involved in a situation that he *clearly* isn't capable of handling." He flashed Garibaldi a brief unsympathetic glance. "In fact, removing Mr. Garibaldi from his position might be said to be for his own good."

Sheridan had seen the look. He snapped, "That won't be necessary, Commander. Your request is denied. Mr. Garibaldi has just been injured in the course of carrying out his duties as head of security, investigating a murder on this station. He has every right to question suspects or witnesses to this crime, whether or not you consider them 'your witnesses.' Particularly since it seems that you've been questioning every other man, woman, and alien on Babylon 5."

Wallace blinked, looked back at Khatib. He seemed uncertain. "What murder?"

"A salesman from Earth was killed recently. A man named Yang."

"Yang?"

"That's right. Why? You don't know anything about this case, do you? This man named Yang?"

Quickly, too quickly, shaking his head, "No. The name means nothing to me."

Garibaldi's head lifted a few centimeters from his pillow, staring at Wallace with avid interest.

Sheridan went on, unnoticing, "Then it won't interfere with your own investigation if the Babylon 5 security office tries to track down his killer? Since the two cases aren't related. As you claim."

Wallace took a slight step backward. "Of course not. I can see I might have . . . been misinformed."

"Yes, you might have," said Sheridan. He looked at Torres, who was standing motionless and looking like she wished she were invisible. "Lieutenant, you can escort the commander from Medlab."

Gratefully, Torres said, "Yes, sir. Commander, if you'd come with me?"

Wallace turned to leave, ignoring Torres, but Garibaldi, sitting up on the treatment bed, couldn't resist. "Say, Commander. If you do come across any leads on the Yang case, you'll let me know, won't you?"

Wallace said coldly, "Of course."

"I'll do the same for you, too. We ought to help each other out, shouldn't we? Seeing as we're in the same line of business."

Wallace didn't answer, but Khatib shot Garibaldi a silent, deadly look.

"That's a nasty one," he thought to himself as they left, followed at a safe distance by the lieutenant.

"Thanks, Captain," he said out loud.

Franklin looked satisfied to see Wallace leaving. "I think we should all leave Garibaldi to get some rest, sir."

"Just a few minutes, Doctor. If I can speak to Garibaldi alone."

"I think I'm feeling dizzy," Garibaldi muttered, closing his eyes.

"Flash it, Garibaldi. And to hell with Commander Wallace. I want to know what's really going on! I talked to Torres, and she says you do think this Yang case is related to the other one. You know something, and I want to hear it!"

"I swear, Captain! I've got next to nothing! Every time I think I've got my hands on a lead, it turns into smoke." Garibaldi paused. "All right, you want to know why I think there's a connection? Because I can't find out a thing! No one will talk.

"This is my station. I mean, I have connections here, people that I can talk to, who'll talk to me. But this time, when I was still looking into the Ortega case, before you ordered me not to, I got nowhere. Nobody knows nothing. They won't talk. All right, so when I started asking around about this guy Yang, I got just the same thing. Nothing. Nobody's talking. They're afraid, Captain."

"Afraid of what?"

"That's what I don't know! Only it all seems to point to Mars. I did find out one thing, that Yang was from Mars. He was involved in something people don't want to talk about. And Ortega was from Mars. He was a suspected terrorist, no one wants to talk about that. He came to Babylon 5, he was killed. Yang came to Babylon 5, he was killed. One more thing. We've got no record of Ortega coming onto the station; the station records on Yang were falsified."

Sheridan said nothing, but he was listening, at least.

"Everything else is just crazy speculation."

But the captain wasn't going to let him leave it at that. "What kind of crazy speculation?"

Garibaldi rubbed his head. "Like, who Yang really was. What he was here for. Look, it's just a crazy theory, all right? But I've been talking with Ivanova. You know how she traced the leaks in that transport routing data back to Mars? Well, she figures there might be somebody from Earthdome in on it, covering it up. So it could be that Ortega wasn't a terrorist, that he found out about the deal, and the bad guys in Earthdome tried to shut him up. So they send an enforcer after him, but something goes wrong, the enforcer gets killed, too."

"And Yang was the enforcer?"

"That was his line of work, from what I've heard."

Sheridan was frowning in thought. "But then, after all the probing around he's done, questioning everyone on the station who's ever been to Mars, why wouldn't Wallace know about Yang?"

"I think he does."

Sheridan looked at him and the shock snapped his eyes wide.

Garibaldi nodded. "Just then. When you mentioned Yang's name. I was watching Wallace's face—and that snake, Khatib's. They *knew*. They knew about Yang, all right. They just didn't think *we* knew. And they weren't happy about it."

For a moment, they both considered the implications of that in silence.

Then Garibaldi went on, "So say we've got Earthforce officials mixed up in something dirty. Some guy finds out about it. He's got, say, names, dates. He's dead, the enforcer's dead, but the information hasn't shown up. You don't know if he's passed it on. So maybe you send another enforcer to find it. An enforcer with authorization—"

"Direct from the Joint Chiefs? Come on, Garibaldi!"

"Hey, didn't I say it was crazy?"

Sheridan paced a step away from the bed, stopped, turned around again to Garibaldi. "I mean, I wondered about Wallace, I admit it. His tactics. Enough to question Earth Central about him. And you saw what I got back! I mean, the Joint Chiefs, Garibaldi. Direct from Admiral Wilson. You're spinning conspiracy theories all the way up to the High Command!"

"Yeah, I know. Why do you think I didn't write it up in an official report? Why do you think I tried to keep the whole Yang business quiet?" Garibaldi sighed. "Only, there's one more side to it."

Sheridan looked as if he didn't want to hear it, then waved for Garibaldi to go on.

"All right, the bad guys send their investigators. They discover that the guy with the information met with a certain Earthforce officer. And it's the same Earthforce officer who just filed a report with Earth Central pointing right to their dirty dealings. And the first thing the investigators do is call for that officer's arrest."

Sheridan clenched his fists. "I *can't* go to Earth Central with this! You know I can't! I've got my orders! Direct from—" He didn't say it. "Dammit, Garibaldi, this *is* crazy! I don't believe it. You said it—you don't have any facts to back this up."

"Yeah, I know." Garibaldi sighed again, rubbed his head where it ached. "And there are other problems.

Like, who just zapped me with a shock stick and stuffed me in that locker? And who killed Yang?''

"The same group?"

Garibaldi shook his head, winced. The drugs were starting to wear off at the edges, letting the pain in. "No. I had a lot of time to think about it, in there. And I don't think so. They could have killed me easy enough, if that's what they'd meant to do. No, it was a warning.''

"You mean, stop asking questions, or you'll end up like Ortega, stuffed into a locker?''

"Something like that, yeah." Garibaldi paused a moment, thought about it. "No. Whoever took care of Ortega was a pro. Whether it was Yang or not. But he didn't care much about the body being found. In fact, he might even have meant it like they did me—as a warning.''

"To someone," Sheridan agreed.

"But whoever killed Yang, they *didn't* want the body found. In fact . . ." he paused again, "in fact, they'd probably be real upset if they knew it was identified. And that somebody was investigating the murder. I'll bet that'd be kind of a shock.''

He met Sheridan's eyes, knew they were both thinking the same thing.

"And that kind of changes everything," Garibaldi said slowly. After a moment, he asked, "So now what do we do?''

Sheridan's jaw tightened. "I don't know about all this other stuff, Garibaldi, all these conspiracies. But we still have an unsolved murder on Babylon 5. That's a fact. And, like I told Commander Wallace, I can't overlook a murder on the station where I'm in command.''

"And Wallace just admitted that the Yang case isn't related to his investigation," Garibaldi added with a certain tone of satisfaction. "So I guess it's up to us to find the killer.''

"And I *won't* tolerate an attack on one of my officers," Sheridan went on, his course firmly set. "That's another fact. Now, first thing is to bring in this witness you were talking to just before it happened. What's his name?" He raised his hand to call security on his link, but lowered it when Garibaldi said, "I don't know."

"Don't know his name?"

Garibaldi shook his head, carefully this time. "The way it was set up, he wouldn't talk if I knew his identity. He didn't have that much to say, anyway."

"So how'd you contact him?"

"Through . . . other contacts. Look, Captain, I'm not sure I want to say who it was. These people talked to me because I promised confidentiality. And they know they can trust me. What am I supposed to do—break my promise? Turn them in?"

"What else do you think they did? They turned you in, Garibaldi! They set you up, they turned you over to . . . whoever it was! You could have been killed. These are the people you want to protect?"

"Yeah, it sounds crazy, doesn't it?" Garibaldi closed his eyes and let his head drop forward. The headache was getting worse again now. And the trouble was, he did want to protect them. Nick, and the others who'd trusted him enough to spill their guts. It was part of being what he was—you stood up for your sources, you didn't give them away. "Look, I'd just rather . . . do this my way. It's my job, after all."

But Sheridan was unmoved. "Your way just almost got you killed. And you're still not fit for duty. No, Garibaldi, this time, things are going to be done my way."

CHAPTER 19

On approach to the docking bay, Escort Wing Alpha pulled back to let the transport enter first, then docked themselves. Ivanova cracked her canopy and climbed out with stiff, cramped legs after hours in the cockpit. She nodded cheerfully to the docking crew and headed to the ready room to take off her flight suit. But first she linked-in to Sheridan.

"Captain, this is Ivanova. We're back, escort mission a success. Transport *Kobold* safely delivered, no casualties or damage, one raider flamed. Would you like me to report for debrief right away?"

"Can we put that off for a while, Ivanova? We have a situation here. There was an attack on Garibaldi—he's all right, he's resting in Medlab. But there are some security-related matters I want to take care of first."

"He's all right? Can I see him?" she asked, alarmed.

"Dr. Franklin says not to worry. But he's tired now. He got kind of banged up. It might be better to let him rest."

Now what was going on? Ivanova wondered. Who had attacked Garibaldi? At least he was going to be all right.

As she went to her own quarters to change, it occurred to her that there was time, then, to meet with the *Kobold*'s pilot. She was curious to know what he had to say.

His name was Pal, a thin, dark man, and he insisted on buying her a late dinner, which Ivanova didn't refuse, as the confrontation with the raiders had restored the edge to her appetite.

"You have no idea, Commander," he said, leading the way to a table in the open-air restaurant, "no idea what a relief it was to come out of the jump gate and find you there waiting for us. Though there were a few seconds— before you identified yourself—that I thought your ships might be the raiders themselves.''

"You were expecting an attack, then?''

"Gods, yes! we were expecting an attack. I'll tell you —things have been so bad lately, the Transport Pilots Union has been threatening an action. Ground all transports until Earthforce starts to do their job and give us some escort through raider territory.'' He frowned, cleared his throat, then said nothing as the waiter came up to bring them plates of pancakes rolled around a mixture of chopped vegetables and spices. Pal poured a generous amount of hot sauce over his, bringing the dish to near the combustion point. Ivanova, familiar with the sauce, served herself a much smaller amount.

After the waiter had left, Pal lowered his voice. "The thing is . . . I'm on the union's Central Committee. And so I happen to know that as of the date we left Marsport, Earthforce was still 'studying our demands.' That's why I said I was surprised to see you out there. They keep telling us they don't have the resources to provide the escorts we need. They say they don't have the ships. So that's why I'm curious. What's going on?''

"I see,'' said Ivanova, swallowing a cautious bite of her meal. Hot, but good. "No, there's been no policy change on the Earthforce Command level, I can tell you that. It was Captain Sheridan, here on Babylon 5, who ordered the patrols, just for the territory we cover in Grid Epsilon. And only for certain transports judged to be high risk.''

Pal's eyebrows raised. "And just what do you consider a high-risk transport?''

Ivanova hesitated. How much should she reveal? "We've done a computer analysis of the pattern of recent attacks. Certain routes seem more vulnerable than others.

Certain cargoes that are particularly valuable on the black market. The computer indicates the transports that are most likely to be attacked, based on that analysis, and we send out an escort wing to meet them. So far, at least, it seems to be working.''

Pal leaned closer across the table. ''And does your computer analysis say anything about data leaks, about routing information being sold to the raiders, about the way they know where these valuable cargoes are going to be coming through the jump gates, and when? Come on, Commander, don't tell me about a random computer analysis! We know better! Someone out there is making a profit by selling us out, making a profit off dead ships and crews! Don't tell me Earthforce doesn't know a thing about it!''

Ivanova swallowed. So she wasn't the only one who'd noticed this pattern in the attacks! ''Mr. Pal, I'm only a wing commander at the moment. Earth Central doesn't confide in me at the policy level.'' She paused. ''But, just personally, I think you're right. I'm sure you're right. The raiders have got to be operating on the basis of inside information.''

''Oh, they know about it,'' Pal said darkly. ''Earth Central. They just won't admit it. Not to us. And after a while, you know, you start to ask why.''

''And?''

''Some of us wonder if they maybe have a reason to look the other way.''

Ivanova put down her fork. She *wasn't* the only one to suspect it! ''Mr. Pal,'' she asked carefully, ''do you have any proof for this accusation? Any evidence?''

But Pal shook his head. ''Not . . . directly. No. But we've made complaints. Many complaints to Earthforce. Nothing is done. Nothing is ever done! So I think—one or two officers, highly placed, in a position to derail an investigation, put questions on hold, file complaints where they won't be found?

"And there's another thing," Pal went on. "Some of us have started to wonder about those cargoes. The ones the raiders have targeted? The ones so valuable on the black market, as you say?"

She nodded. "Strategic metals, primarily, these days. What you were carrying—iridium, morbidium—"

"If that's what we really are carrying. Some of us would like to go back in our holds, crack open those crates, see what's really inside. Is it strategic metals—or slag?"

"Slag?"

"Worthless mass." Pal was using his fork now to punctuate his remarks. Ivanova had forgotten about hers, about her meal. "Think about it, Commander. How much is an ingot of iridium worth? A whole crate of ingots? A ship's hold full of them? What insurance value would you place on a cargo like that?"

"I believe the value is determined by Earth Central, isn't it? The price of strategic metals is restricted."

"Exactly!" Pal exclaimed, stabbing the table. "And if you have this commodity to sell at the official price, and the price on the black market keeps going higher and higher, what do you do? How can you make a greater profit?"

"So they sell to the black market? They bribe Earthforce officials to overlook certain shipments? But what does this have to do with the raids?" she asked, intrigued but confused.

"This is what we think," he said, leaning closer across the table. "For each cargo, there are two ships. One with the real cargo. The other with slag. They pay the raiders to take the false shipment. The real one, they ship to the black market. They get the higher price for the metal, and, for the false cargo, they collect the insured value.

"Simple, isn't it?"

Ivanova, who had already suspected much of this herself, was speechless for a moment. "What does your insurance company think about this?" she wondered finally.

"They also have their suspicions. I've been in contact with the insurance agent here on Babylon 5. We've discussed possible measures to confirm what we suspect." He frowned. "I'm telling you this in confidence, Commander."

"You have my word."

"When we reach our destination, we intend to have the crates unsealed, the contents checked before we deliver it. The insurance agent is trying to arrange for this now. If you like, I'll let you know what we find."

"I would appreciate that," Ivanova said eagerly. "I'd really like, personally, to get to the bottom of all this."

Pal's expression went grim. "Well, I warn you, Commander, the union won't stand for it much longer! Our people are dying out here—ships and crews are being sold out to satisfy the greed of rapacious corporations and corrupt officials! We're not powerless, Commander Ivanova. They're making a mistake if they think they can get away with this!"

By this time, Pal had raised his voice, and half the tables were looking in their direction. Ivanova quickly stabbed her fork into a slice of pancake in an attempt to pretend the conversation was of no particular importance. But her hand froze as she lifted it. There in the restaurant doorway, glaring at her, was Lieutenant Miyoshi.

"Uh-oh," murmured Ivanova. "There's trouble."

But it was too late now to pretend nothing was going on.

In a spirit of defiance, she turned back to her dinner companion. "I think I'll have some more of that hot sauce, Mr. Pal."

Because things were certainly getting hot enough around here lately.

An hour or so later, after meeting with the captain, Ivanova came into Garibaldi's room in Medlab to find him seated on the edge of his bed, contemplating the floor. "I thought you were supposed to be resting."

"So I rested. I feel fine now. Time to get back on my feet."

She looked him over. "You don't look so fine. What's that on your head?"

His hand went to the place. "This? Oh, that's nothing, it looks worse than it is. I just hit my head when I fell."

"When they zapped you with a shock stick."

"I guess you've been talking to someone."

She nodded. "The captain."

"What else did he tell you?"

"Not too much. Somebody grabbed you, stuffed you in a locker. Made it look like the way we found Ortega. He thinks it's a warning not to go around asking questions. Thinks it was a terrorist group. Only . . ."

He heard the hesitation in her voice. "What?"

"Well, I found out something today. If it's true. I still don't know what to think. But I just had dinner a while ago with the pilot of that transport we brought in this evening. His name is Pal, he's some kind of official with the Transport Pilots Union. They're suspicious of the raider activity, too. *And* a cover-up. But . . . they think it's some kind of major fraud on the part of the mining corporations. That certain transports are set up with a fake cargo, something that has mass but no real value. Then they file a false insurance claim and sell the real cargo on the black market. Garibaldi, if he's right, the profits could be in the millions! More than I ever thought.''

''He has proof of this?''

She shook her head. ''That's the problem, he says they don't. But they're going to try to get it. Crack open the cargo crates and see what's really in there.''

''Isn't that illegal?''

''I think they're trying to arrange something with their insurance company. Anyway, I got the impression they don't much care by now. All the raids, all the losses they've taken, no one doing anything about it.''

Garibaldi sank back onto the bed. He rubbed his head. ''They're going to open up the crates? But wait a minute. That doesn't make sense. They couldn't count on every raid being successful, could they? So what happens when these fake cargoes get to where they're going? What happens when the buyers open the crates and find junk? Wouldn't that expose the whole scheme?''

Ivanova's expression sobered. She hadn't considered that. But . . . ''Unless the buyers were in on it?''

''Maybe,'' Garibaldi admitted.

''But the main thing is, they suspect the same thing we do. Someone is selling out those transports. And somebody from Earth Alliance is covering it up.''

''Yeah,'' Garibaldi agreed, ''but it still doesn't tie in the rest of it: Ortega, Wallace, Yang.''

''Yang?''

''The other guy who was killed, remember? I told you about him. We found his foot in the recycling system?''

He briefly explained the recent confrontation with Wallace and his discussion with Sheridan afterward. ''He thinks the whole thing sounds crazy. You've got to admit, a conspiracy going all the way up to the Joint Chiefs?''

But Ivanova had seized on one fact. ''Wait a minute! If this Yang worked for the mines—so did J. D.! He was a mining engineer, I think. So, you see, there *is* a connection!''

"Maybe," Garibaldi admitted slowly. "I don't know. My source wasn't what you'd call real reliable. But there's one more thing."

"What?" Ivanova demanded when he didn't say anything.

"Wallace made a mistake," Garibaldi said slowly. "He was caught by surprise when the captain mentioned Yang's name, and he said he'd never heard of him. And he was lying. I'll stake my career on it, he's lying. But the thing is, he denied there was any connection between Yang and Ortega, between the two cases. We've got orders from high up in Earth Central not to interfere with the Ortega case. But Babylon 5 security is free to track down whatever we can find out about Yang."

Garibaldi started to get to his feet, but Ivanova put out her hand to stop him. "What do you think you're doing?"

"They hid my uniform somewhere around here."

"You're not leaving here?"

"No! I just want something in one of the pockets."

Ivanova told him to stay put and searched out the uniform herself. "All right," she said, handing it to him, "what is it?"

"This," he said, pulling out the holo card with Yang's picture. "I meant to ask you before if you could identify this guy."

She activated the viewer and gasped suddenly as Yang's holographic image coalesced. He was a man with Oriental features, middle-aged, with a heavyset face and dark eyebrows. "That's him! That's the man in the ready room! He brushed right past me as he came out of the head!"

"Where he'd just left Ortega's body," Garibaldi said,

nodding. "This is it. This is the guy who killed him. Now we know for sure."

Ivanova snapped the image off, shuddering. "If I could only just *remember*," she said in a whisper. "If I only knew what J. D. was trying to tell me. Then we'd know."

"But we don't. We don't know for sure. Not yet." Garibaldi's face was set into lines of grim determination. "But I'm going to find out."

CHAPTER 20

"Commander Ivanova!"

She looked around to see who was calling her. It was the next morning, she was just crossing the Zocalo, and the first thought she had was a recollection of Garibaldi's warning. But she dismissed the thought of assassins attacking her in the middle of the most public place on the station.

And the person approaching was an unlikely assassin, wearing a business suit, a young woman with severely cut black hair, with the look of the up-and-coming junior corporation soldier, putting in her time in space to earn a transfer to the seats of power on Earth. "Commander Ivanova?" she asked again.

"Yes, what can I do for you?"

"I'm Luz Espada, agent for Universal Underwriters here on Babylon 5. Could I speak with you about an important matter? I think Mr. Pal has already mentioned it to you. Perhaps if I could buy you a cup of coffee?"

Even without the offer of coffee, Ivanova would have agreed at once. Espada got them a secluded table in a small, expensive cafe.

"Commander," she got right to the point, "I spoke last night with Mr. Pal, and he suggests you might be able to confirm some suspicions which have come up lately concerning the raids on shipping. That there may have been insurance fraud on a very large scale."

"That's possible, yes," Ivanova admitted cautiously. "You understand, though, anything I say is unofficial, unconfirmed by Earthforce. In fact, they might even deny it."

"Which makes the whole situation rather more complicated, yes," Espada agreed. "But anything you can contribute would be appreciated."

Briefly, Ivanova outlined the data search that had led her to conclude that information on shipping routes was being sold or transmitted to the raiders. "It wasn't really very hard to dig this out, once I started asking the right questions," she concluded. "That's when I started to wonder if there was any official involvement, someone in Earthforce in on the deal, helping cover it up."

"Yes," Espada nodded, "that's essentially the same conclusion we're starting to reach."

Ivanova frowned, confused about something. "If I'm right, the pattern I found shows that this has been going on for at least a year. Would it take the insurance companies so long to start to notice a pattern of fraud? I thought your industry was on the watch for this kind of thing."

"Well, of course we are. But as a matter of fact, the *Kobold*'s cargo would have only been the third such loss for Universal within the last year. Two losses would have been consistent with the general level of raider activity lately. I don't believe there was an investigation. Or, if there was, it was inconclusive. Three times, though. That starts to look like a pattern."

"You only insured the cargo? Not the ship itself?"

"That's correct."

"Is that usual? To have the ship insured by one company and the cargo by another?"

"Oh, very common." She tapped her wrist link, a design very similar to the Earthforce model. "Computer, do we have the data on the *Kobold*?"

"The cargo transport vessel *Kobold*, 1,500 tonnes, is owned by Instell Shipping, Inc., a subsidiary of Aegean Enterprises. It is insured by the TransGalactic Assurance Corporation."

"And who shipped the cargo?" Ivanova asked tensely.

Espada queried her computer and got the answer, "Property of AreTech Consolidated Mines."

"Is that a Mars corporation?" Ivanova asked.

"Their operations are all on Mars," Espada told her. "The company headquarters is on Earth."

"What about the other two raider losses you mentioned? Did their cargoes both include morbidium? Were they shipped from AreTech, too?"

Espada looked at her. "As a matter of fact, they were."

"But Universal doesn't insure all AreTech's cargoes, does it?"

"No, I don't believe so." Espada pulled out a portable data screen from her case and plugged it into her link. Figures scrolled onto the display. "No," she said slowly, "it seems that AreTech deals with a number of different companies."

"Is that . . . usual, too?"

"It's not unusual, no," Espada said. "In cases of cargoes so valuable, and vulnerable, a company might ask several insurance carriers to bid on the coverage of each shipment, to minimize costs. Also, from our side, it tends to minimize the risks, spread them out."

Ivanova had a strong sense that she was onto something, that any moment now it was going to break through—the key to the whole situation. "Then no single insurance company would be likely to notice a suspicious pattern of losses?"

"Not unless they compared figures," Espada agreed. "And industry policy is to keep that information confidential. To keep the other companies from undercutting our bids."

"So a company like AreTech Mines would know about this policy?"

"I'm sure they would be aware of it, yes."

"Ms. Espada, what Mr. Pal spoke to me about involved a rather . . . far-reaching conspiracy, if it's true. He mentioned selling strategic metals on the black market. How much money might be involved in that? An amount large enough to bribe Earthforce officers?"

"Commander, the current official price of a single ingot of morbidium is twelve hundred credits. On the black market, you could probably get six times that price today. And we're talking about tons. Shiploads."

"I see," said Ivanova.

Espada's lips compressed with worry. "Commander, unsettled times are very bad for the insurance industry. And lately, things aren't looking very settled at all. There are governments preparing for war. Alien races attacking each other. The demand for strategic materials is likely to be insatiable, and that will keep driving the prices higher. This doesn't look good."

Ivanova was about to agree wholeheartedly, but before she could say so, a voice came over her link: "Commander Ivanova. Security wants you to come to docking bay 18 right away. There's an incident with the crew of a transport, and they've asked for you."

"I'll be right there." Then she asked, "What transport is it? The *Kobold*?"

"That's it, Commander."

"I'm on my way." She stood up quickly. "Excuse me, an emergency."

"Of course," said Espada. As soon as Ivanova had turned to go, Espada returned her attention to her data screen and started to go through the figures again.

Ivanova took the tram down to the docking bay, wondering how serious the disturbance was, if she ought to stop and get riot control gear—a flak jacket, at least, or a weapon. But the security officer in charge, Ensign Torres, told her over her link that it wasn't necessary.

"The situation isn't violent—not yet. But they want you here. The transport's crew asked for you specifically. As an intermediary, I suppose."

She could hear the uproar almost as soon as she reached the docking area, angry voices raised, echoing in the vast spaces where the largest ships were docked. There was a security detail on the scene, she saw when she came closer, but none of them had weapons drawn, which was a good sign. Ivanova was glad to see that Garibaldi hadn't somehow dragged himself out of his bed in Medlab to take charge of the situation. They probably had him sedated.

Torres beckoned her over, looking relieved. "Glad you're here. Do you know what this is all about?"

"No!" She had to shout to be heard over the shouts of the ship's crew, gathered at the cargo hatch in an attitude of repelling boarders, do or die. "What's going on?"

Torres pointed across the bay to the dark, menacing figure of Lieutenant Khatib. "He's got orders from Commander Wallace to search the transport's cargo. But the crew claims we've abducted their pilot and they won't let him into the ship. Khatib orders his own security detail to use force, but the detail won't do it without confirmation from Babylon 5 command. Khatib says it's mutiny. I think he'd shoot the whole squad if he could."

Mutiny? Ivanova thought. "Where's the captain?"

"He's in conference with the Narn ambassador. There's been another incident with the Centauri. They're talking about declaring war or something. The captain's mediating."

"And Garibaldi's in Medlab." *And I'm no longer in the chain of command,* Ivanova added to herself, but Torres certainly understood the situation well enough. "So you're in charge?"

"I'm senior security officer on duty. But *he*—Khatib —won't take my order to leave the docking bay. He wants me to order my team to attack the transport. Of course, I won't do it. And *they*—the transport crew—refuse to disperse. They're armed, Commander, but so far they haven't done anything. And they've been asking for you.''

"Right." Ivanova nodded, grasping the situation in its simplest terms: one more crisis. Fine. She knew how to deal with a crisis. "Who's their speaker?"

"The tall dark guy. Copilot. Name's LeDuc."

"Right." Ivanova said again, advancing past the security line to confront the *Kobold*'s representative. "Mr. LeDuc, I'm Commander Ivanova. You asked for me?"

"Commander! Yes! I'm glad you're here. Mr. Pal said he trusted you. Now they've got him somewhere. What's going on around this station?"

"I'm not sure yet. But I'm trying to find out. What happened to Mr. Pal? Who's got him where?"

"Security! They took him away!"

"Under arrest, you mean?"

LeDuc pointed in Khatib's direction with a look of open hostility. "He comes up to Pal, says he's from security, a special investigator, wants to ask a few questions. Pal says he doesn't have time, we've got a scheduled departure, we're already off schedule, he's already talked to one of the officers on the station, he doesn't have anything more to add.

"*He* says that doesn't matter, his questions are different, and if Pal doesn't cooperate he'll order our departure canceled. Can he do that, Commander?"

Ivanova frowned. "Not on his own authority, no. Not directly, at least."

"That's what Pal told him, told him to flare off. Then this guy says Pal's under arrest, and he grabs him like *this.*" LeDuc demonstrated, bending his own arm back. "Some of the crew was with him, they say, hey, what's going on, but this security guy pulls a weapon and says if they interfere, they're under arrest, too, for obstructing justice.

"So they go back to the ship, I call the security office to protest, they say they'll check on it, but I don't get any answers, just a runaround, you know what I mean, Commander?"

Ivanova nodded.

"So, about an hour later, *he* shows up at the ship with this security detail, and now he says he's going to search the *Kobold*. Well, *I* say he's not going to set one foot on our ship until we get our pilot back, and our clearance for departure, because, I tell you, Commander, you saved our butts out there at the jump gate, and I was glad to see you then, but now I can't wait to get off this station, if you know what I mean."

Ivanova thought she felt the same way, sometimes. This might be one of them.

But LeDuc went on, "So *he* says the ship isn't leaving this docking bay 'til he checks out the cargo, and *I* say he's not coming on board the ship until they release Pal—"

Ivanova figured she had the general picture. "So what we have here is a standoff, right?"

"Right. And we decided to call you in, because Pal said you could be trusted, at least."

"Right."

Ivanova looked across the security cordon at Khatib, who glared back at her. Right. "Look," she told LeDuc, "the officer who arrested Mr. Pal isn't in charge here, the ensign over there is. And she's not going to order our security forces to do anything drastic. There won't be any violence unless you start it."

LeDuc shook his head fervently. "We don't want trouble, Commander, we just want our pilot back and our clearance off this place."

"Fine. I'll see what I can do." Without much hope of

success, she went up to Wallace's aide, who stood with folded arms as close as he could get to the ship's cargo hatch. "This isn't getting anyone anywhere, is it, Lieutenant Khatib?"

Khatib sneered down at her from his superior height. "You have no authority here, Commander Ivanova. You're not in command."

"No, I'm not, but neither are you, Lieutenant. Ensign Torres is the officer in command here, and I know she's not going to order Babylon 5 security to use force in a situation like this. So it seems to me that it's time to negotiate, and the crew of the *Kobold* have asked me to speak on their behalf. They want to know where their pilot is and they want him back with all his working parts in order, if you know what I mean."

"The pilot will be released when Commander Wallace is finished with him. And *after* I've searched this ship. I have my orders, and they don't include negotiation."

"And just what kind of questions does the good commander have for Mr. Pal, anyway?"

"The subject of our investigation is confidential," Khatib sneered.

Ivanova wished Captain Sheridan were there. Only Sheridan outranked Wallace, and even so she wasn't sure he had the authority to order him to release his reluctant witness. She walked over to speak to Torres again. "I'm going to try something. But first I need to know, has the *Kobold*'s clearance for departure actually been canceled?" It rankled to have to go through the ensign for the information that should have been hers with a single query through her link, but Ivanova was determined to play this by the book as long as Khatib was watching her.

"I'll check, Commander," Torres replied, and opened her link. "No, they're still set for departure, as far as C&C is concerned."

Ivanova nodded. Good. She knew C&C would never

revoke the *Kobold*'s clearance on Wallace's orders. It would take someone on the command staff, and the command staff was thin on the ground right at the moment.

She went back to consult with LeDuc. "I have a tactic to propose," she told him. "Now, as you know, your pilot Mr. Pal confided in me about some very sensitive matters. Do you know what I'm talking about?"

Gravely, the copilot acknowledged that he did.

She went on, "Because of what he told me, and because of other incidents that have happened here on Babylon 5, I'm concerned about leaving Mr. Pal in the hands of these particular Earthforce officers. Concerned about his safety."

"I know! That's why we're protesting this!"

"Yes," Ivanova agreed, "but, because of other things Mr. Pal told me, I think he wouldn't object, himself, to having a thorough search made of the cargo. Would he?" LeDuc's eyes widened in comprehension as she went on, "Of course, it would be illegal for anyone else to break open sealed shipping crates, but it's different in the case of a search conducted by the proper authorities, right? In that case, the broken seals would be accounted for."

"I see what you mean," LeDuc said slowly.

"So it's probable that if Mr. Pal were here, he wouldn't actually object to this search."

"Yeah, I see what you mean."

"Now, this is the hard part," Ivanova went on. "If I'm right, then the investigators who are holding Mr. Pal want to examine this cargo very badly. I don't know why, exactly, but I know they're looking for something and they think it might be on this ship. It's a risk, but I'm willing to bet that they want to search the ship even more than they want to keep Mr. Pal for more questioning. The question is—are you willing to take that risk?"

"What do you mean?"

"I mean that I'd like to offer Lieutenant Khatib over

there a deal. If he produces your pilot, free and unharmed, you'll let him and a security detail onto the ship
to search it. Uh, I'm assuming you don't have anything
to hide?''

"No! We've got nothing to hide. This is a straight-up
transport ship, we don't do smuggling deals on the
side.''

"Good, then.''

"But what if he doesn't go for it?''

Ivanova grimaced. "That's the hard part. You take
off.''

"Without the pilot? No! We're not running out on
Pal!''

"Listen,'' Ivanova urged him. "It's a bluff. I *think*
Khatib will give in. If I'm right, they want something on
this ship more than they want Pal. But you've got to
convince them you mean it. You've got to be ready to go
through with it. No backing down, not even at the last
minute, not even at the jump gate. You go through.''

"And what happens if you're wrong, Commander?
What happens then? To Mr. Pal?''

Ivanova took a breath. "All right. Good question. In
the first place, Captain Sheridan isn't available now, but
when he knows what's going on, I'm sure he'll take steps
to make sure Mr. Pal is safe. I guarantee, myself, to make
every effort to see that he is.''

"Can you guarantee it'll work?''

She shook her head. "No. But this is the alternative:
to keep the standoff going, to wait until Captain Sheridan
is finished mediating a dispute between a couple of alien
races, however long that takes, to wait while he tries to
negotiate with Commander Wallace, the officer who's
holding Mr. Pal. It's a matter of time, don't you see? If
we take the risk, we stand a chance of getting Pal out of
there *now*. Not tomorrow, or the day after that.''

''I see what you mean,'' LeDuc said again. ''I got to talk to my crew.''

He stepped back to the hatch, and there was a brief huddled discussion. Then LeDuc nodded to Ivanova. ''Go for it, Commander. I'll go heat up the engines.''

''Right.'' Back to Khatib. ''This is the deal, Lieutenant.''

''My orders don't include deals,'' Khatib said loftily.

''The deal is—you get in to inspect the ship, search the cargo, whatever you have in mind. As soon as the pilot is released.''

Khatib scowled. ''I don't have the authority to agree to that.''

''Then why don't you get on the link to your boss and ask for the authority, Lieutenant? Because this is the rest of the deal. If you don't produce Mr. Pal, unharmed, in twenty minutes, you can forget about searching the cargo because the *Kobold* will be departing Babylon 5, on schedule.''

''You can't do that!''

''I'm not doing anything, Lieutenant, I'm just a speaker for the *Kobold*'s crew. This is their offer.''

''I'll revoke their clearance to depart!''

''No, you won't. You don't have the authority, Lieutenant Khatib. Commander Wallace doesn't have the authority. And I'll just bet that by the time you find somebody who does have the authority, the *Kobold* will already be through the jump gate and gone. So what's it going to be, Lieutenant? Do we negotiate, or do you stand here until that ship takes off?''

''You wouldn't dare.''

Ivanova raised her eyebrows. ''Me? I told you, Lieutenant, I'm just an intermediary here. Lieutenant, I'm not involved. This is the *Kobold* crew's decision.''

''They wouldn't dare. We have their pilot.''

Ivanova's brows lowered. ''That wouldn't be a threat,

would it, Lieutenant Khatib? You wouldn't be planning to harm Mr. Pal?''

Glaring at her, Khatib stepped back and toggled on his link. She could hear him briefly describing the situation to Wallace, and at one point he raised his voice a little: ''I *can't*! I've tried, but C&C won't take my orders! All right, you try it.'' Interested, she tried to hear more, but Khatib had lowered his voice again and all she could catch were snatches: ''Twenty minutes . . . no, she won't take my orders either . . . I can't! . . . dozen people watching . . .''

''Commander Wallace is considering the matter,'' he finally snarled to Ivanova.

Her lips quirked in a half-grin, knowing that Commander Wallace was probably on the comm right now, trying to browbeat C&C into revoking the *Kobold*'s clearance. But she knew Torres had briefed the duty staff on the situation, and she didn't think they'd give in. They weren't eager to take Commander Wallace's orders. He hadn't endeared himself to Babylon 5 personnel during his stay on the station.

Ivanova waited. Torres waited. The security cordon, still alert for trouble, waited. The transport's crew continued their preparations for departure.

Several minutes later there was another heated exchange between Khatib and Wallace over the link. Khatib shut it off and glared again at Ivanova. ''You say they agree to allow the search?''

''After Mr. Pal is safely onboard the ship.'' She added, ''And they want Ensign Torres, as security officer in charge, to be present, to make sure there are no irregularities. And representatives of the crew, since they're legally responsible for the condition of the cargo. And the agent of the company insuring it.''

''Agreed,'' Khatib snapped. He took a step toward the

cargo hatch, but Ivanova held up a hand to stop him. "*After* Mr. Pal is onboard."

"The commander is on his way."

"He'd better hurry," Ivanova remarked casually. "In . . . eleven minutes this bay will have to be cleared for takeoff. I don't think you want to be standing here waiting for him after the blast doors are sealed shut."

Khatib made an inarticulate sound of rage in the back of his throat. Ivanova grinned smugly back at him. Enjoying this.

But a few minutes later they could see Wallace approaching, accompanied by a security man and a smaller figure between them whose walk was slightly unsteady. Ivanova stepped up to take him from them and saw that Pal's expression was somewhat glazed, his pupils wider than they should have been. *Drugs,* she thought. Drugs and a telepath. They weren't leaving anything to chance, were they?

Wallace recognized her, drew back, made a gesture as if he were about to drag Pal back, but there were clearly too many people watching for him to pull out of the deal now. "Commander," he said coldly, "I didn't know you were involved in this. But I should have realized."

Ivanova smiled at him politely. "I'm simply here to speak for the *Kobold*'s crew. At their request. They were concerned about Mr. Pal." She grasped the pilot's hand reassuringly and led him toward the crew hatch, where his copilot was waiting.

"Are you all right?" she whispered urgently.

"Fine," he said, "but I talked, I told them things. They . . . gave me something."

"It's all right," she said, hoping it was. "I think he'll be fine once he sleeps it off," she told LeDuc, "but he's in no condition to be on the bridge."

Wallace and Khatib had been consulting. "Now I suppose there will be no objection to our searching the hold?'' Khatib asked.

''No objection,'' Ivanova agreed. ''Ensign Torres, you'll be an official observer? And the crew representatives?'' She had already called Espada, who was on her way down.

''Our purser, Mr. Kim. And Commander Ivanova.''

''She's not a member of your crew!'' Wallace objected.

''She's still our representative,'' LeDuc insisted. ''And I will be present as well.''

But Wallace didn't seem to care who else was in the hold as long as he got in to search it. Khatib, picking up a bag of equipment, followed him as the ship's purser solemnly unsealed the door of the hold.

Ivanova's first reaction on stepping into the space was —*How are they going to check out all this!* Hundreds of sealed cargo containers filled the hold. Cargo was usually shipped in containers—crates or canisters or drums—for ease of loading and unloading, for load stability. And for reasons of security, since most goods sent through space were valuable, most containers were sealed. But Wallace and Khatib seemed to know what they were doing. With their instruments, they scanned the crates, one by one, followed by the attentive purser, Mr. Kim, with his notebook listing each container's contents, owner, port of origin, and other pertinent data. Espada, at his side, compared her own records to his. Ivanova, Torres, and LeDuc trailed after them, as if they fully understood what was going on.

Wallace stopped, pointed to a particular crate, and said, ''This one.''

Kim stepped up and cracked the seal, making a note in his records. As Wallace and Khatib inspected the contents, Ivanova looked over her shoulder at Espada's display. *Container # 7794. Contents: morbidium ingots, approx 96% pure; property of AreTech Consolidated Mines; port of origin, Marsport . . .*

She exchanged glances with LeDuc, who held a whispered consultation with Kim. What did an ingot of pure morbidium look like, anyway? she wondered. How could you distinguish it from an ingot of, say, tin or iron?

Kim made more notes. Wallace and Khatib continued their search, looking dissatisfied. It took quite a while. It took a very long while. The cargo crew eventually had to be summoned with equipment to shift the crates. For each one they opened, Kim the purser made his own inspection, and another note in his records. LeDuc had a consultation with his bridge crew, relaying a query from Babylon 5 C&C. No, he didn't have any idea how long this would take, departure would have to be delayed indefinitely.

When he was done with the hold, Wallace insisted on searching the rest of the ship, including the bridge and crew quarters. But it was finally done, and Wallace, looking as if he'd just swallowed something bad, retreated from the *Kobold,* followed by an equally dissatisfied Khatib.

"Whatever it was, I don't think they found it," Torres remarked, sighing.

"No," Ivanova agreed thoughtfully. Whatever it was. But she had a good idea. Something that might have been passed on from J. D. Ortega, to her, to the transport pilot. Something Wallace had been terrorizing the station's population trying to find.

But it was LeDuc who looked the most relieved. "Now we can get out of this place! Not to accuse you of inhospitality, Commander. But I want the first slot for departure *off* Babylon 5!"

"I understand. But what about the cargo? Is it genuine?"

Kim looked up from his notebook. "Morbidium. Every crate they opened contained morbidium. Between ninety-four and ninety-eight percent pure metal. Every ingot I checked.''

"Well," said Ivanova, slightly disappointed. "So much for that theory."

"Apparently so," Espada agreed. "I still want to thank you, Commander. Your insights have been very helpful."

"Then you'll continue to investigate?"

"Oh, yes."

"Tell Mr. Pal that I'm sorry for all his trouble," Ivanova said to LeDuc.

"I will. And thank you, Commander Ivanova. You got him out of there."

But not in time, Ivanova thought to herself as she left the ship with Espada. Whatever Pal knew, everything she'd told him—Wallace probably knew it all now.

Occupied with her thoughts, Ivanova heard a familiar voice call her name as she left the *Kobold*'s docking bay. She looked up. There was Captain Sheridan on the deck, in consultation with Ensign Torres.

She went over to them. "The ensign tells me that this situation is under control now. I'm glad to hear it," Sheridan said. "I understand you were of some assistance in the negotiations."

"I was just a speaker on behalf of the transport's crew," Ivanova said again. "It wasn't much trouble. Really."

CHAPTER 21

"So now we know," Ivanova admitted, setting down her tray on the table in the mess hall. "Damn, I was *so* sure that Pal had to be right! The insurance fraud scheme and everything! But the morbidium cargoes aren't fake, after all."

She went on glumly, "And now Wallace has pumped Pal full of drugs and found out about the whole thing."

"Except that what he found out is wrong," Garibaldi added.

"Some comfort." Ivanova looked at her breakfast with distaste. "And the captain is still convinced that whoever knocked you on the head was involved with the Free Mars movement?"

"Yeah." Garibaldi gingerly touched the healing contusion on his forehead. "What do you think"—he grinned—"does it give me that romantic, wounded look?"

"It'd help if you lost your appetite and went all pale and thin instead," she replied with a pointed look at the amount on his tray, rapidly being diminished.

"Forget it, then," Garibaldi said firmly. "I'm probably not the type, anyway."

Ivanova finished her own meal, looked up to see him assessing what was left, rolled her eyes. He was the incorrigible type, is what he was.

"Going back out on patrol?" he asked.

"Right." She sighed. "I know this raider thing was my idea, but if things ever get back to normal around here, you won't hear me complaining about lack of flight time for a while."

"It's good for you," he remarked. "Keeps your reflexes sharp. People won't sneak up on you, zap you with a shock stick. Especially not while you're off somewhere in space."

"I'll remember that," she said dryly. And left Garibaldi the tray.

He pulled it over to him, but once Ivanova had left the mess hall he showed no real interest in the fruit or biscuits she hadn't eaten. In fact, he pushed his own tray away. It was hard, he thought, having to live up to your image all the time, what people expected of you.

There across the room, at a table by herself, was Talia Winters sitting over a cup of some synthetic coffee-substitute. She looked thin. She ought to eat more, but he didn't know how to approach her to tell her so. Which was really dumb, he told himself, because she was a telepath, she'd *know* how he felt. Still, he didn't trust himself not to say some stupid thing.

Besides, he decided, abruptly getting to his feet, he had work to do. See what kind of a mess had piled up in the security office while he was flat on his back over in Medlab.

There was, as he'd suspected, a backlog of messages, memos, and reports waiting for him. Garibaldi sighed, sat down in front of the display, and called up the first ones. A few moments later his eyes met a familiar name on a list of persons detained within the last twenty-four hours. "Hey! What's Nick Patinos doing in the lockup?"

The computer obligingly replied, "Nick Patinos is being held for questioning."

"On whose orders, dammit?"

"The detention was ordered by Captain Sheridan."

He called over to the clerk on duty at the lockup, "Kennealy, what do you know about these arrests?"

The clerk looked up from his own display. "The captain ordered them. He said he was personally taking over the case while you were in Medlab.''

''What case?'' Garibaldi demanded, exasperated. Who did Sheridan think he was, taking over his job? Maybe he'd like it on a permanent basis?

But to Kennealy it was self-evident. ''Your case, Chief. The case of whoever zapped you with that shock stick. Assault on a station officer. The captain was really flamed about it, that's for sure.''

''I see.'' Garibaldi went back to sit at his console and try to think this through. The thing was, he'd meant what he'd told Sheridan about confidentiality. His sources. It was a basic thing, underlying all his work in security, all throughout his career. If your source couldn't trust you —trust you to go to the wall before you'd say a word to implicate him, to break his cover—then you didn't deserve his trust. It was that simple. He'd done a lot of things he wasn't proud of, but that wasn't one of them. He'd never given up the name of a contact.

And Nick—he'd gone back a long way with Nick Patinos. Would even call the man a friend, an old friend. Now what was Nick going to think of him? How could he ever ask Nick to trust him again?

And where had Sheridan gotten Nick's name from, anyway?

Kennealy didn't know. He'd just processed the order, then the record when the man was brought in. That was all. Why, was there a problem?

''No,'' Garibaldi said curtly.

Yes.

He was halfway ready to call up Sheridan and ask him what the hell he thought he was doing, detaining his contacts, violating their confidentiality, breaking his *word,* dammit. But he hesitated, because Sheridan wasn't his old friend Jeff Sinclair, and it might mean his job.

Sheridan was a different type of commander. Garibaldi remembered what the captain had said back in Medlab yesterday, that he wasn't going to tolerate assaults on his station's officers. It meant something to Sheridan—his officers, his people. Slowly, Garibaldi thought about the last time he'd been hospitalized, only then he was in a coma, dying—or so Doc had told him, later. And Sheridan had been the one who'd saved his life, donating his life-force to a man he'd never met but who was one of his officers. Sheridan had done that, the very first day he set foot on the station.

It was a somewhat subdued head of security who finally called up his commanding officer. "Captain, there are some names on the detention list that I didn't authorize. These are sources of mine. I promised to protect their identities."

Sheridan's expression on the screen was firm. "We had this discussion already, Mr. Garibaldi. I respect your position, but I want you to appreciate mine. I have reason to believe these individuals had knowledge of, or possibly participated in, a wanton assault on my head of security. I can't, I won't tolerate it. Now, if you don't want to conduct the investigation in this case, I can assign it to someone else. But I'm going to find these people, Garibaldi, and this station is going to see that they can't get away with this kind of act."

"Yes, sir, I do appreciate your position. I'd just like to know this, though—where did you get the names? How did you find these people? I didn't . . . in Medlab, with the drugs, I didn't say anything, did I?"

Sheridan paused, and a look of understanding crossed his face. "I see. No, you didn't give anything away. I asked some of your officers. I had them go through your files. Quite a few names surfaced, and we ran them through a computer analysis. And, Chief, I'm not charging them with anything, not yet. For the moment, they're just being held for questioning."

"I see." *Which one of my officers?* Garibaldi wondered. *Torres?*

"Will you be wanting me to assign this to someone else?" Sheridan asked. "It might be better, considering your involvement."

Garibaldi shook his head firmly. There was no more pain. "No, sir. I'll take care of it myself."

"That's your call."

"It's my job."

Garibaldi stared for a while at the blank screen. It occurred to him that maybe the captain was right and he was wrong. That if he'd been set up—but, hell, of course he'd been set up! Who else could have done it? He'd been asking people to trust him, but didn't that have to go both ways? Who'd betrayed whom?

He finally pulled the witness files from the computer and started to go through them all, one by one.

Nick Patinos gave a short, bitter laugh on seeing who'd just come into the lockup. "Well, Mike. I wondered when you'd be showing up. Hey, if you'd wanted to talk, you could have sent an invitation. Or, hell, I'd have invited you to my place."

"And how many guys with shock sticks waiting for me when I got there, Nick?"

Nick looked down, muttered, "You weren't supposed to get hurt. It was a warning. That's all."

Garibaldi said heatedly, "So you were in on it! You set me up!"

"I didn't—"

"*Dammit,* Nick! I thought you . . . I didn't think you'd—"

"*I didn't know!*" Nick shouted. Then, looking away from Garibaldi again, "I mean, I didn't know what was going to happen, what they were going to do." He looked up again to meet Garibaldi's accusing eyes. "I told them. I said, you weren't a part of it, you weren't working with those other bastards. But Earthforce is Earthforce, Mike. That's what it comes down to, doesn't it? And you're Earthforce." He shook his head. "I told them, I didn't want to know about it, whatever they were going to do. Just to make sure you weren't hurt. And that's what they said, it was just to warn you off."

Nick clenched his fist, then brought it down on the table between them. "You couldn't just let it go! You had to keep coming around, coming back, asking more questions. Dammit, Mike, I tried to warn you, I told you what was going on. But you had to keep coming back!"

But Garibaldi's anger was equal to Nick's. "Yeah, I had to keep coming back! That's my job! There's been at least two people murdered on the station and a lot of transport crews murdered out in space, there's a good officer with her career ruined, there's God-knows-what kind of conspiracies and collusions maybe all the way up to Earth Central. So, what, I'm supposed to forget about all this just because my good buddy Nick says people don't feel like talking about it? I'm in charge of security around here. I have responsibilities! I can't just forget about things like that."

"No matter who it hurts?"

"You think people aren't being hurt now? You really believe these guys when they tell you nobody'll get hurt? Nick, I thought you had better sense than that!"

For a few moments they just stared at each other, the atmosphere between them heated by high emotions. Nick was the first to lower his eyes. Finally he said, "Look, Mike, I don't know about the rest of it, but I am sorry it had to be you." A shorter pause. "I hope it wasn't . . . you know . . ."

"I've had better experiences." Garibaldi struggled with himself—the friend versus the security officer. "Oh, I guess I'll live."

"For what it's worth," Nick's voice was earnest, "I really didn't know what they were going to do. I just hope you can believe that."

Garibaldi said nothing. He wasn't sure if he could or not. Maybe it'd take time.

He took a breath. "The thing is, Nick, I'm going to have to have their names."

Nick drew back, stiffened, and the friend became the prisoner, the man on the other side of the divide. "Nothing doing, Mike."

Garibaldi hadn't supposed he would say anything else. Still, he had to ask. "All right, then, Nick. But I can't let you go, at least not until this thing is over. Understand— it wasn't just me who was assaulted, Mike Garibaldi—it was the head of Babylon 5 security."

"I guess you've got to do your job," Nick said coldly.

"That's right. I do." Garibaldi turned to leave, then stopped. "I want you to know one thing, though. It wasn't my order to have you brought in. It wasn't me they got the names from. That's all I ask you to believe."

But his old friend Nick said nothing in reply, only turned his back.

The guy from the machine shop was named Williams, Val Williams.

Garibaldi had dug out the name himself, the way he'd question any witness—going through the computer, having it sort through the files for men of the approximate physical description of the man he'd met with in the machine shop. It hadn't even taken very long, less than an hour, until he recognized the guy's face out of the hundreds of faces the computer pulled up and displayed. He noted that Williams didn't work in the machine shop, after all.

Garibaldi figured it was better this way. He hadn't wanted to have to resort to forcing the name from Nick or anyone else who'd trusted him, once. Not unless he had to.

Yeah, it was better this way.

He closed down the computer search without flagging Williams's file, then sent out a team of security agents to bring the suspect in. But the man's assigned quarters were empty, and he hadn't been seen at his job since the meeting in the machine shop. Garibaldi wasn't surprised. He sent out an alert to check departing ships and went through the passenger lists of ships that had already left since the attack. Nothing. So, if he was lucky, Williams was probably still hiding on the station somewhere.

By this time, Ensign Torres had come on duty again. "It's good to see you back, Chief," she told Garibaldi, a bit uncertain in her manner.

"You did good, Torres," he reassured her. "You used your best judgment under the circumstances." He grinned. "You were probably even right."

She still seemed uncomfortable. "About those names. Of your contacts. Captain Sheridan ordered me to track them down."

"I understand." Garibaldi didn't blame Torres. He didn't even really blame Sheridan. They were only doing their jobs. Neither of them had made a promise to the men they'd brought in, and no one had breached a confidence.

It was true, his contacts would probably never believe it. Never trust him again. Nick Patinos, maybe—he might. One of these days. But at least Garibaldi knew he hadn't broken his word.

But it was done now, and Torres had done a good job getting all those names. He told her so, adding, "I hear you did great handling that incident down in the cargo bay, too. It could have turned into a riot."

"It was Commander Ivanova who settled it," she said, deprecating her own efforts.

"But you were in command," he insisted. "I'm going to make sure it goes into your file."

"Thanks, Chief," she said. "Um, what about my report? On Yang? Did you get a chance to read it?"

"Damn!" Garibaldi almost slapped his forehead, caught himself in time. With everything that had happened, he'd forgotten all about it. "Sorry, I was interrupted by a shock stick and it completely slipped my mind. So what did you find out?"

She shook her head. "Well, I checked with all the merchants, all the import-export agents. None of them had seen him. His credit record—nothing. Almost no transactions. He paid for his quarters, had his meals there. Whatever the man was doing on Babylon 5, he didn't leave a trail."

Garibaldi nodded. "Which tells us what we thought all along. This guy was no import-export merchant. If he was here on business, it was the kind of business he didn't want anyone to know about."

"The only thing I did find out is, he's not from Earth. We ran a routine identification request to try to find a next-of-kin, and they couldn't find a record of any Earth resident matching the ID we have for Yang."

"That helps, Torres, that helps a lot. Good work."

"So now what do we do?" Torres asked, more confidently now.

"I'm going to check out our Mr. Yang with Earthdome on Mars," he told her. "As for you, how'd you like to go track down Val Williams? Here's all the stuff we have on him. According to the records, he hasn't left Babylon 5."

"But according to Yang's records, he'd already left the station, when he was here, dead. I mean, we can't really trust the records, can we?"

"You're right," he agreed, adding to himself, *And who had access to the records, who could have changed them?* "So let's not count on them, but let's assume he's still here. Make sure everyone in Security sees Williams's picture, that they can identify him by sight, *not* just to rely on the ID scanner, that he might have a counterfeit identicard. Check all outbound passenger ships—and transports. You know what to do."

"Right, Chief. And thanks." She left, confident and eager to be on the hunt. Garibaldi envied her enthusiasm. But that was youth. He used to have that, too. When he was Torres's age. It was unsettling to realize the size of the gap that lay between his age and Torres. She was young enough to be his daughter—if he'd ever had one.

Dismissing *that* unwelcome thought, he got back to work, calling up a communications channel to Mars and contacting Earthdome to put in a request for all information on a Yang, Fengshi, known to have arrived from Marsport on the *Asimov* on 04/18/59. He advised them that possibly the information given on Yang's ID might be incorrect.

After that, he got down to all the work that had accumulated while he was laid up: the messages, memos, reports, the requests that needed his authorization, all the chicken tracks a bureaucracy ran on.

There was Torres's official report on Yang in the queue, and he read it through, just in case there might be one piece of data in there that might match up with some other piece and amount to a clue. There wasn't. The man had moved on Babylon 5 like a ghost, leaving no tracks to follow him by. Or rather, Garibaldi corrected himself, like a pro. And a pro, almost by definition, is working *for* someone. So who was it? Was he working for someone in Earth Alliance? The AreTech mining company? The Free Mars organization?

The call from Mars came in much sooner than he'd expected, interrupting this well-worn train of speculation. He answered, "Garibaldi here. What do you have for me?"

But the face on the screen didn't belong to a mere data clerk. This was an Earthforce major, security. "I'm sorry, Mr. Garibaldi," she said, "but your request for information has been denied. That file is classified."

"What?" He recalled himself, lowered his voice. "Excuse me, Major, but what do you mean? I'm head of security on Babylon 5, I have an ultraviolet clearance to see classified files."

The major shook her head. "As I said, I'm sorry, but not this file. It's classified ultraviolet eyes-only."

"Well, just whose eyes are we talking about, Major? This isn't just a casual request, you know. I'm conducting a murder investigation here. This Yang character was killed, chopped into little bits, and shoved into the recycling system. Now, I'd say that constitutes need-to-know, wouldn't you?"

The face on the screen looked grave, even concerned. "I don't know about that, Mr. Garibaldi. It sounds like you have a point. But I just can't release this information without authorization."

"Whose authorization? Who ordered this file classified, anyway?"

"I'm afraid that information is classified, too."

Garibaldi controlled himself. He didn't swear out loud. "Well, I'm putting in an official request for access to the files on Yang. Take it as far up as it has to go. This is a murder investigation and it may involve other illicit activity, too."

"I'll make that request, Mr. Garibaldi. Through the official channels. But until I receive authorization, there's nothing else I can do."

Garibaldi thought for a moment. If Ivanova was right, someone in Earthdome, someone most likely in

Earthforce security, was involved in a cover-up. Was this major part of it? Or was she just following orders?

"Can you tell me this: how long has that file been restricted? What's the date on that eyes-only classification? Or is that information restricted, too?"

A slight smile lit her face, and there was a look in her eye that Garibaldi liked. She checked something on a screen out of his sight. "No, that information is not classified, Mr. Garibaldi. The file was restricted as of 22:45 hours, 04/26/59, Earth standard time."

Garibaldi felt his heartbeat quicken. Yes! Yang's file had been restricted less than an hour after Wallace had declared in Medlab that he knew of no connection between that case and Ortega's. Commander Wallace had made one big mistake—and now he was trying to cover it up!

"Can you tell me," he asked the major on Mars, "whether the classification of this file was requested by a Commander Ian Wallace?"

Garibaldi wasn't a telepath, but he could see the major's eyes go to the unseen terminal and open in surprise. "I'm sorry, that information is classified."

Oh, he thought, *but you've given me the answer, anyway.* "That's all right, I understand. You've been very helpful, Major. I want to thank you for your cooperation."

"And good luck with your murder investigation, Mr. Garibaldi."

"You'll transmit that request?"

"Right away."

"Thanks again."

Garibaldi signed off, then leaned back in his chair to consider the implications of what he'd just found out. First, it was true—Wallace had lied about Yang, that he didn't know anything about the case. He'd lied, then immediately acted to cover it up. "That's your second mistake, Wallace," he said softly to himself. "You should have classified that file from the beginning."

So why hadn't he? Because a classified file was like a red flag, telling everyone who saw it that there were secrets inside. Wallace hadn't wanted anyone to know there was a secret about Fengshi Yang. As far as he figured, no one ever had to know Yang existed. But what he hadn't counted on was—someone finding the body.

Just one stroke of bad luck.

It would have certainly stayed a secret, otherwise. For one thing, Yang's secretive ways worked against him. There were only the bare records of his arrival and presence on Babylon 5. He might almost not have existed. Certainly, there was no reason for anyone to notice him missing, to report it to the authorities. Especially if his records said he'd left the station—who would doubt it? Who would suspect that someone would have altered those records?

There were still questions—too damn many questions. Who had Yang been working for? What had he known— or found out—or failed to find out?

Ivanova thought Yang must be an agent of the corrupt officials in Earthdome, but Garibaldi wasn't so sure. Yang had certainly killed Ortega, but who had killed Yang? Wallace was covering up evidence, but whose side was Wallace on? Captain Sheridan refused to believe in a conspiracy that went all the way up to the Joint Chiefs. And what was Garibaldi, as head of security, supposed to do about all this? Hand over his evidence to Wallace? Arrest him, for obstructing justice in the Yang case? What kind of proof did he have, what kind of evidence? Is it evidence when the suspect has the evidence classified?

Garibaldi knew when he was in over his head. Normally, he supposed, the thing to do would be to call Internal Investigations. Maybe, if he had a case. But he didn't have a case. He had part of a body, a file he couldn't access, and a big pile of suspicious circumstances, but that wasn't a case.

Yeah, he could just hear it, the kind of questions *they'd* ask him: "And how do you know Commander Wallace was lying, Mr. Garibaldi? Isn't it possible that he felt you simply weren't entitled to know the details of his investigation? How can you claim you know that the commander ordered Yang's file to be classified? Do you have clearance for that information? Don't you think you're overstepping the bounds of your authority, Mr. Garibaldi? Weren't you given explicit orders not to get involved in the Ortega case, Mr. Garibaldi?"

Yeah, he'd be the one ending up in the lockup, after all that.

So what could he do? Nothing? At least until he could find some proof. Do nothing, while Wallace still didn't have whatever he was looking for and in the meantime there'd been two deaths . . . at least two deaths . . .

Garibaldi tapped his link. "Torres, this is Garibaldi."

"Torres here."

"What's the status with Williams? Any fix on him yet?"

"Negative, we're still searching, but we haven't found anything yet. Um, we have had an encounter with the competition."

"Commander Wallace?"

"His aide, that Lieutenant Khatib."

"Keep looking, Torres," Garibaldi said grimly.

He shut down his console and got to his feet. A few moments later he was in the lockup, confronting Nick Patinos. "Look," he said urgently, "maybe you know something I don't, maybe you have reason to know that Val Williams is safe in hiding on Luna Colony and everything's fine. But security hasn't found him yet, and I'm starting to think about what happened to the last missing person we found on this station. At least, we found a piece of him. That's all that was left. One piece of him.

"So unless you're sure, Nick, unless you're very sure that Williams is safe and sound someplace where neither Wallace nor I can get at him, I strongly suggest you tell me where you think he is. Or the name of someone else who knows. Unless you'd rather see him melted down to sludge in the recycling system and coming back as breakfast in the mess hall. Because if I don't find him, I'm afraid someone else is going to. And if he does, I don't think anyone will ever see him again."

Nick paled. "I can't tell you that, Mike," he said finally, but it was obviously hard.

Garibaldi's jaw tightened. "If that's the way you want it. Your choice. I thought maybe you might have figured out the difference by now between me and that bastard Wallace—"

"Dammit . . ."

"Your choice."

"All right!" Nick held his head in his hands. Then he looked up at Garibaldi. "His real name is Nagy. Josef Nagy. He might try to get off the station using his own ID."

Garibaldi frowned. "What else?"

"That's it, Mike. All I know."

"The truth?"

Eyes met. "The truth."

Garibaldi nodded, toggled on his link. "Torres, this is Garibaldi—" Then he stopped himself, remembering Wallace, the possibility of a bug in communications. This was one name he couldn't afford to leak to the opposition. "I have some information for you. Hold on." He was going to have to run it down to her himself.

He looked at Nick. "You'd better hope we find him first."

CHAPTER 22

"**D**istress call coming in, Commander!"

"Get the coordinates, Alpha Two!" Ivanova ordered Mokena, picking up the call.

The signal came through unevenly. ". . . raiders . . . We're under attack! . . . help! Is anyone out there?"

Ivanova immediately transmitted, "Vessel under attack, this is Earthforce Commander Susan Ivanova. Give me your location."

"Earthforce? Is it Earthforce out there? We need help! Raiders attacking!"

"They must be having communications problems," Ivanova sent to Alpha Two. "Did you get that? Can you get a fix on them?" But what ship was it? They were out here to meet and escort the *Duster,* another ore carrier out of Marsport, but it wasn't scheduled to come through the jump gate for another hour.

To the ship under attack she sent again, "This is Earthforce. We're trying to help you! Transmit your coordinates!"

"I've got it, Alpha Leader! Coordinates Red 477 by 36 by 10."

"Heading to Red 36," she ordered her patrol. "Keep formation. Thrusters on max burn. We've got raiders out there. Be ready to open fire on my orders."

With a surge of power from her engines, Ivanova's Starfury shot forward, changing course for the location of the endangered ship. The ready indicators for her weapons array glowed red. As one, the other fighters in the patrol turned with her, maintaining the formation.

After a moment, she established clear communication with the ship and asked for their ID.

"This is Earth transport *Cyrus Mac,* out of Luna. We've got raiders on our tail! How soon can you get here, Earthforce?"

"We're on our way, *Cyrus Mac*! I estimate eighteen minutes. How many raiders? Can you hold them off? Is your ship crippled? Are you having communications problems?"

"Four . . . no, five of them! They're closing in fast! They're almost in range. Hurry, Earthforce, or we may not make it!"

Ivanova swore under her breath. She wondered if the raiders had made a mistake, pouncing on a ship that had come through the jump gate ahead of the *Duster.* Just how accurate was their information?

Or was this a diversion?

"Alpha Wing, stay alert!" she warned her patrol. "This could be another trick."

But the pilot or communications officer, whoever was transmitting from the *Cyrus Mac,* seemed on the verge of panic now. "They're firing! They're . . . we're hit! Earthforce, we're hit!"

With a firm grip on her fighter's controls, silently cursing the raiders, Ivanova pressed for more power, but the Starfury was already burning at the maximum. Damn! It was going to happen again. She knew it. They were going to be too late again. She *hated* this helplessness, knowing that only a few minutes could make the difference between saving a ship or losing it, and there was no way to get there any sooner.

Alpha Two reported, "Alpha Leader, we've lost communications with the transport."

But she'd already heard the channel go to background static. Damn!

They could only keep going, in the hope there might

be something left to save. In a few more minutes Ivanova picked up the image of the transport on her tactical screen. No raiders. They must have picked up the Starfuries on the way. "I've got the ship," she said. "Alpha Two, check the transport. The rest of you, wide scan, see if you can pick up the raiders."

"No sign of life, Commander," Alpha Two reported. "That ship is dead."

As the patrol came closer, the image of the transport clarified. Ivanova swore again. Wreckage. Crumpled, blasted, twisted metal. No sign of life, no survivors.

"Commander, I've picked up the raiders!" came a transmission from Alpha Six. "Heading 120 by 19."

Automatically, Ivanova started to give the order for pursuit. No, wait. Heading 120 by 19 was away from the jump point. This was another diversion. She was sure of it. Again, she scanned the wreckage of the dead ship. Dead and cold. It radiated no more warmth than the dark, empty space surrounding it. No telling how long it had been drifting here lifeless—days or months or maybe years. But it had been a lot longer than ten minutes.

"No pursuit," she ordered her patrol. "This is Alpha Leader, I repeat, no pursuit. It's another trick. This wreck is cold. We're heading back to the jump point."

After marking the wreck with a beacon for the salvage team, she spun her ship, and the Starfuries reversed direction, re-formed, and followed their commander toward the rendezvous with the *Duster*.

They knew we were going to be here, Ivanova thought to herself. The raiders had their diversion planned in advance, knowing exactly when we'd show up. It sure looked like their information was up-to-date.

Only the deception hadn't worked, and now it was too late for the raiders, for a change. But that was enough to give Ivanova an idea. The raiders weren't the only ones who could set a trap. "Alpha Two," she sent, "this is

Alpha Leader. Proceed to the vicinity of the jump gate with Four and Five and meet up with the *Duster*. Alpha Three and Six, you stay with me."

If this went the way she planned, then the raiders lurking near the jump point, ready to pounce on the *Duster,* would think their deception had worked, that Ivanova had split the patrol and sent half the Starfuries off in pursuit of the attackers of the dead *Cyrus Mac*. She hoped it would make them overconfident. She hoped she was right.

She was using the jump gate itself as a shield, coming around it from the other direction, hoping the residual tachyon emissions would mask the presence of her fighters on the raider's tactical displays. She kept a channel open to Alpha Two, but they maintained radio silence in case the raiders were monitoring their communications lines. So she heard: "I've spotted them, Alpha Two. Raider ships! Must be, nine . . . ten of them!"

"Any sign of the transport yet?"

"Negative, Alpha Two."

"They're coming in! They're attacking!"

Ten of the raider ships against three Starfuries. The odds just barely favored the raiders. But Ivanova was about to change that. She led the rest of Alpha Wing into the fight from around the other side of the jump gate, coming in from the rear of the raiders, trapping the pirates between them. She and the two fighters on her wings each took out one of the raiders before they had time to react to the sudden appearance of another enemy attacking, and now the odds that had prevailed just a few minutes ago were reversed. One-on-one, the Starfuries had the decisive edge.

The dogfight was a fast, furious action. It took quick reflexes and a cool head to be a fighter pilot. Both sides had computer-assisted targeting, but even so, with twelve ships involved in the fight, there was always a chance for one to get flamed by friendly fire.

Several of the raiders spun around and tried to flee the action, but those were shot down almost instantly. The rest, seeing what chance they had, formed up and tried to defend themselves. A couple of them were good, Ivanova noted with that part of her brain that always remained cool and detached in a firefight.

But the rest of her was fully engaged in the combat mode. "On your tail, Four!" she shouted, and the raider ship fired, but Alpha Two took it out before it could take another shot. Alpha Six, on her wing, blasted another raider coming in from above. Space around them was filled with incandescent metallic gases and flying, glowing shards.

Then Ivanova saw two more of the raiders converging on Alpha Two. Alpha Four, his wingman, was engaged with another of the enemy, but Six fired, got in a strike that sent one ship spinning away. Two's weapons were still operational and he got in a shot that finished the raider off. But it was his last. The second raider, coming in on his other side, turned the Starfury into a glowing ball of death only seconds later.

Ivanova saw her wingman's ship explode, saw him die, and rage boiled up in her throat, a scream she couldn't release. She bore down on the raider with her weapons burning hot, fully charged. Six followed after to back her up, but Ivanova sent through clenched teeth, "He's *mine*!"

The raider fled, with nothing but black space ahead of him and Ivanova on his tail like divine vengeance. No matter which way he turned, twisted, ran, he couldn't shake her. The Starfury's thrusters were burning at max, closing the distance, and Ivanova counted down the seconds he had left to live. Her tactical display showed him in range, she locked on the target, fired, and scored a direct hit on the raider's right wing. Superheated plasma fused the discharge tubes, the wing buckled, crumpled, and the ship went spinning crazily, out of control.

"Got him!" Ivanova exulted in a fierce whisper, diving after her prey, heading in for the kill.

She had him in her sights again, her weapons locked on, her hand closed on the firing control, when she suddenly heard the signal for surrender coming from the raider's ship. "Eat plasma, you bastard!" she shouted back, and fired. But at the very last instant, she pulled her aim and the shot only grazed the tip of his other wing as she went streaking past, so close she had a clear sight of the ruined ship on visual. One wing was gone, the other twisted and half-melted away. It was completely helpless, unable to move under its own power or fire its weapons. Only the cockpit looked as if it might be intact. Maybe.

Ivanova circled back in a tight loop, cutting power to her thrusters. In the distance, Alpha Six had turned back to the fight, now that Ivanova had taken care of the enemy. She scanned the raider. The cockpit wasn't quite intact, after all. Atmosphere was boiling out of a crack. But there were life signs. The bastard was still alive. Still sending the surrender code. *Damn!*

Her guns were still hot. She wanted to fire. She wanted, very simply, to kill the bastard, to blast him into superheated steam. For vengeance, for the sake of all the dead ships, for the *Cassini,* for the cold wreck still drifting out there with the salvage beacon on it. And most of all for Lieutenant Gordon Mokena, her wingman. For the sake of Alpha Two.

There were no witnesses. No one would ever know.

She circled back again, almost drifting now, the damage to the raider ship stark and violent ahead of her. Scan showed the cockpit atmosphere almost dissipated, and as it came into view, she could see the raider himself, suited and helmeted. She wondered how much oxygen he had, how long he'd last if she fired up her engines, took off, and left him there alone to die.

But the surrender signal was still going. Then the raider opened his comm channel. "Well, Earthforce, what's it going to be?"

Ivanova swore again to herself and opened the channel. When she spoke, her voice was crisp, as if she were handling routine traffic in the Observation Dome back on Babylon 5. "This is Commander Susan Ivanova. You have five seconds to say why I shouldn't melt down what's left of your ship with you inside it."

"How about Earthforce regs, Commander? Like the one about not firing on a disarmed enemy who wants to surrender?"

"Those are the Articles of War. They apply to an honorable enemy, not a glob of scum like you." But she already knew she wasn't going to do it. Maybe no one would ever know—but she would, and she'd never forget it, either.

But she did, for her own satisfaction and to make sure all his weapons really were disabled, put one more shot on her lowest power setting through the remaining half of the wing. The wreck of the raider's ship lurched and spun in reaction, and over her comm channel Ivanova could hear his choked-off curse, then the gasping intake of his breath as he realized he was still alive.

"Hey . . . Commander. Look. Maybe we can make . . . a deal?"

Though Ivanova had no intention of firing again, she paused before answering. "What kind of a deal?"

A shaken laugh. "Hell, any kind of deal you want, Earthforce! You want to know where our base is?"

Contemptuously, "You'd sell out your own side?"

"Hey, like you say, I'm scum. They're all scum. What difference does it make to you, one piece of scum more or less?'' And when Ivanova didn't answer, ''So c'mon, what do you say, Earthforce?''

The tone of his voice was almost enough to make her regret her decision not to shoot. But this was an opportunity she hadn't looked for. Slowly, she replied, ''That'll do for a start. Then I want to know where you get your information about the transport schedules. How you know what ships are going to be coming through the jump gate and what they're carrying. Where the information originates, how you receive it, how the targets are picked—all of it.''

A pause. ''You don't think small, do you, Earthforce?''

''Well, c'mon,'' she mocked him, ''what'll it be?''

He exhaled in resignation. ''So what do you want to know first?''

CHAPTER 23

The first thing Garibaldi did after leaving Nick in the lockup was make sure the rest of security was notified about Josef Nagy's real identity. But he was interrupted by a call from Mars.

It was his security major from Earthdome, and her expression was very stiff, even grave. "Mr. Garibaldi, in response to the request that you made, I'm afraid the answer is 'No.'"

"Just like that, so fast? Just 'No'?"

"I relayed your request up to the highest levels. The information you want is restricted *to* the highest levels."

"By 'the highest levels' you mean . . ."

"The very highest levels. I'm sorry, Mr. Garibaldi."

Even the fact that the Joint Chiefs office itself had disapproved his request was classified. Garibaldi shook his head in disbelief. Maybe something was going on he had no idea about.

"I'd like to ask one more question, if I can?"

"Of course. If the information isn't classified," she replied with a faint return of her smile.

Garibaldi sighed. She had a sense of humor, his major on Mars. "I'd like any information you have on a Josef Nagy. May have been involved in the Free Mars movement. Age, oh, between twenty-five and thirty." He played a hunch. "He may have worked in the mining industry."

Out of his view, she checked her records. "Yes, we have a file on a Josef Nagy. Wanted on suspicion of membership in a terrorist group, wanted for sabotage, wanted for conspiracy to commit treason. Is this Nagy on Babylon 5?''

''We have no record of him on the station,'' Garibaldi didn't quite lie. That was according to the rules of this game. ''His name was brought up in the course of an investigation into another matter. I figured I ought to check it out. Of course, without the file, I have no way of knowing if it's the same Josef Nagy. I don't have ID on him, just the name.''

''I'll send you the file right away.''

''Then this one isn't classified?''

She smiled. ''As head security officer on Babylon 5, your clearance is sufficient. Is there any other way I can help you, Mr. Garibaldi?''

''No, that's it for today. Maybe we can talk again sometime, though. Thank you, Major.''

The screen blanked to the BABCOM logo. A few moments later, the computer notified him, ''Data file arriving, transmitted from Earthdome on Mars. The file is restricted, please input password.''

He tapped out ''bastard'' on the keys of his console, having changed all his passwords since Wallace released the station's files.

''Access granted.''

Immediately a man's image appeared on his data screen. It was Williams. That is, Williams was Nagy, all right, although the longer hair and mustache he'd worn on Mars made him look younger than the bitter, suspicious worker Garibaldi had interviewed in the machine shop.

He scrolled down the rest of the information and exclaimed aloud, ''Yes!'' A year ago, Nagy had been employed by AreTech Consolidated Mines as a data analyst. During last year's insurrection on Mars, there'd been a system crash which wiped out a number of the company's personnel records. Nagy was a prime suspect. An alert had gone out for his arrest, but he remained missing.

Garibaldi switched from Nagy's file to the list of scheduled departures from the station. The passenger liner *Heinlein* was scheduled to depart, but that was too obvious. He knew Torres would check it out, of course, anyway. Also departing: the Minbari ambassador. A Narn cargo ship. The *Redstone 4,* a supply transport heading back to Earth by way of Mars and Luna. The name struck him, made him think of Mars. He called up more data on the transport and hit it immediately. Red Stone Shipping, Inc. And the pilot, Edwin Cooper— from Mars Colony.

Garibaldi quickly got on the link to Torres. "The *Redstone 4,*" he said, "have you checked it out?"

"Not yet. Departure isn't scheduled for another eight hours."

"I'm going down there. I'll meet you. I've got a feeling about this one."

"I'll be there."

They arrived at the loading dock while the *Redstone 4* was still taking on cargo. Garibaldi briefed Torres on the situation and then, accompanied by a team of security agents, they asked for permission to board the ship and speak to the pilot.

He met them on the bridge. Torres stepped forward. "Mr. Cooper, I'm Ensign Torres, Babylon 5 security, and we'd like to take a look through your ship. We have reason to believe there might be some contraband items on board."

Cooper scowled. "I hope this doesn't cause a delay, Ensign. As you can see, we're busy loading."

"I certainly hope it doesn't, Mr. Cooper. Now, if I could see your records, the bill of lading, customs statements . . .''

Garibaldi, standing back with the rest of the security

team, could observe Cooper while Torres went briefly through the records. The man looked itchy, nervous. Like he wanted them off the bridge. Torres logged off the ship's computer, having gone through the items mentioned plus the roster of the crew. She shook her head slightly. "Everything seems to be in order, Mr. Cooper. Now we'll just take a look around." But as a precaution against the pilot calling to warn Nagy—if Nagy were in fact on board—she left one security man on the bridge as a guard.

"He's not on the crew roster," she said, once they were off. "Under the name of either Williams or Nagy. But they could have just smuggled him on board. How should we do this?"

"Why don't you check the holds, and I'll take crew quarters," Garibaldi suggested.

The men and women who crewed the *Redstone 4* did not live in luxurious quarters, but they were better than some barracks Garibaldi had occupied during the varied course of his career. Bunks were fold-down, wardrobe space adequate, entertainment systems minimal. The rooms were all quiet, apparently empty, which was normal with cargo loading underway. All hands would be at work. All legitimate crew members, at least.

Garibaldi went up and down the corridors, checking each room with his scanner for life signs. One room, another, another. Then he was picking up something. Not from this room, but the one next door, marked Laundry. And with departure only a few hours away, this was definitely not the time for someone to be washing out his unmentionables.

Garibaldi took out his PPG, adjusted it to the lowest power setting. He didn't want to blast this guy Nagy, he wanted him alive for questioning. On the other hand, Nagy was probably desperate and might be armed. Garibaldi took a breath, then abruptly kicked open the door.

There was a gasp of breath, a movement in one corner, and Garibaldi had his gun trained on the man backed into it, partly hidden behind some bags of dirty clothes. "Hold it! This is Babylon 5 security! Come on out of there—slow."

The man in the corner froze for a few moments, as if Garibaldi might have not seen him, or might have meant someone else. Then he slowly straightened, and Garibaldi got a good look at his face. It was Williams, all right. Or rather, Josef Nagy. "Put your hands up," he ordered him. "Step out here."

Nagy did it, taking one step, then another into the center of the narrow laundry room. But Garibaldi saw his eyes darting wildly—to the PPG, to the corridor behind him. He was prepared for the desperate lunge, the last-ditch, futile attempt to break away. He sidestepped, turned, and met the onrushing fugitive with a fist in the gut. Nagy's breath exploded out of him. He folded up and collapsed onto the deck, where Garibaldi pinned him.

But the fight seemed to have gone out of Nagy. He'd taken his chance and lost it. Garibaldi opened his link. "Torres, this is Garibaldi. I've got him."

He pulled his prisoner to his feet. "Come on, Nagy, let's go have another little talk."

Torres and her men showed up when he was halfway down the corridor. "Should I take him to the lockup?" she asked.

But Garibaldi had been thinking about that, and other things, like classified files and who had access to them, even with new passwords. "No, I don't think so. I'll do it." He went on, looking hard at each one of them at a time, "Look, I know this is irregular, but I'd like this arrest kept quiet. No official file on it. No prisoner named Nagy in the lockup. I think you know why. Can I count on your cooperation?"

After a moment's hesitation, Torres said he could count on her, and the others agreed.

Garibaldi marched Nagy out with him through the *Redstone 4*'s cargo hatch, toward the lift tube. "You can't do this!" his prisoner protested in a low voice that lacked real conviction. "You can't get away with this!"

"Shut up," Garibaldi told him without rancor. "I'm doing this for your own good, whether you believe it or not."

Nagy clearly didn't believe it, but he shut up anyway and went without a struggle, the path of least resistance. He seemed completely defeated as Garibaldi brought him into an interrogation room and shoved him down into a chair, taking the seat opposite.

"All right. *Now* we're going to talk. For real this time."

Nagy said nothing, looking around warily, as if he were wondering when the instruments of persuasion, the drugs, the Psi Corps were all going to materialize.

Garibaldi knew he had to shock him into speech. "First of all, where's the real Val Williams? What'd you do with him—knock him over the head, take his ID?"

Nagy's head jerked up. "No! I mean, there is no real Williams. It's just a name. Made-up."

"Where'd you get the ID, then? From your terrorist pals in the Free Mars group?"

"That's a lie!"

"That was a *question*."

"Free Mars isn't a terrorist organization! I'm not a terrorist!"

"So what are you, Nagy? Why did you come to Babylon 5, anyway? What were you planning to do here? Sabotage? Blow up the station, maybe?"

"No! I'm a patriot! Only my homeworld is Mars, not Earth! Is that so hard to understand?"

"I don't get paid to understand. I get paid to enforce

the rules and stop trouble. Right now I'm getting paid to figure out why two men are dead here on this station. And at least one of them was a suspected terrorist from Mars. J. D. Ortega. Funny thing. He worked for the mines, too, just like you."

Nagy shook his head.

"What does that mean?" Garibaldi prompted him.

"Ortega was no terrorist, either. He wasn't even part of the organization."

"You knew Ortega?"

"Who he was. He worked for the company."

"What company? AreTech?"

A nod.

"What did he do there? Wasn't he an engineer, something like that?"

"Metallurgist, I think. One of the guys in white coats, worked in the lab. I don't know exactly what he did, I was just a clerk. I kept the records."

"Do you know why someone would charge him with being a terrorist?"

A shake of the head.

"Why someone was trying to kill him?"

"No. I don't know about any of that stuff. Look, when you worked for the company, you didn't want to know about anything that wasn't your business, all right? You didn't want to ask questions. There was always talk— about under-the-table deals, bribing the safety inspectors, closing down the whole mine. But if they found out about it . . ."

"Would that maybe be when a guy named Fengshi Yang would step in? Company enforcer? His job to keep the workers in line, stop the rumors? That kind of thing?"

A sullen nod.

"So if Ortega had gotten into trouble with AreTech, they might have sent somebody like Yang after him?"

Another reluctant nod.

Garibaldi pressed on, "So Ortega could have come to Babylon 5 because he was in trouble with the company, not because he was a terrorist."

"If they sent Yang after him, yeah."

"But you didn't think it was a good idea to tell me about any of this when we talked before in the machine shop, before you had me mugged. I suppose you knew there was a team of special investigators nosing around the station, probing into Ortega's death. But you talked to me. Why?"

"They took Sonia! And . . . I heard . . . that you weren't part of them. The ones who arrested her."

"So you decided to talk to me. But right after that you decided it was a real good idea to send a hit team of your friends out after me, to stuff me into that locker. Just like Yang did with Ortega's body. You knew about Yang, didn't you? You knew he killed Ortega."

A very slight nod.

"So the question is, who killed Yang? Was it you, Nagy?"

"No!" The prisoner's face paled with shock.

"Then who did? Someone else who worked for the company? Some more of your patriot friends from Mars? Did they kill the company enforcer, chop up his body, stuff him into the recyclers?"

"I don't know! I swear! I don't *know* who did it!" Now Nagy was volubly eager to talk, to deny it. "All anybody knew was, he was here on Babylon 5. He'd already killed one guy, no one knew who else he was after. Anybody could have done it!"

Garibaldi nodded in understanding. "So somebody figured they had to get rid of Yang. But I kept coming around, kept asking questions. Better get rid of me, too. Isn't that right?"

There was a slight new sheen of nervous sweat on

Nagy's forehead. "Like I said, some people said you weren't part of it. That you were . . . all right. But, then, you knew about Yang, about the mine . . ."

"Part of what?" Garibaldi asked.

"The whole thing! The company! Earthforce! All of you! You're all in it together! God knows what they've done with Sonia—"

"That's right. Your friend. From the assay office. The one they took away. Did she know about you? Your background?"

"No! God, I don't think so, I was careful. If she knew, I'd have been dragged in days ago. She . . ." Nagy dropped his head into his hands for a minute, then raised it, took a breath. "I never knew her on Mars. We only met after I got here and started to work. As far as she knew, I was Val Williams, from Earth, I was a clerk for a survey company."

"She never worked for AreTech?"

"No, she worked in the assay bureau. That's a government office."

"What about Ortega?" Garibaldi asked. "Do you know how he came onto Babylon 5? Did he have a fake identicard like you did? Under another name? Where do you think he might have gotten such a thing if he wasn't mixed up in the Free Mars organization?"

"I don't know." A pause. "Maybe. If he knew the right people."

"What right people?" But Garibaldi's link interrupted him. "Mr. Garibaldi, you're wanted at the Shuttle Bay. There's been another killing. It's Lieutenant Khatib."

Khatib? Murdered? As if things weren't already complicated enough!

Jumping up, he said, "I'll be right there." But he

paused, turned back to Nagy. "You're a lucky man, Nagy. He was out there looking for you, too. And, take my word for it, you're glad he didn't find you before I did."

CHAPTER 24

"Alpha Leader, this is Alpha Three. Are you all right out there?"

"Everything's under control, Alpha Three. I'm just stopping to pick up a piece of . . . salvage. What's the situation there?"

"Raiders are all scragged. Alpha Four sustained minor damage, but Moy is all right. And we've made contact with the *Duster*, we're going to rendezvous with her now." He gave the coordinates.

"I'll meet you there, Three."

Ivanova returned to her work, making the grapples fast between her ship and the raider. She meant to tow the crippled hulk over to the *Duster*, now that it had shown up, and transfer her prisoner to the transport for the trip back to Babylon 5. She was worried that her prisoner's sudden willingness to talk might take on less urgency, now that he was no longer at immediate risk of being hosed with charged plasma.

Not, she thought sourly, that he'd stopped talking yet.

"Say, Earthforce, how long's this little trip going to take? I haven't got all the oxygen in the universe, you know. Even scum like me needs to breathe. What are you going to do if I start to run short on air?"

"Watch you turn blue," Ivanova snapped, which she regretted a moment later. It only seemed to encourage him.

"Kinda hard to talk without air, Earthforce."

"Then why don't you start saving it?"

"I got a lot to say, you know. About our operations,

contacts. It'd be too bad if I ran out of breathing room before I got a chance to tell you all about it.''

But when she no longer responded, the raider eventually went silent. In fact, he was quiet for so long that Ivanova finally started to worry: maybe it hadn't been a bluff, maybe he'd really run out of oxy. She ran a quick scan, saw he was still alive. And the *Duster* was just ahead now, just about ten minutes away.

''Alpha Three, this is Alpha Leader, how do things stand?''

''This is Alpha Three. The *Duster* has room in its shuttle bay, so we're stowing Alpha Four in there for the trip back.''

''You say Moy is all right?''

''She's fine, Commander. But her ship's got one wing that doesn't look like it wants to take a lot of stress.''

This suddenly appeared to Ivanova as a solution to her problem. ''Do you think she's in shape to fly my ship home?''

''One minute, Alpha Leader, I'll check.'' A moment later, ''She says no problem. Are you all right, Commander?''

''I'm fine. I just want to stay with my salvage on the way back to the station.''

''We'll be expecting you, Alpha Leader.''

A few minutes later, Ivanova cut thrusters and came in on a slow approach to the *Duster,* with the three intact Starfuries clustered around its bulk. The *Duster* was definitely in the supersized class of carriers.

She opened a channel to the transport's bridge. ''This is Earthforce Commander Susan Ivanova, from Babylon 5. I'd like to speak to the pilot of the *Duster.*''

''This is Bogdonovich, Senior Pilot. We were sure glad to see your reception committee.''

''Glad to hear it, Mr. Bogdonovich. I understand you're taking one of our crippled ships onboard?''

"We've got plenty of room, Commander, it's no problem."

"Good. I'd like to know if you also have some kind of secure room onboard that I could use as a lockup."

Bogdonovich had obviously scanned the wreck of the raider ship she had in tow. "Prisoner, Commander?" he asked curiously.

"Let's say an item of salvage, Mr. Bogdonovich."

"If you say so. Sure, I have a place where you can stow your salvage. You can dock and bring it onboard through cargo hatch D."

"Good. And be careful loading it. I suspect it's still hazardous."

"I read you, Commander."

Ivanova opened the channel again to the raider ship. "This is Commander Ivanova. We're going to be bringing you onboard the transport shortly. This is just a reminder not to try anything. If you still want to keep on breathing."

"Whatever you say, Commander."

The raider's voice was a whisper now. Maybe he was really short of air. But Ivanova didn't waste time wondering about it. With practiced efficiency, she let loose the grapples to the raider and docked with the transport ship. She'd let the experienced crew handle the job of taking on the cargo. Before leaving her fighter, she took out her handgun and powered it on.

Moy was waiting, suited and helmeted, at the lock. "You're sure you're all right?" Ivanova wanted to know. "No problem with flying my ship back?"

"I'm fine, Commander. No problem at all."

The transport's crew had already gotten the hulk of the raider's ship onboard through a cargo hatch when Ivanova arrived. She noted with satisfaction that she wasn't the only one armed. The crew seemed to have a security officer, that was good. She nodded at him, and he came over, spoke to her through his helmet radio, since the cargo bay was still unpressurized. "I'm Massie, Commander. Anything I can do to help?"

"Thank you, Mr. Massie. Just keep an eye on him for now."

While they were securing the wreck of the raider's ship and closing up the cargo hatch, Ivanova spoke to her prisoner again. "All right, as soon as your ship is secure, you can climb on out of there. Just remember, everyone here has more than sufficient reason to want to blow you out of that cockpit."

There was no reply, but the canopy of the pirate ship slid open slowly. Ivanova watched with her PPG trained on the cockpit as a helmet emerged, then the rest of the suited figure. He hung for a moment at the edge of the canopy, hesitating, then jumped down. For a moment his knees didn't seem to be able to hold him, then he grabbed hold of the remains of a wing strut and pulled himself upright with one hand. As soon as he did, he unlatched his helmet and pulled it off, taking great gasps of air, despite the fact that Ivanova's indicator showed the air pressure in the hold wasn't quite completely equalized yet. So maybe he did almost run out of air, she thought. The business end of her PPG still didn't waver in its aim, even when she unlatched her own helmet, handing it over to a crew member. "Can you keep this for me?"

"Sure, Commander."

She stepped up to the raider, who saw her approaching, straightened up, and turned to her with a wan, bloody grin. "So you're Ivanova, huh? Hey, from what I'd heard around, I was figuring on an old ice-axe. I'm Zaccione, but everybody calls me Zack."

Ivanova had no trouble recognizing his type and dismissing it. "Are you in need of medical attention?"

He waved a hand nonchalantly. "Hell, no. Just a

scratch, like they say.'' But with his other hand, he was still clutching the base of the wing strut.

The transport's security officer had come up on the other side of the prisoner so they both had him under guard. ''Commander Ivanova? What do you want done with him?''

''Does your ship have a medic?''

''Yes, we do.''

''Good, we can get him patched up and scanned to make sure he has no hidden weapons.''

''I have a scanner here with me.'' Massie ran the instrument up and down the raider's body. ''Nope, he's clean.''

''Good,'' Ivanova said again. To the prisoner, ''Last chance. Do you want to see the medic, or not, before we talk?''

''If you insist.''

Zaccione's injuries proved to be cracked ribs and a broken nose. ''Clean him up,'' Ivanova ordered, ''but don't be too generous with the painkillers. He's got a lot of talking to do and I don't want him nodding off.''

''Thanks a lot,'' the raider said, wincing as Massie secured his wrists in restraints.

''Mr. Massie, I understand you have a secure room?''

''That's right.''

''Let's go, then.''

Massie was reluctant at first to leave her locked up alone with the raider, but he made no more objections after she told him the subject of the interrogation was classified and might in fact be dangerous to know.

''So now we're alone together, huh, Earthforce,'' Zaccione said, grinning up at her with a set of very white, even teeth.

''Let's get this clear, scumball,'' Ivanova said tightly. ''You're facing a short walk out into some very cold vacuum as soon as we get back to Babylon 5. For a man who likes to breathe as much as you do, you're wasting a lot of air with this line of crap."

"I thought Earth Alliance law reserved the death penalty for treason and mutiny."

"You've attacked Earthforce ships, and that's treason enough in my book." Ivanova wasn't sure if this was so, but she managed to sound convincing anyway. She wasn't concerned with penalties at the moment, she was concerned with information.

"Whatever you say, Commander. So what is it you want to know?"

"How do you pick the particular transports you attack? Where do you get your information? Is it always morbidium?"

"You've been doing homework, Commander. Yeah, that's it."

"Why morbidium? Why not some other strategic metals?"

He started to shrug, then stopped himself. "I dunno. The deal is for morbidium, that's all. If there's something else shipped with it, that's dessert, right? Hey, it's all right with us. You know what that stuff's *worth*?"

"I have a rough idea, yes. So what do you pay for the information?"

"Used to be, we'd pay the fixed rate. You know, the official price. Lately, with the price going up, the price we get, they've been wanting more. Greedy bastards. They turn around and collect from the insurance, too."

"Just what greedy bastards are you talking about?"

"The mine."

"Your information comes directly from the mine?"

"Yeah, that's right."

"That's the mining corporation, the owners? Not just some clerk that you're dealing with?"

"Yeah, they're selling out their own cargoes. Don't ask me why."

"So they sell you the information at the fixed rate, then collect the insured value. And you get the rest of the profit?" Ivanova recalled Pal's suspicions. "Some people have wondered if maybe the cargoes are just slag—empty mass. That all this is just part of an insurance fraud scheme."

"Hey, Earthforce, this isn't what you'd call a low-risk enterprise, is it? We'll pay for the information, but the cargo has to be worth it. We're not going out after slag!"

"All right, let's get back to where you get the information. From the morbidium mines. Just one company, or all of them? Just who's passing it to you? I want names."

The raider wasn't grinning anymore. "Look, Commander, like you said, once you take me in, all I see waiting for me is an open air-lock and a lot of vacuum. If I tell you everything I know now, then what kind of a guarantee do I have?"

"The only thing I guarantee right now is that you'll keep breathing long enough to make it back to Babylon 5," Ivanova said grimly. "Then you won't have a choice whether to talk or not. There's a team of special investigators waiting for you. They'll suck every scrap of information out of your mind and leave it as empty as a broken eggshell. They'll throw what's left out the air-lock and you won't even be in there to know it."

The raider blinked at the threat. He searched her face —did she mean it?

Ivanova stared back. "Or you can talk to me now and have it on record."

"AreTech," he finally, reluctantly, said.

"The big mining company? They're the only one?"

"Right. The information comes from their main office on Mars. We have an agent there. He passes it on. We know where the cargo's routed, when it's scheduled to come through the jump gates, when we can hit them. It's real convenient. Or, at least, it used to be.''

Ivanova thought about what Espada, the insurance agent, had told her, about the shipments all being insured by different companies, to divert suspicion. ''You never wondered why they were doing this?''

He shrugged, winced. ''Uh, Commander, you know those painkillers the medic talked about?''

''Later,'' she said, pitiless.

''Look, all right. We're always on the lookout for data. Makes our job easier, you know what I mean? So, one day a while back, this guy makes contact with one of our agents. He says he's got information, routing details on a real valuable shipment of strategic metals. Are we interested? And the best thing is, he doesn't want anything for it. Just for us to hit the transports where and when he says.

''So, well, sure everyone automatically thinks this is some kind of trick, the guy's an Earthforce agent, you know? Too good to be true? But our guy checks him out, he's legitimate, works for the mining company and all that. Some of us decide, well, we'll check it out. The ship comes through, just like the guy said it would. We hit it, get the stuff, sell it, and suddenly this is looking like a good idea. So we're in business, we make a deal with the guy for regular information. It's worth what we pay for it. By now we're one of the major suppliers of weapons-grade morbidium in eight sectors.''

''Who do you sell to?''

''The highest bidder, who else?''

''Aliens? The Narn, maybe?''

''Hey, it's a free market! Not like Earth. Supply and demand, you know. Right now, demand is real high. We've got buyers for every shipment we take.''

''Why don't they just sell the morbidium on the black market themselves, then?''

"Don't ask me, Earthforce. Maybe it's the E A inspectors, the way they check each shipment, count every ingot before they seal it up. I don't know."

"Wouldn't it be easier to just bribe the officials? Would you know anything about that? Earthforce officers on the take? Covering this business up?"

"I've heard . . . maybe they've got somebody paid off, yeah. But I don't really know. What I've heard is, people around the mine who start asking questions don't last very long. You know what I mean?"

"I still want names. Does the name J. D. Ortega mean anything to you? Was he involved in any of this?"

"Never heard of him."

"How about Yang? Or Wallace?"

"Look, Commander, I said I don't know. Not any of those names. I'm not involved in that. I'm just a fighter pilot, just like you are, that's all."

Ivanova almost hit him. "Don't you *ever* say that," she said fiercely. "Don't you ever say that again."

"Whatever you say, Commander."

CHAPTER 25

Sheridan and Garibaldi waited, watching while the shuttle pilot brought in Khatib's body. On the other side of the bay were Wallace and Miyoshi, rigid, speaking to no one.

Under his breath, Garibaldi remarked, "Would you believe I didn't think this situation could possibly get any worse?"

Sheridan only looked angry and muttered something about not planning to tolerate any more murders on Babylon 5.

Garibaldi raised his eyebrows. "This one is going to be a lot of fun, I can tell you. Khatib was a real, real popular guy. I can't think of anyone on the station with more people who had reason to want to do him in. I guess I'm lucky I'm such a nice guy, or else I might have been out the air-lock instead of just shoved into that locker."

The shuttle door opened, and the pilot emerged, looking around for someone to help him bring out the body. Dr. Franklin and one of his medics were standing by, but Commander Wallace shoved them both out of the way.

Sheridan swore and moved to intervene, with Garibaldi following after.

"This man was my aide," Wallace was insisting with particular vehemence. "This murder is connected to my investigation and no one—"

"Commander Wallace!" Sheridan glared at him. "Are you a licensed medical examiner or forensic pathologist? If not, you *will* stand back and let Dr. Franklin take the remains to Medlab for a proper examination.

Whatever questions you have, I'm sure he can answer them.''

As Wallace sullenly moved back to let the medics at the body, Sheridan got a good look at it. Not a pleasant sight. The limbs were frozen into contorted, outflung positions, the jaw hung open as if Khatib was still screaming aloud when his murderers shoved him out the air-lock. But when Sheridan saw where Franklin's attention was focused, he doubted that Khatib had had a chance to scream at all. Dark-red crystalline blood had filled a distinct depression in the side of the dead man's skull. As they moved him, sparkling flakes of it fell from his hair onto the deck.

While the body was being transferred to Medlab, Wallace objected again to anyone but himself having access to the results of the examination. At that, Garibaldi protested, ''Hey, wait a minute! This is the third murder on this station in the last ten days! If that's not a matter for Babylon 5 security, I don't know what is!''

''I can't allow interference with my investigation! The information is restricted!''

Garibaldi snorted angrily. ''Just what is it you've got to hide, Wallace? You know, it's getting awfully suspicious when records and evidence start to disappear whenever you show up, or files are all of a sudden reclassified the minute somebody tries to take a look at them. Maybe we'd better check for blood on your hands, too, while we're at it.''

At that, Wallace went white with anger, but Captain Sheridan stepped between the two before they were at each other's throats again. ''No one is going to be interfering with the results of this examination. I want the truth out in the open for once.''

Wallace started to protest again, but a glance at the expression on Sheridan's face stopped him. He paused, pulled Miyoshi away from the rest, and gave her some orders in a low voice that Sheridan couldn't make out.

"All right, *Captain,* as you so often point out, you're in command of this station. At the moment."

Sheridan ignored the threat. He was heartily sick of Commander Wallace, his constant threats, his investigation, his disruption of the station. In fact, he briefly allowed the subversive thought: if anyone had to be put out the air-lock . . .

Garibaldi could tell that Dr. Franklin wasn't real happy at all the witnesses gathered around his examination table. "What is this, a medical-school class?"

It took a short while to restore the body from its flash-frozen state, during which Franklin made a number of superficial observations, something about whether Khatib had already been dead when they put him out into space. Wallace, Garibaldi noticed, kept having to avert his eyes from the corpse. Squeamish, he thought. Sheridan watched the proceedings without outward emotion. Garibaldi supposed that the captain had seen enough of the effects of decompression on human flesh during the Earth-Minbari war.

But his thoughts kept returning to the murders, the pattern of them—whether there was any pattern. Three bodies, he thought. If you're the killer, what do you do with them? One in a locker, one recycled, and one out the air-lock. Three different sets of killers? Or different circumstances?

Ortega had been killed by a pro. The deed had been premeditated, but rushed, and the body left as an example, if Nagy was right, to other employees who might dare defy the AreTech mining company. Yang's killer, on the other hand, had gone to a great deal of trouble to try to keep the body from being discovered.

And now Khatib. Again, this one had the look of a

rush job. The killer wasn't a pro, if Garibaldi knew anything about it. Just hit the guy over the head, dispose of the result any which way, as soon as you can. A human body floating outside a station like Babylon 5, with its heavy traffic load, wasn't likely to go overlooked for very long.

Garibaldi was distracted from this line of thought as Wallace got a call over his link. From Miyoshi, Garibaldi supposed. Whatever the news was, Wallace seemed agitated. He stepped back away from the examining table, all the way back to the door, where he continued the whispered exchange. Garibaldi wondered what was going on, but his attention was drawn back to the examining table when the medical tech picked up a laser and started to cut away the victim's clothes. Garibaldi took a step closer, picked up the pieces of Khatib's uniform and quickly ran his hands over the pockets, recognized the familiar shape of a hologram viewer card in one.

He glanced over in Wallace's direction again, but the investigator was still distracted. Good. He carefully shook the contents out of the pockets, to seal the items away in evidence bags. What was on the viewer? He turned it on and saw the familiar face of J. D. Ortega materialize. No surprise there. But there was more information on the viewer. He scrolled down, saw files appear, personnel files, clearly marked as the files of AreTech Consolidated Mines. But on the bottom? Whose signature was it? He turned up the resolution.

"Give me that!" Wallace reached to grab the viewer.

Garibaldi automatically pulled it away. "Watch it! This is evidence!"

"This information is classified!" Wallace screamed. "You have no authority to view that! Hand it over!"

"This is evidence," Garibaldi insisted again. "Evidence in a murder investigation. What happens if I hand it over? Does it just conveniently disappear? Will it ever show up in court? Or will the court ever be allowed to see it?''

''That's none of your concern, Garibaldi! This is *my* investigation—''

Garibaldi appealed directly to the commanding officer. ''Captain, this evidence has a direct bearing on the Yang murder case. Which, if you remember, Commander Wallace and Lieutenant Khatib claimed to know nothing about. Well, this proves they lied. It may prove a lot more.''

''All right, I'm taking custody of all this material,'' Sheridan said decisively. ''Commander, if you want to appeal my decision, go right ahead. All the way to the Joint Chiefs. But I'm getting just a little bit tired of people getting killed every other day on this station and nobody admitting they know what's going on!''

''You'll be sorry,'' Wallace started to threaten, but his link interrupted him again.

''What?'' he shouted. Then, lowering his voice only slightly, ''Not right now, Sumiko! . . . What? Well, can't you handle it yourself? Get more security?''

''What about more security?'' Garibaldi demanded, but just then his own link cut in.

''Mr. Garibaldi! Can you come up to Red Central right away? There's trouble here, a crowd of people—it looks like it might turn into a riot!''

''I'll be right there!'' Garibaldi glanced at Sheridan, but the captain had heard. His expression was grim.

''Dr. Franklin, can you keep these items of evidence secure here in Medlab?'' he asked.

''Completely secure,'' Franklin assured him.

''Then let's go,'' he told Garibaldi.

There was, indeed, a near-riot in progress by the time they came on the scene, both Garibaldi and Sheridan in black combat armor. Security agents had their shock sticks out and were using them where necessary. The crowd as far as Garibaldi could see amounted to about a hundred, all human, and as far as he could tell mostly station workers. And they were clearly worked up to a mad froth about something. Shouting, they surged forward in waves against the cordon of security agents, clashing, falling back to regroup and gather their fury for another advance. Things were being thrown, too—sections of grid panels wrenched off the walls, chairs, components of shattered comm screens.

Garibaldi grabbed the nearest security man he could reach. "What's the situation? Are any of them armed?" he shouted over the noise of the mob.

"No, sir, at least we don't think they have guns. But they've got pipes, conduit, tools—they're starting to tear things up, throw stuff."

At which point a metal shard came flying overhead, close enough that Sheridan swore out loud.

"Do you think we're getting it under control?" Garibaldi asked.

"No, sir, I wouldn't say so, not really. Orders are not to use guns, not unless it looks like somebody's going to get hurt. But if this keeps up—"

The agent broke off his remark and went after a pair of rioters who were trying to drag down another security man. Garibaldi and Sheridan ran after him, and the rioters retreated, yelling curses.

The two security agents returned together, breathing hard. The second one had a visible bruise discoloring the edge of a cheekbone. He recognized Sheridan and Garibaldi. "Getting mean out here, sir."

"What's this all about?" Sheridan demanded.

"Not quite sure, sir. They're demanding the prisoners be released, that's all I know."

"What prisoners?"

"I heard there was some kind of sweep, lots of arrests, bunch of people started to protest—it turned into this."

Sheridan shook his head. "There were no orders—"

But Garibaldi said curtly, "Wallace!"

"Damn!" Sheridan swore. He toggled his link. "This is Captain Sheridan, get me the senior security officer assigned to Commander Wallace."

"Contacting Lieutenant Kohler," the computer voice serenely replied.

Almost at the same time, "Kohler here," came through Sheridan's link.

"Lieutenant, what's going on? How'd this get started?"

"Sir, I got orders from Commander Wallace to bring in a long list of people. Suspects in the murder of Lieutenant Khatib. There was a confrontation. One group on the docks tried to keep us from taking a suspect out. That seems to be what started all this. I guess it must have moved up to Red."

"Lieutenant, you take no more orders from Commander Wallace, not unless *I* order it. Is that clear?"

"Yes, sir!"

"Damn!" Sheridan said again.

Garibaldi felt a twinge of alarm. He told Sheridan, having to raise his voice to be heard, "That may not be the only thing going on. I just arrested that guy who set me up to get zapped the other day. He admitted it. He's involved with the Free Mars movement somehow. I was just questioning him when the news came through about Khatib. Could be his arrest has something to do with all this, too. And those other people you had brought in for questioning."

"Well, it's time to get it stopped," Sheridan said decisively. He started to edge toward a more central location where he could be seen by the whole crowd, and Garibaldi went with him, shotgun position, trying to keep himself as much as possible between the station's commander and the furious mob.

It was hard going, ducking the thrown missiles that came flying from the hands of the angry rioters, but eventually they reached a place where Sheridan could swing up on a catwalk and be several feet above the heads of the surging throng. Unfortunately, it would also make him a target for every hand holding something to throw, or even a weapon. Garibaldi pulled the captain back. "Let me get their attention first."

He picked a convenient nearby power junction, aimed his gun, and the sudden blinding flare of sparks caused by the high-energy plasma burst did indeed get the instant attention of the mob.

Sheridan lost none of the opportunity, immediately climbing up to the catwalk and shouting, "I'm Captain John Sheridan, commander of Babylon 5! What the hell is this disturbance all about? If you people have a grievance, tell me about it! Now! So what's going on?"

Several dozen people began yelling all at once. Sheridan shook his head, waved for silence. After a few moments the voices quieted down and a couple of people stepped forward. "We want all the arrests stopped! All the prisoners released!"

Someone from farther back in the milling throng yelled, "Or else we take this station apart to get them out!"

Several dozen of the crowd cheered that remark, and Garibaldi took a firmer grip on his PPG.

"What prisoners? What arrests?" Sheridan demanded again. "You want me to release murderers, is that it? Traitors?"

"Not criminals! Innocent men and women!" There was even louder agreement with this statement, but a few voices also added, "Patriots! Not traitors!"

Garibaldi reached up to get Sheridan's attention.

"Nagy," he explained. "The guy I arrested, the guy with Free Mars. That's what he called himself, a patriot."

"This isn't getting us anywhere." Sheridan took a worried look at the restless mob. Raising his voice again, he said, "I want to meet with your representatives. Bring me a list of names. If innocent people have been arrested, I'll personally see that they're released."

There was a long moment as the speakers in the front of the crowd turned back to consult with the others. People were shoving forward to try to be heard, calling out names. Some were angrily demanding more concessions. One man yelled, "It's like a police state!" and that comment again was greeted with approving cheers.

Garibaldi tensed, and security agents braced themselves, but there was no new outbreak of violence. Sheridan got on his link and contacted Kohler again. "Lieutenant, meet me in briefing room three with that list of people you just arrested. And bring Commander Wallace with you!"

Four people stepped forward again, three men and a woman, and one of them said, "All right, Sheridan, we've got the names. Let's meet. Let's see what you do about this!"

A cordon of guards cleared the way to the briefing room, with the crowd surging behind them, willing for the moment to wait to see what came of the meeting. Garibaldi wondered how long their patience would last and hoped they could resolve the issue quickly.

The foremost spokesman was a man Garibaldi recognized as Hank Ndeme, proprietor of the largest food-service operation on Babylon 5, and a native of Mars. He got right to the point before Sheridan could say a word, holding out a notebook in his hand and shaking it in the faces of the Earthforce officers. "Here are the names!

I've got them all right here! Now let's see them released!''

"*If* they're innocent," Sheridan reminded him. "Let
me inform you, in case you don't know it already, that
there've been three murders on Babylon 5 in the last ten
days, plus an assault on the station's chief security officer. If you think I'm going to tolerate that, you're going
to find out otherwise."

"Is that any excuse for turning this whole station into
a police state?" Ms. Connoly, the Dockworkers Union
Rep, demanded, repeating the phrase. "Is that any reason
to pull men and women out of their quarters, off their
jobs?"

"I'm checking into that right now," Sheridan told her.
"There may have been excesses. If so, they'll be recti-
fied."

But Ndeme shook his head. "This has got to *stop*," he
insisted. "Every man, woman, and child from Mars on
this station is treated like a criminal, like a terrorist.
What is it, a crime to be born on Mars? You come from
Mars, you've got no rights? Is that how things are?"

"Not just from Mars," Connoly protested. "They
took three people from my section, none of them ever set
foot on Mars—"

Garibaldi interrupted, "Let's hear those names."

Ndeme activated the recorder. The first couple of
names no one recognized; the third was "Val Williams."

Garibaldi said, "Val Williams is a pseudonym for
Josef Nagy, who was taken into custody earlier today.
Mr. Nagy has confessed to complicity in the attack on an
Earthforce officer."

Ndeme seemed taken aback by this information, but
only for an instant. "What about Allen Rodgers, then?
Irene Hardesty? Nick Patinos?"

"None of these people is currently being charged with

any crime. They were taken in for questioning in the case of the assault on Mr. Garibaldi,'' Sheridan said.

"Taken in for questioning, under arrest—what's the difference?" Ndeme demanded. "All we know is, security comes and drags them away to the lockup. You ask why, and no one gives you any information, everything is classified, and then they start to ask: What connection do *you* have to the suspect, anyway?"

Sheridan and Garibaldi looked at each other, both thinking the same thing: *Wallace.*

Sheridan looked irritably at his link, but just then the briefing room door opened and Lieutenant Kohler came in, looking agitated and slightly the worse for wear. With him was a hostile and truculent Lieutenant Miyoshi. "Sorry, sir, I couldn't reach the commander. I did bring the lieutenant, though."

Sheridan's jaw tightened. "C&C, this is Captain Sheridan. I want Commander Wallace to contact me *now,* and that's an order!" To Miyoshi, he said, "Where's your superior, Lieutenant?"

Defiantly, "The commander doesn't want to be disturbed!"

"Lieutenant Miyoshi, you *will* get on your link and contact Commander Wallace."

"You don't have the authority—"

"Or I'll have you under arrest for insubordination and refusal to obey a direct order."

Miyoshi, glaring at Sheridan, toggled her link. "Commander, this is Miyoshi. Captain Sheridan has ordered me to call you. Are you there, Commander?" She looked up from her wrist with a smug and bitter expression of triumph. "He doesn't answer."

"You'd better hope it's not because someone shoved him out an air-lock," Garibaldi said uncharitably.

But Sheridan decided to give up on Wallace for the

moment. He asked Kohler, instead, "Do you have that list of names?"

"Yes, sir." He took out a data crystal, handed it to Sheridan, ignoring Miyoshi's shrill protest: "You can't do that! Those names, all that information is classified!"

"To hell with that!" Sheridan said decisively, inserting the crystal into the reader. The list of names appeared on the screen, and Ndeme and the other representatives crowded around it, saying, "Yes! That's him! There they are!"

There were at least fifty names. "These were all arrested in connection with Lieutenant Khatib's murder?" Sheridan asked Kohler.

"Well, no, sir. That's just the list of suspects. We didn't bring all of them in yet. The disturbance broke out—"

But Sheridan had already found the second list, the names of people actually in custody. "There'll be no more arrests," he reminded Kohler, and Miyoshi as well. "Not without my express order. No more people dragged in for questioning without my authorization."

"I understand, sir," said Kohler. Miyoshi said nothing.

Sheridan went back to the first list, muttered to himself, "This is too much."

Garibaldi added, "If you wanted to bring in everyone on this station who might have wanted to shove Khatib through an air-lock, you couldn't hold them all in the main docking bay."

"All right," said Sheridan. "Lieutenant Kohler, I'm ordering every person on that list to be released, immediately. Monitor their whereabouts, but let them go." To Miyoshi, anticipating her protest, "If Commander Wallace can show any cause to connect them with Khatib's murder or any other crime, we'll pick them up again."

"I think, with Nagy in custody, we can release these

others,'' Garibaldi added, meaning Patinos, Hardesty, and the rest brought in for questioning about his assault.

The civilian representatives, skeptical, were still going through their list, comparing them with the names on the screen. ''There's still more,'' Ndeme insisted. ''More names aren't on that list.'' He named some of them. Connoly added several more.

Sheridan took a breath. ''I have to explain something. Commander Wallace and his aides, from Earth Central, have been conducting an independent investigation into a terrorist incident which occurred on Babylon 5. The specific details are classified, but I know that they include at least one murder. You understand, the commander is operating directly under the authority of the Earth Central. If Commander Wallace has authorized arrests, I don't have direct knowledge of them. All I can promise you, and I *do* promise you, is that I'll do whatever I can to find out what's happened to these people.

''But I warn you, I'm not about to let the murderers of an Earthforce officer get off free. This crime will be investigated and the guilty parties will be punished according to the law. I hope that's clear.''

The representatives consulted with each other. Finally, ''I guess that'll do, Captain,'' Ndeme said.

''*If* the rest of these people are released,'' Connoly added.

''They'll all be released unless we find specific, concrete reason to hold them,'' Sheridan promised. ''And there'll be no repetition of today's incident. All arrests in connection with this investigation will have to be authorized by me.'' He fixed Miyoshi with a hard stare. ''Do you understand me, Lieutenant?''

''I'll inform Commander Wallace,'' she said stiffly.

''Mr. Garibaldi, will you take those names?'' Sheridan ordered.

In a few moments more it was done, the lists of names

recorded and cross-checked, everyone but Miyoshi agreeing that they were satisfied for the moment.

As the civilian representatives left the briefing room, Garibaldi held Sheridan back for a moment. "Sir, you're taking quite a risk, aren't you? Wallace is bound to try to take your head for it."

"I did what I had to in an emergency," Sheridan insisted. "To disperse a riot. This damned witch-hunt of his is disrupting the entire station, interfering with normal operations. There's got to be a limit."

"Well, I have some information that I think will help." He explained, "I just found some of this out. Anyway, you remember, when we found Yang's . . . remains, that Wallace said he knew nothing about the case? And I said he was lying? Well, it seems that Yang was an enforcer from a company on Mars, looking for J. D. Ortega. In fact, the evidence points to Yang as the one who killed him."

Garibaldi took a breath. "Just now, when I was going through Khatib's uniform, I found a holo card with Ortega's personnel file, taken from the company he and Yang both worked for. And the signature authorizing the transfer of the file was *Fengshi Yang*." A pause. "There's only one way Khatib could have come into possession of that card."

"So Yang killed Ortega, then Khatib . . ."

"Killed Yang. I'd put my money on him, anyway. And Wallace knew about it, at the very least. That's why he lied, so we wouldn't connect him with the murder."

"So that's murder and complicity, and concealment of the crime," Sheridan said. "But is it proof?"

"We'll have proof for sure if we find Yang's prints or other traces of him on that card, as soon as we can do a forensic scan . . ." He stopped as the thought occurred to him, only an instant before it occurred to Sheridan, too: the evidence implicating Wallace, still in Medlab.

Where they'd left Wallace. And Wallace, nowhere to be found.

Garibaldi had his link on first. "Dr. Franklin! This is Garibaldi! It's an emergency!"

"This is Franklin, what is it, Garibaldi?"

"The evidence! Khatib's effects! Are they still secure? Listen, whatever you do, don't let Commander Wallace—"

"You're too late, Garibaldi, he was already here."

Only the tone of amusement in Franklin's voice kept Garibaldi from cursing out loud. "And the evidence? Is it safe?"

"Come and see for yourself."

"I figured it must be important, whatever it was, the way you and Wallace were fighting over it," Franklin was saying. "So I put it in the most secure place around here, the biohazard lab. Not too long after you left, Wallace pulled out a gun and demanded I turn over the evidence. He said he was the only one authorized to have access to it. Well, I don't argue with a gun in my face, so I opened the lab and let him in."

Franklin was grinning. Neither Sheridan nor Garibaldi quite got the joke. "You might remember, I just recently upgraded the security for the biohazard lab."

"Yeah," said Garibaldi, "I remember you said something about adding more fail-safes."

Franklin nodded. "Now there are two sealed air-locks, each one leading into the next compartment. Unless you activate the override sequence, the locks don't open until the person in the chamber has undergone a prescribed decontamination procedure and put on an environment suit. And if someone doesn't wait for the procedure and tries to force the lock . . ."

Now Garibaldi was grinning. "And you didn't hit the override switch when you sent him in there, did you?"

Franklin looked pleased with himself. "I don't much like it when people force their way into Medlab and wave guns in my face, no."

The air-lock door with the biohazard warning was clear, and Sheridan looked through, then Garibaldi. Commander Wallace lay unconscious on the floor. The inner seal of the air-lock showed signs that it had taken and withstood a direct burst from a PPG.

"That's one seriously sealed lock you've got there, Doc," Garibaldi commented.

"Biohazard contamination is a serious potential problem on a space station," Franklin replied in a humorless tone of voice. "The knock-out gas is released automatically when someone tries to force the seal. And that's the outer compartment. If someone tries to leave the inner chamber without going through decontamination, the gas that's released is lethal."

Garibaldi gave him a look of respect. "And the evidence bags are in there?"

Franklin nodded, stepped to a console, and input a command. "Of course, with the system deactivated, there's no risk. Do you want to go retrieve the evidence?"

Garibaldi hesitated. "You wouldn't want to go first? Just in case?"

CHAPTER 26

"Commander Ivanova, we're cleared for docking at Babylon 5. ETA twenty minutes."

"Thank you, Mr. Bogdonovich. Could you get me a clear channel to the station?"

"Here you are, Commander."

Ivanova was on the *Duster*'s bridge, her prisoner under guard back in the ship's small medlab. When the channel opened she said, "This is Commander Ivanova, could you put me through to Mr. Garibaldi?"

But C&C replied, "I'm sorry, Commander, but Mr. Garibaldi isn't available at the moment. There's a disturbance on the station."

Ivanova swore to herself in Russian.

"What was that, Commander?"

"Never mind. Can you contact me with someone in security, then? Ensign Torres, possibly?"

"I'm sorry, Commander, but there's really no one available in security right now."

"How big of a riot is it?"

"It's sort of a big one, Commander, from what I hear. Unless you have an emergency—"

"Not an emergency, exactly, no," Ivanova admitted. "But it is important. I suppose the captain is unavailable, too?"

"Sorry, Commander."

"Well, please have Mr. Garibaldi contact me onboard the *Duster* as soon as he's free."

"Trouble, Commander?" the transport's copilot asked.

"Some trouble on the station, it looks like. I don't have the details. A disturbance of some kind."

"I hope it doesn't mess up our docking."

"I doubt it. They wouldn't have cleared you if there was trouble in the docking bays." She thought a moment. "Could I borrow your guard after the ship docks? Massie, that's his name, isn't it? I'd like some more security when I take the prisoner onto the station, especially if there's trouble going on."

"Duke Massie, sure. Go right ahead and borrow him, Commander. If it weren't for you and your fighter squad, we probably wouldn't be docking now or anytime."

Things got busy then on the bridge as the crew prepared for docking. It was no simple maneuver with a ship as large as the *Duster,* and for a while Ivanova watched Bogdonovich's work on the bridge with professional interest. But halfway through the process she left to take charge again of her prisoner.

The raider didn't look so very dangerous in the custody of Massie, whose size had probably been one important qualification for his job. Zaccione wasn't so subdued, however, that he couldn't look up when Ivanova came into the room. "Hey, Earthforce, you're back! Missed me, did you?"

"Shut up, slimeball," said the guard.

Ivanova ignored both of them, saying to Massie, "I'd like you to help me take the prisoner to the lockup after we've docked. There's a disturbance on the station, and no security available."

"Sure, Commander, be glad to. He won't give you any trouble while I'm along."

"Thank you," she said uncomfortably, a little stiffly, while the raider grinned.

Ivanova uncharitably observed that his swollen, broken nose rather negated the intended effect of his boyish charm. She counted the minutes until the transport was docked and she could get rid of both prisoner and guard. She stood quickly when the announcement came over the comm system: *Docking procedures completed. Passengers may begin disembarking now.*

"That means us," she said briskly. "Let's go."

"Let's go," Massie repeated to the raider, gesturing with his weapon.

Zaccione got more stiffly to his feet. "Whatever you say."

The *Duster* did in fact carry a few passengers in addition to freight. Ivanova encountered them on the way to the boarding hatch. When the civilians saw the armed Earthforce officer, the massive armed guard, and the prisoner between them, they quickly stepped back to give them plenty of clearance.

The Babylon 5 customs guard also raised her eyebrows at the sight of them. "Welcome back, Commander." She looked at the prisoner, the guard.

"Nothing to declare, Fitch," Ivanova said briskly. "Just a worthless piece of salvage. How are things on the station now?"

"Settling down. Cleaning up to do yet."

"Thanks." Ivanova frowned, wondering why Garibaldi hadn't contacted her if the disturbance was over. Had he gotten her message?

Once they got to the lift tube, she raised her link, not taking her eyes from her prisoner. "Garibaldi, this is Ivanova. Are things under control?"

"Ivanova! You're back!"

"Can you meet me in Security Central? At the lockup? I think you'll want to see what I brought back."

"I'm there now. I think you'll want to see what I've got, too."

She frowned, recognizing the amused tone in Garibaldi's voice and wondering what surprise she had waiting for her this time.

Getting off the tube at Red level, she was shocked to see the condition in which the riot had left the place. Wall panels had been battered, even quite a few of them ripped off. Lights were smashed, equipment broken, and debris littered the floor. A maintenance engineer was up on a scaffold doing repairs to a power junction that looked as if it had been blasted with fire from a PPG. Which, knowing Garibaldi, Ivanova figured it probably had.

The raider emitted a low whistle. "Some wild parties you guys must have around here, Earthforce."

Ivanova gritted her teeth. Without comment, she led the way to Security Central, back to the lockup area, where both Garibaldi and Sheridan were waiting for her. "Captain," she said in slight surprise. Then, gesturing at Zaccione, "Garibaldi, will you please have someone take this off my hands? Mr. Massie, thank you for your assistance."

A guard came to lead the raider away, but Zaccione turned to call back, "It's been fun, Earthforce!"

Garibaldi rolled his eyes back. "Who's that?"

Ivanova exhaled in relief. "One of the raiders who hit us out there. I managed to run him down and persuade him to surrender." Then, turning back to Sheridan and straightening to attention, "Sorry, sir. Mission was completed successfully. Transport safely escorted to dock. Nine raider ships shot down, one captured. But we lost Lieutenant Mokena."

Captain Sheridan's face seemed to tremble for an instant, before his expression set. He'd heard those words too many times, too many men and women under his command gone to their deaths. "Any other casualties?" he asked at last.

"No, sir, just slight damage to Alpha Four. Moy brought in my ship, and I came back in the transport with the prisoner."

The dead pilot's memory hovered like a ghostly presence among them, reducing speech to set formulas. Finally Garibaldi asked, "And your prisoner? Sorry, I got your message, but I didn't have time to contact you before this. We had a few problems on the station."

"So I saw," she said dryly. But then she recalled a little of the excitement of finding out what Zaccione knew. "The prisoner, right. I got him to talk. He knows *all* about the morbidium deal! It's a company called AreTech behind it."

"AreTech Consolidated Mines?" Garibaldi asked with great interest.

"They pass the routing information on to the raiders. It's a scheme to sell morbidium on the black market. I'm sure there are Earth Alliance officials involved, too. To keep the whole dirty mess quiet."

"And this guy knows about it?"

"He knows a lot. More than he's already said, I'll bet on it."

"So that's what it was all about," Sheridan said, shaking his head.

"And that must have been what Ortega knew, the reason they wanted him killed," Garibaldi added.

Ivanova looked at him. "Ortega? You found a connection?"

"Oh, I forgot, you don't know. J. D. Ortega worked for AreTech mines. The guy who killed him, Yang, worked as an enforcer for the mining company."

"That's what Zaccione said! People who asked too many questions about the mining operations would turn up missing."

"Yeah, that sounds like Yang, all right," Garibaldi agreed.

"So that's it! That was the information they were after!" Ivanova's excitement heated with hope. They had the answer! Finally!

"And then Wallace's gang came onto the station to find out what Ortega knew, who he'd passed the information on to. They found out about Yang, took care of him—"

"Commander Wallace killed Yang?"

"Actually, it was probably Khatib, if you ask me. At any rate, we found evidence decisively linking Khatib to Yang's death."

"Has he confessed?" Ivanova asked doubtfully.

"He can't. He's dead," Garibaldi said.

"Khatib is dead?" Ivanova shook her head. "Wait a minute. Just what exactly has been going on around here while I was gone?"

Garibaldi grinned. "It all started when I got a lead on that guy who set me up to get zapped. I put him under arrest—he has an interesting story to tell, too, by the way —and I tried to keep it quiet, but apparently word got out. Some of Nagy's Free Mars pals panicked. They must have figured somebody talked and they were next to be arrested. They killed Khatib—I guess they didn't like him as much as me—and shoved his body out the airlock. We retrieved the body, took it to Medlab, and that's where we found the evidence linking him to Yang's murder."

"That's all?" Ivanova asked, eyebrows raised.

"Not quite. So when Wallace found out Khatib was dead, he went a little unhinged. He ordered a general sweep, started to pull in people from all over the station —people from Mars, people who'd worked with Nagy, people who had any connection to mining. And that was just the last straw. People had just had enough of the arrests. Somebody tried to intervene, it turned into a fight, the fight turned into a riot.

"And while we were all busy trying to put out the flames, Wallace sneaks back into Medlab to try to steal the evidence linking Khatib to Yang."

''And did he?'' she asked, ready to believe anything by this time.

Garibaldi's grin widened. ''Nope. But he did manage to give us sufficient cause to charge him with complicity in Yang's murder. After the fact at the least.''

Ivanova slowly understood. ''You mean—''

''That's right. Wallace and his little mouthpiece Miyoshi are locked up right down the hall from your pirate.''

CHAPTER 27

The raider wasn't cooperating. He wasn't joking anymore, either, at least.

"He insists on seeing the Ombunds," Sheridan told Ivanova. "Says he's not saying a word unless he does. Says he's got the right."

"He has the nerve to talk about *rights* . . ." she fumed.

"Well, he does," Sheridan told her. "And the fact is, he doesn't have to talk at all, if it comes to that. If we want his testimony, that's how we're going to have to play it."

"Put him out on the other side of the air-lock, see how long it takes him to decide to talk," Ivanova said stubbornly. "I've got it all on record, what he told me on the transport."

"That's another point," Sheridan said firmly. "It could be argued—and when he goes to trial and has a lawyer it probably *will* be argued—that everything he said at the time was coerced. That you threatened him. Now, I understand how it was—Mokena getting killed, the heat of combat. You got carried away. But if we want his testimony to hold up this time, we've got to do it by the book."

"So he gets to see the Ombunds. To cut a deal." Ivanova was disgusted.

"We need what he has to say," Garibaldi said, looking up from the display where he was going over the raider's records. "We're all pretty far out on a limb here if Earth Central wants to start sawing. J. D. Ortega still officially has the status of a wanted terrorist, and you're still under suspicion as his associate. We have to prove those charges were false, that Earthforce officials on Mars were corrupt, that Wallace was engaging in a cover-up, not a legitimate investigation."

"Or else we're in for a long, hard fall," Ivanova said under her breath, reverting to pessimism.

Communications broke in. "Captain Sheridan, there's a Gold level transmission for you, from Earth. Admiral Wilson."

Oh-oh, Garibaldi's expression said, and Ivanova nodded agreement as they both stood to leave the briefing room and give the captain privacy to take the call.

Sheridan faced the comm screen alone, like a man facing an execution detail. He straightened his shoulders, said, "Put the admiral through."

Wilson's face was high-colored with agitation. "You've really done it this time, Sheridan. You had your orders. *Explicit* orders. You were warned. *Not* to interfere with Commander Wallace's investigation in *any way.* I thought I made myself clear. You've exceeded your authority this time, Sheridan."

"With all due respect, sir, I believe I have not. I believe that my actions were justified. Sir."

"*Arresting* the investigating officer? For murder? For conspiracy?"

"Sir, if my authority in commanding this station does not include the authority to place a murder suspect under arrest, given adequate cause, then I hereby tender my resignation, immediately."

"Now, you just hold it, Sheridan. What are you talking about?"

"Sir, we have proof that Commander Wallace's aide, Lieutenant Khatib, murdered a man named Fengshi Yang. We have additional evidence that the commander knew about this murder, that he abused his authority in order to cover it up, and that he finally tried to destroy the evidence, pulling a lethal weapon on my senior medical officer.''

Wilson looked dubious. "This is a serious accusation. You said you have *proof*?''

"I hope so, yes, sir. We do have proof of the murder, and who committed it. And in addition, we may have additional evidence that involves the commander in a another conspiracy which has cost the lives of over one hundred transport crew members over the last sixteen months.''

Now Wilson snorted in disbelief. "Wallace? In a conspiracy?''

"Sir, we have strong evidence that AreTech Consolidated Mines has been engaged in a systematic conspiracy to sell out its own cargoes to raiders, in order to profit from the increased price of the metal. We believe Earth Alliance officials were part of this conspiracy. We have reason to believe that the actual purpose of Commander Wallace's investigation was not to pursue Free Mars terrorists but to eliminate a threat to this conspiracy.''

Wilson's face slowly lost its color. "You say you have evidence of this?'' he asked slowly. "This conspiracy?''

"We have some evidence. In the case of the murder, conclusive evidence. Our investigation into the other matters isn't concluded yet.''

Wilson looked grave. "Captain, you've stumbled onto matters you know nothing about. It may be that you've uncovered some valuable information. I'm going to consult with my superiors about this. I'm not authorized to disclose any further details. In the meanwhile, let me warn you—this information is to go no further than it's already gone. Is that understood?''

"Yes, sir. And what about Commander Wallace? He hasn't yet been officially charged with murder—''

"Forget about that, Captain. You do nothing about the

commander. It will be taken care of. A ship will be coming to take him back to Earth."

"I understand."

"I'll get back to you about the rest of this. Wilson out."

The screen blanked. Sheridan sat for a moment watching the BABCOM logo scroll across it, as if it carried a message for his execution. Finally he stood and went through to where Garibaldi and Ivanova were waiting for him, both looking concerned.

"Do we keep our heads," Garibaldi was the one to ask, "or not?"

"We keep them." But before the expressions of relief could take hold, he added, "For the moment."

"And Wallace?" Ivanova asked.

"Gets shipped back to Earth." Sheridan glanced around at security agents coming and going, making reports and taking calls. "Maybe we'd better talk about this back inside."

"He's going to get away with murder?" Garibaldi demanded with some heat once they were back behind the closed doors of the briefing room.

Sheridan answered him slowly. "I get the distinct feeling that Earthforce Command thinks a single murder is insignificant, in comparison."

"To what?" Ivanova asked.

"To what they won't say yet." Sheridan paused to remember what Wilson had said: "We've stumbled onto matters we know nothing about. That we're not supposed to know anything about, either."

"So what are we supposed to do, then?" Ivanova demanded.

"For one thing, not to let this information, whatever it means, go any further than it already has. That's an order. And the other thing is, if we have any chance of finding more evidence, we'd better find it now."

Ivanova sighed. "In that case, we'd better call in the Ombunds."

Ombunds Wellington's position on the matter was quite firm. The station's chief civilian judge might be old and white-haired, but his air of authority was sufficient to transform the utilitarian setting of the interrogation room into a court.

"No matter what you might think of Mr. Zaccione's alleged crimes, nothing he could have done negates the fact that he still has the right not to incriminate himself. And it seems clear that what you're asking him to do, to testify about these matters you can't disclose, would in fact require him to admit to his involvement in a number of crimes that carry the highest penalties our law allows —short of the death penalty, that is," he added, with a reproving look at Ivanova.

She flared back, "I don't need his confession. I have enough proof to convict his tail a dozen times over. I *saw* him flame my wingman—"

"But that isn't the point, Commander, as we all know," Sheridan reminded her. "It's not Zaccione we want to convict. Not now, at any rate."

She exhaled sharply. "I know. Of course. Sorry. It's just the thought of that scum, getting off—"

"You don't want to convict him now," Wellington reminded them, "but Mr. Zaccione has to consider that he will be put on trial later, in the future. When what he says now can be held against him."

"What's the deal, then?" Garibaldi asked, getting as usual to the bottom line. "If he thinks he can just walk—"

"I managed to convince him that option was unrealistic," Wellington said dryly. "As Commander Ivanova points out, the evidence against him is quite overwhelming. He has agreed to testify for you under two conditions: first, that none of his testimony will ever be used as evidence against him in a court of law. Second, that you agree not to seek either the death penalty or brainwipe if he's convicted of any crimes.''

Ivanova was about to protest, but Sheridan said, ''Remember, Commander, from what Admiral Wilson said, I don't think it's likely that Earth Central will allow the facts to be made public in a trial, no matter what. And if we have any hope of proving . . . what we need to prove, your raider is it.''

''I know. I know. All right. If it's the only way.''

''Tell him it's a deal,'' said Garibaldi.

''No, wait!'' They all looked at Ivanova. ''All right,'' she said through clenched teeth, ''it's a deal, but I want something else. I want a guarantee that his testimony is really the truth. I want a telepath to scan him during questioning. I want the truth out of him, no matter what.''

Garibaldi stared at her. ''You want to call in the Psi Corps?''

''Ivanova has a point,'' Sheridan agreed. ''Can we get Ms. Winters in to scan the raider while we question him?''

''I'll see if she's available,'' Garibaldi said, lifting his link. ''This is Garibaldi, get me Ms. Winters.''

But he still couldn't quite believe Ivanova had asked for her. Not Ivanova.

Two guards brought the prisoner between them into the briefing room, sat him in a chair, and at a nod from Garibaldi, left the room.

The raider looked around, from one of them to another, and when his eyes lit on Ivanova a faint grin came onto his face. ''Hey, Earthforce, I guess you missed me, huh?''

But the joke was halfhearted and fell predictably flat

in the company present. Garibaldi took the place of the guards, leaning back in the corner with his arms crossed, watchful eyes on the prisoner.

Captain Sheridan, ignoring the remark, began the proceedings by sitting down opposite the raider. "Mr. Zaccione, this session is being recorded. You've freely agreed to make these statements on the condition that they won't be used against you in any future legal action, is that correct?"

"Yes, that's right," he replied.

"The woman standing next to you is Ms. Talia Winters, registered telepath. She'll be scanning you during the questioning to monitor the truth of your statements. You've freely agreed to this, is that correct?"

"Right."

"Mr. Zaccione," Talia took over, "I want you to relax and try not to think about my presence. Simply answer all the questions openly. Remember, I'll only be scanning the surface level of your thoughts, just far enough to determine whether you're telling the truth. You probably won't even be aware that I'm here, unless you attempt to lie."

"Oh, I think I'd always be aware of *you* in my brain, Psi Corps," he said, turning the grin on the telepath, who ignored it.

"I'm ready, Captain."

"All right, Zaccione, you can start by telling us everything you know about the scheme by AreTech Consolidated Mines to have its cargoes apprehended by raiders. How did you obtain the shipping schedules from the company?"

The raider went through the entire story again, essentially what he'd already told Ivanova on board the *Duster:* how a contact from AreTech had met with an agent of the raiders to pass on the shipping routes and schedules, the company selling out its own cargoes. But Sheridan pressed for more details:

"How often did your agent meet with the company representative?"

"Did you know the names of the ships? The exact nature of the cargoes? The exact tonnage?"

"How many freighters did you attack every month as a result of this information? How many in total? What was the total tonnage of cargo lost?"

Most questions the raider answered, occasionally saying he didn't know the exact details Sheridan was asking for. In a few cases, he seemed reluctant.

"The name of the AreTech representative who supplied this information to you?"

"I'm not sure . . ."

"Previously, you told Commander Ivanova that your organization had verified his identity."

"Forrester, I think. Or maybe Forrestal—something like that."

"Ms. Winters?" Sheridan asked.

"I believe the name Forrestal is correct, Captain. As far as he knows."

"And the name of your agent on Mars?"

Zaccione shifted uncomfortably in his chair. "I . . . don't—"

"That's not true, Captain," Talia said crisply. "He does know the name, but he's reluctant to disclose it."

"Answer the question," Sheridan ordered.

The raider's eyes shifted from Sheridan to the telepath. "You'd better answer, Zack," she told him. "It'll be a lot easier on you than if I have to go in after the name."

"King," he finally said in a low voice. "Wally King. He works as a shipping clerk in a freight office in Marsport."

"That's the truth," Talia confirmed.

"Good. Now," Sheridan went on, "do you believe there were Earth Alliance officials connected to this conspiracy? Officers in Earthforce?"

"Somebody had to keep Earthforce off our backs." He glanced briefly, resentfully at Ivanova. "They were supposed to, anyway."

"What are the names of these corrupt Earthforce officials?"

Zaccione shook his head. There was a noticeable increase of tension in the room. Ivanova held her breath. Garibaldi leaned forward.

"I don't know."

"Their names," Sheridan insisted. "Ms. Winters?"

She looked over at the captain. "He's not lying."

"Go deeper," Ivanova insisted. "Dig them out of him."

"He doesn't know their names," Talia said firmly.

Sheridan scowled. "Does the name Yang mean anything to you?"

"Yeah, but he's not Earthforce. He works for the company. Leans on people who ask questions."

"To your knowledge, did Yang ever kill to keep people from asking questions?"

"One time I know of, at least. Guy from an insurance agency came around. They found him outside the dome without his breather."

"And what about the name Wallace?"

The raider shook his head.

"He doesn't know," Talia supplied.

"Are you sure?" Ivanova demanded.

"Quite sure. He doesn't know the name."

Sheridan's expression was worried. He looked at Ivanova, shook his head. He continued the questioning a while longer, eliciting a few more facts about the raiders' operations, but no more details about the Earth Alliance officials who were supposed to be involved in the cover-up. Zaccione didn't know their names. He'd never been in direct contact with them. They worked behind the scenes, he explained.

Eventually Sheridan pushed back his chair. "I guess that'll be all," he admitted.

Garibaldi left his corner, led the prisoner away, back to the lockup.

"I'm sorry," Sheridan said to Ivanova. "I don't know how much this will help. Without the names. Without a direct connection to Wallace."

"Oh, well." She grinned weakly. "I guess you can't get turnip juice from a stone. We tried."

"We did the best job we could," Sheridan agreed. "And thank you, Ms. Winters, for assisting."

Ivanova hesitated a moment, then stepped closer to Talia. "Yes, thank you. I know it had to be unpleasant, stepping into that kind of mind."

Talia shook her head, produced a faint smile. "Oh, he wasn't so bad. Not compared to some."

Ivanova's brows raised. "Scum like him? With what he said to you?"

"Oh, a lot of people say that kind of thing—men, especially, when they're trying to mask anxiety. It didn't mean anything."

Ivanova looked skeptical. "Anxiety? Him?"

Now it was Talia's turn to hesitate. "I know you don't . . . care for what I do, Commander. But I've learned that most minds really aren't evil. Some of them—yes, some of them are. But mostly what I see is fear. And loneliness. And self-doubt. I know that this raider shot down your wingman, that you must be very angry. But there was nothing you could have—"

Ivanova held up her hands in front of her face, shook her head. "No," she said, "you don't know that, you don't know anything about it . . ."

She rushed from the room.

Talia sighed in dismay. "I'm sorry," she apologized to Sheridan. "I almost thought there, for a moment, that she could accept what I am, that I'm not a threat to her."

"It's all right," Sheridan said. "It didn't take a telepath to see it. It's hard when you lose a wingman, you know. Even when you know there's nothing you could have done, there's still this voice inside you, saying if you just could have been there a little sooner, tried a little harder."

Talia turned to a different subject. "Is it true? Has Commander Wallace been arrested?"

Sheridan frowned. "I supposed you'd know sooner or later. It's true. But that's confidential."

"Of course." She nodded slowly. "I'm glad. Doing this for him, invading all those poor people's minds while he questioned them . . . Their consent was coerced, you know. He threatened them with arrest, shipping them back to Earth. In some cases, they never consented at all."

"Well, he won't be doing it anymore," Sheridan assured her. "Not on Babylon 5."

CHAPTER 28

"Captain Sheridan, there's a Gold level communication, from Admiral Wilson."

Sheridan had been expecting it. "Put him on."

It was in fact an Ultraviolet level transmission, which required Sheridan to input his code before it would commence. Then Wilson's face appeared on the wall display. "Well, Sheridan, I expect that Commander Wallace and his aide will soon be on their way back to Earth."

"Yes, sir, their ship leaves Babylon 5 in about half an hour."

"Good. And I'm sure you'll be glad to know that your recent actions have been reviewed by the Joint Chiefs, and they've decided that under the circumstances, you were justified in what you did. It seems on further examination that Commander Wallace didn't conduct his investigation with the greatest possible amount of discretion."

"And the other charges against him?"

The admiral cleared his throat portentously. "I've been authorized to disclose certain facts which were previously restricted—with good reason. The conspiracy involving AreTech Consolidated Mines is indeed quite real. In fact, your investigation into the matter will prove quite helpful in tracking down a number of matters you don't need to know about. But some arrests have already been made on the basis of what you've sent.

"However, your suspicions concerning the involvement of Commander Wallace, no matter how well founded they might have seemed in light of your limited knowledge of the situation, are incorrect. Commander

Wallace is an agent of the Joint Chiefs office. The matter which he was sent to investigate is something that must remain classified, but it involves information of vital importance to Earth's defenses. Vital importance.

"This information is believed to have been obtained by the man named J. D. Ortega, who was employed by AreTech. We still aren't sure what he intended to do with it. Suffice it to say that he could have gotten any price— any price he wanted to name—for it. AreTech sent their agent to get the information back. Our agents were searching for him at the same time. As you're aware, the agent from AreTech got to him first.

"Commander Wallace's orders were to retrieve that information by any means necessary. Naturally, his suspicion centered on the AreTech agent, Yang. Unfortunately . . . well, you know what occurred. At any rate, the information has never been recovered. We can only conclude it must have been destroyed—or that it's already gotten into the wrong hands. This is unfortunate, but there doesn't seem to be any value in pursuing it further."

"Then the investigation is over?"

"I'm afraid it is. But you'll be glad to know that there will be no reprimands for you or your staff. We understand that you had to proceed according to the information available."

"Yes, sir, that's very good to hear. Then I assume Commander Ivanova will be reinstated as second-in-command here?"

Wilson frowned. "At this time, the Joint Chiefs don't think such an action would be advisable."

Sheridan stood halfway up in his chair. "What? It was Commander Ivanova who uncovered the conspiracy—"

"True, Captain. The Joint Chiefs have taken this into consideration."

"Into consideration of *what*?"

"The possibility of terrorist associations—"

"There *was* no terrorist activity involved! You just admitted it yourself. J. D. Ortega was taking some secret information from AreTech Mines, he wasn't a terrorist!"

"Captain, you're out of order!" Wilson's color rose as his scowl deepened. "As the evidence from your own security department clearly shows, this Ortega did have a connection to the Free Mars movement. It was this terrorist organization that arranged for him to leave Mars and come onto Babylon 5 with false credentials. It was individuals connected with this organization who conspired to attack your head of security and who most probably murdered Lieutenant Khatib, in order to protect their own identities. Isn't this correct?"

"But that has nothing to do with Ivanova!" Sheridan insisted vehemently. "She had nothing to do with J. D. Ortega. He was her flight instructor, years ago—that's all."

"That may be true, but nevertheless, the decision of the Joint Chiefs is that it would be best if Commander Ivanova did not occupy the rather sensitive position of executive officer of Babylon 5. At this time, at least. The matter is scheduled for a review."

"A review? When?"

"A decision on that has not yet been made. You'll be informed of the results in due course."

And with that, he cut the transmission while Sheridan could only sit and swear at the logo on the screen.

The worst part was—he still had to tell Ivanova.

The liner Asimov *will be departing for Earth at 09:00 hours, with scheduled stops at Mars and Luna colonies. Passengers can now proceed to boarding area. We hope you've enjoyed your stay on Babylon 5.*

Sinclair nodded absently at the announcement. Sometimes it was reassuring to hear the normal sounds of the station going about its regular routine—business as usual, no emergencies, no disturbances.

The lift tube opened, and a pair of security guards stepped out, escorting a prisoner in prison coveralls and wrist restraints, Garibaldi following them. Sheridan watched the raider Zaccione being taken past the customs guards and into the ship before the regular passengers. Garibaldi stopped to join him. "Lucky guy," he commented.

"Not too lucky. He'll be spending the rest of his life in prison on Earth."

"Better off than brainwiped," Garibaldi insisted. He rubbed his forehead. "But sometimes I think Ivanova's got the right idea, just shove them out the air-lock. Easier on everyone."

"Maybe," Sheridan said. "When you've seen enough good men die, it's hard to get real worked up about a bad one. But I think she's taking it all fairly well. Considering."

Garibaldi nodded. "She was fine at the trial. I was glad to see that. For a while, I was worried she was kind of obsessed with this raider."

"I know. He was the one who killed Mokena. And, you know, it's a lot easier when you have someone to take the blame, instead of wondering if there was something else you could have done."

"Yeah, but a good commander always does."

Neither of them said anything else for a while, just stood there, watching the traffic moving through the station.

"It was a raw deal they gave her," Garibaldi said finally, meaning the Joint Chiefs, not the raiders.

"When I could send her out on those escort patrols," Sheridan agreed, "it was one thing. A mission. Something she could get her teeth into. But now—they could have reassigned her. But to just leave her like this . . ."

"I could use her in security, but that's no job for someone with her rank. It's just a raw deal," Garibaldi said again.

But there was nothing either of them could do. There was no higher level where the decision could be appealed. They were both aware that promises of a future review were just that—empty promises. Earth Central would simply let Ivanova wait until she finally got tired of hanging in the vacuum and turned in her resignation.

"Commander! Commander Ivanova!"

Ivanova turned around. It was Espada calling to her, the insurance agent. She waited until the other woman had caught up.

"Commander—Oh, I'm out of breath!—Commander, I just wanted to thank you and let you know Earthforce has finally released the information we needed for our case against AreTech Mines! We have proof now that we can take to court—AreTech *was* feeding the shipping routes to the raiders! We're suing to invalidate all their claims." Espada was beaming with elation. "I don't know how you knew it, but you were right. They've already stopped trading in AreTech stock. They say the corporation directors are all going to be indicted, not just the officials directly involved."

"I suppose Universal stock would be a pretty good buy now, then?" Ivanova asked wryly.

Espada suddenly sobered. "Well, strictly speaking, to say that would be a violation of the statutes on disclosing insider information. But if anyone deserves to profit from all this, it's you!"

"Well, I'll certainly keep that in mind when the next big financial windfall drops at my feet," Ivanova replied. She apologized for having to rush away, citing urgent duties and deeply feeling the irony of the lie. *"Urgent duties,"* right. As urgent as polishing the silverware in the mess hall. Taking an inventory of the inventory-control forms. Or maybe the forms for officers tendering the resignation of their commissions. Which she was afraid it was going to come to, sooner or later. Couldn't go on like this forever, that was for sure.

What was on the agenda for today? Another training flight?

She knew she couldn't blame Sheridan for her situation. He had his orders. And part of the problem was, by capturing that raider, she'd just smarted herself out of her own job. Taking out those escort patrols, going head-to-head with the raiders, that was one thing. But routine training flights, day after day?

She went to her locker in the ready room, started to suit up. Still no replacement for Mokena, she noted as the others pulled on their flight suits.

No, she couldn't blame Sheridan. The fact was, and she knew it, Earth Central just didn't trust her. And it was nothing to do with terrorists on Mars, either, though they still used that convenient excuse. They still thought she knew something, had something to do with that secret information Ortega had—whatever it was, if there ever really was secret information. Maybe it was lost, maybe it wasn't. No one knew. All Ivanova knew was that Ortega wanted to pass it on to her, have her save it for him—something. And that *damned* note. "Hardwir," she said out loud. Never had figured out what it meant.

Climbing into the cockpit. Sealing the canopy. Instrument check. "Alpha Flight, power on."

The routine she could do in her sleep. Training flight. Close-formation flying. Basic maneuvers. She dropped back and let Moy take over the leader position, give her some experience, see how she did with it. Then back to the warm red tunnel of the docking bay, back to Babylon 5.

That damned note was still on her mind. "Hardwir."

What was it supposed to mean? Why had J. D. thought she'd remember? Earth Central probably thought it was a secret code.

Back in the ready room. The place was a mess, as usual. The little old woman mopping the floor wasn't doing a very good job cleaning up.

Maybe Sheridan would let her have that job—scrubbing floors.

It sure didn't look like she was ever going to get a better one here on Babylon 5.

Garibaldi was still on duty when he wandered into the casino, just to check things out. Ivanova would have been on duty, too, in better times. At the moment, though, she was out of uniform—very much so, in fact. Hair down, red dress obviously cut with display in mind, drink in her hand.

And the guy next to her had his hand where Garibaldi had rarely ever seen a guy put his hand—and survive the experience. But Ivanova was laughing. Laughing a little too loud. And leaning back against the guy, so his hand slid farther down, across the surface of one breast . . .

Garibaldi's eyes narrowed. He didn't like this. Ivanova could take care of herself, under normal circumstances. Hell, he'd seen her close down the bar, just because some idiot made a remark suggesting he might like to do what this guy was doing right now. Garibaldi thought he'd frankly almost rather see her exorcising her demons that way, in a good brawl, not like this.

He wandered purposefully in her direction. Forcing a cheerful tone, "Hey, Ivanova! This a friend of yours, is he? I don't think we've met."

"Garibaldi! Hi! This is Rick." She blinked through an alcoholic haze. "It is Rick, isn't it?"

"Sure is, Susie. Rick Morrison, remember?"

Garibaldi almost boggled openly as the guy stroked

her throat, and downward, where the dress invited it. *Susie?!* Ivanova? As Londo would say, *Great Maker!*

"Pleased to meet you," Garibaldi managed to say with the minimum necessary civility.

But a few moments later, when Ivanova had briefly left the table, he had his chance. Taking the guy by the elbow hard enough to let him know he meant business, he said, "Look, *friend,* I just want you to know something. Susan Ivanova *is* my friend. And I wouldn't be happy to hear that she ends up doing something she's going to regret the morning after. You understand me?"

"Hey, what's it to you? I'd say the lady's old enough to know what she wants. What are you, anyway? Her keeper? Her father, maybe?"

That one hurt. But if Garibaldi was maybe old enough to be Ivanova's father, he could at least show this slimy punk how easy it would be for the old man to break his arm. The guy blanched as he applied just a little more force to his elbow. "I'll tell you who I am. I'm head of security on Babylon 5, that's who. Now, maybe you're right and Ivanova's old enough to choose who she wants to party with. That's fine with me. But is she sober enough? That's the question. So I tell you what. You can either pretend to be a gentleman and walk her back to her quarters and shake her hand good night. Or you can take your chances. But if you hurt her, you'll by God wish you were never born."

He released the arm just as Ivanova came back to the table. The guy pulled it away and rubbed his elbow, looking frightened. Ivanova had a glazed look in her eyes. "I'm getting kind of sleepy, Dick, I think I'd like to go back to my quarters and go to bed."

The guy swallowed nervously. "I'll walk you back there," he said.

Garibaldi watched them go. So maybe he'd been out of line, maybe Ivanova was entitled to a little harmless fun. Maybe this Rick Morrison or whoever was really a nice guy.

And maybe the Narn and the Centauri would kiss and let bygones be bygones.

God, he hated to see Ivanova like this! But how else could he help her? What could he do?

Commander Ivanova, the time is now 06:05 hours.

The mercilessly cheerful computer voice repeated the time again. Ivanova moaned.

"Commander, your reply was not understood. Would you repeat?"

She tried to raise her head, moaned again, and finally managed to form a couple of semicoherent words: "Go away."

"Acknowledged, Commander. Have a nice day!"

Ivanova hoped that if she only lay very, very still, she wouldn't be sick. Or was it that she'd already been sick and was just waiting to die? She hoped in that case it wouldn't be long.

There was a foul taste in her mouth, her stomach was threatening to heave itself inside out, and her head refused to lift itself off the pillows. She made herself think of the medical dispenser in the bathroom. Relief, if she could just get herself there without being sick on the way. She managed to sit up, to stand, to grope her way across the room, because opening her eyes would have been too much.

"Sobertal," she groaned, and clutched the tablet released by the dispenser. She swallowed it dry, stood holding herself upright, waiting for the pill to take effect.

At last she could open her eyes. She confronted her image in the mirror and quickly shut them again. Oh, no!

What was I doing last night? she asked herself.

A cold shower helped some. Enough to get her brain powered up to remember the night before. Going to the casino. By herself. Feeling *damned* sorry for herself. A sympathetic someone. His nice, warm hands supporting her as he brought her to the door . . .

Only suddenly the notion didn't seem all that nice at all. The conviction that she'd been acting like a fool was taking firm hold in her mind.

On her way back across the room she almost tripped over the dress lying on the floor. The red dress. Ivanova closed her eyes. Why did I decide to wear *that*?

Sober enough by now to feel completely disgusted with herself, she got into her uniform, braiding her hair as tightly as possible until it felt like it was pulling the remains of her headache out by the roots. She ignored the rest of the crowd still in the mess hall for a late breakfast and headed mindlessly to the line for coffee, only remembering at the last minute as the bitter, chemical-flavored synthetic poured into her cup that there was no real coffee.

She shuddered, but took it, unable to face this particular morning without something containing caffeine. At least it was hot. And equally unable to stand the thought of company, she sat down at a table by herself.

She only glanced up when her half-lidded eyes caught sight of a cheerfully replete figure heading in her direction. She closed her eyes completely. *No, not Garibaldi, not this morning!*

He grinned wickedly. "Well, Ivanova, how was your night out?"

She didn't look up. "I don't want to hear about it, Garibaldi, I really don't."

"Really?"

There was something in his tone. Now she did look up. "What did I do? Take off all my clothes? Challenge the Minbari Wind Swords to a duel? Has the casino got a warrant out for my arrest?"

His voice went more serious. He pulled out a chair and

sat down across from her. "Nothing like that. Really. I was worried about you, that's all. That guy you were with—"

"What guy?" she demanded defensively, vaguely recalling that there was some guy or other, but not who.

"Hey! I'm sure he was a perfect gentleman! Look, I'm not saying you can't go out and have a good time. You've earned it. I just . . ." He hesitated. "I just remember when I started thinking that a few drinks might help me face my problems. I don't like to see you . . ."

He looked down at the table; she stared into her coffee mug. Finally, "He was a perfect gentleman, huh?"

"After I promised to break his arm." He paused, saving the best for last. "He was calling you 'Susie.' "

Ivanova winced, took another sip of black synthetic stuff. "Thanks," she said at last. "For caring what happens to me now. Sometimes . . . I'm not sure I do, anymore."

He stood up with a squeal of chair legs. "That's horsehockey. And you know it." And left her there to think it over by herself.

Alone again, she watched the last tendrils of steam from the mug die away. Garibaldi was right, she still cared. That her career was ruined, yes, there was nothing she cared for more than that. If there was only something she could *do* about it . . .

As she stared glumly into the black sludge in the mug, she saw another figure sit down at a solitary table with her tray. Talia Winters. Garibaldi's polar opposite in the food department. She probably had two pieces of dry toast on her tray, at the most. And these days she was looking so thin she was almost gaunt.

But now Ivanova recalled what Garibaldi had said about what Wallace had put Talia through, what a strain on her the ordeal had been. At least they had one thing in common, she thought—neither of them could stand Wallace. Guiltily, she remembered how she'd added to the telepath's workload, insisting that she should scan Zaccione, the raider. And how she'd reacted, afterward.

She lifted the mug, shuddered, put it down again and went back to the line for a fresh mug. She stopped at Talia's table. "Do you mind if I sit down?"

The telepath looked up sharply, startled. "Uh, why, no! Please do. You're just having coffee?"

"If you can call it that." Ivanova stole a glance at Talia's tray. Two pieces of toast. Not dry, though, there was some kind of spread on it. And a dish of fruit.

"I want . . ." Ivanova's throat closed up. This was hard. "I want to thank you again. For helping out during that testimony. I'm sorry I . . . reacted."

"That's all right, I understand. I didn't mean to criticize. Your personal life."

"No. I guess I was thinking, if I could just drag the truth out of that guy, it'd all be solved, all the conspiracies, everything. It'd all be *over*. Make up for everything. And then, it wasn't."

"I'm sorry it didn't all work out. I mean, for you."

"For my career. I know. That's what I want . . ." She swallowed. "I want to ask you. If you could help me again."

"If I can, yes, of course," Talia said, puzzled.

"I suppose you know that Earth Central doesn't want me reinstated. I think it's because they don't trust me, because of Ortega, because of that note he wrote, the information nobody's ever found—I think they still think I know something about it." Ivanova's speech was hesitating. She wondered if she was making any sense at all. Normally, with Talia, she did everything she could to push her away, away from her mind. Now . . .

"What I want is, what was on that note. It was just one word. I'm sure it should be something I remember, but I just don't. And the harder I try, the more it just doesn't mean anything. And I was wondering . . ."

Her hands were sweaty, and she put down the coffee mug before she dropped it. She could feel the rapid stutter of her heartbeat, the nervous tingle of fear. "I was wondering if you might be able to . . . find it . . ."

Talia spoke very softly, carefully. "I think I probably could, yes, if it's part of your memory. The mind retains many, many memories that the consciousness can't access." She looked dubiously at Ivanova. "But it would require something more than a simple surface scan. With Zaccione, for the most part, I was only skimming the outer surface of his thoughts. In your case, in the case you're discussing, I'd need to go deeper than that. Do you understand?"

Ivanova couldn't speak. If she could, she would have wanted to scream, to run, or strike out with every power she possessed: *Keep out of my mind!*

But instead, she stiffly nodded that she understood.

"It would be best to do this in a place where we can have complete privacy, with no interruptions. May I suggest my quarters?"

Ivanova nodded again, managed to whisper, "That would be fine."

Talia looked down at the half-eaten breakfast on her tray. "Do you want to go now?"

"No!" Ivanova took a quick, nervous sip from her mug. "Finish your breakfast. Please. I still have this coffee." Anything, she thought, to put it off, just another couple of minutes. She took a deeper drink from the mug and shuddered. *God, this stuff is awful!*

Ivanova had never been in Talia's quarters, and she looked around with some curiosity while she moved around the room, adjusting the placement of pillows, pulling a dead leaf off a plant. The telepath seemed almost as nervous as she was.

"Well," Talia finally said, "should we start this?"

Ivanova would have rather stepped out the air-lock. But it was her career. The only thing that could save it. "Yes," she said.

Talia gestured to a couch. "I think this would be the best place." As Ivanova stiffly sat down, Talia began, self-consciously, to remove her gray gloves. "Direct touch makes the mental contact easier," she explained, slightly embarrassed.

Ivanova nodded as the other woman sat down next to her. "Sit back, please. Try to relax. Close your eyes. Try not to resist my presence." They were almost the same words that Talia had used when preparing to scan the captured raider, but this time her tone was different, less impersonal.

The telepath carefully placed a hand over Ivanova's. It felt warm and slightly damp from the glove. Talia closed her eyes for a moment. "Now, I want you to think of the time you spent with J. D. Ortega. Don't try to remember any specific thing. Just picture his face in your mind, listen to some of the things he used to say to you. He was your flight trainer. Think about the time you spent with him in the cockpit of the training ship. Think about learning to fly. Yes, that's good."

Ivanova kept her eyes closed. Talia Winters's voice was very soft, a soothing voice. There was no reason for her to be nervous about this. She was going to help her remember, that was all.

She couldn't quite discern the moment when the spoken voice ceased and gave place to the voice in her mind. The touch of Talia's hand was warm, comforting, and reassuring. It was as if Talia were sitting with her in the cockpit of the training ship, with J. D. in the copilot's seat. Talia's bare hands were on the ship's controls, but they were also her own. They were wearing the gray cadet uniform instead of those long, concealing dresses that Talia always wore. *You don't like the way I dress? I'm sorry. I've always been sorry you didn't like me, Susan.*

Next to them, J. D. was talking about the use of the tactical screen. "You all know how to use a computer screen. But you can't use this the way you do an ordinary data screen."

He's really quite good-looking, I think. Too bad he was so much in love with his wife.

"You don't see the screen, you don't see through the screen. You see *with* the screen. It's like your eyes—do you stop and think about how to use your eyes? You don't, you simply see. Well, the screen is your eyes and the screen is your brain. The processing has to be immediate, instantaneous. You don't have time to stop and think."

He was a good pilot. But he didn't like the military. Just the flying.

"You know how they're saying that one day there'll be a direct interface hardwired between our brains and the ship's computer? Well, here's the secret: you have to learn to fly as if there already were—hardwired into the ship, all together."

Susan, isn't that it? The key to the message? Hardwired?

And now Ivanova heard the words, distinct from the thought in her mind: "Susan, isn't that it? The key to the message? *Hardwired?*"

Talia Winters's hand squeezed hers tightly. Ivanova jerked it away, jumped up. "Yes! Yes, that's it! I remember now!"

"I'm so happy for you! What does it mean, though?"

"It means . . . it means the secret is somewhere in my ship! My fighter! On the tac screen! It means he put it someplace where a pilot would see it and not really see it!''

She was almost at the door before she turned around and said awkwardly, ''Thank you. Thank you—very much.''

CHAPTER 29

Ivanova ran all the way to the Cobra bay, barely able to stand still while the lift tube descended. *No wonder,* she was thinking, *no wonder I couldn't remember.* "Hardwired." It was J. D. who was always interested in strange new technologies, things like direct ship/brain interfaces. In those days, all she could think of was getting into the cockpit of a fighter, somehow taking over from her brother and avenging his death all mixed up together in her mind.

She ran past the startled dockworkers, who yelled, "Hey, Commander! Is there an alert on?"

"No, it's nothing!" she shouted back. "Is my ship ready?"

But there was no need for them to answer, she could see it there, the familiar ship in the familiar cradle. She had a thought, turned around to see the shift foreman looking at her with a concerned frown. "Everyone knows which one is my ship, don't they?"

"Why, Commander?" A look of sudden alarm. "Are you thinking of sabotage?"

"No! I mean, there's been no sabotage threat or anything like that. I was just wondering."

"Good. Then there's nothing wrong?"

"No, I just wanted to check out something I forgot last time I was out."

She slid into the seat inside the cockpit, stared around her at the controls and display screens, more than familiar, almost extensions of herself by now. The tac display was dark. She closed her eyes, then opened them again.

She switched on the computer, and the screen glowed

into life: rows of controls, the targeting array. J. D. had been desperate. He wouldn't have had much time. Whatever he'd hidden, it was too dangerous to keep it on him, too valuable to risk its loss . . .

Suddenly, she knew. "Computer, keyword search: Hardwired."

"No file accessed."

She thought an instant. "Keyword search: J. D."

"Accessing: file J. D."

"Display file."

But what flashed into sight on her screen was nothing she could comprehend. A diagram of some kind. A code. Maybe the map of a new star system. So complex that the pattern only emerged after she fined down the resolution. It meant something, certainly. But she had no idea what, and the tactical computer knew no more than she did.

So this is it, she thought. *J. D., this is what you died for? And the rest of them? What secret could this possibly be to be worth so much?*

He'd known she was on the station, somehow found out which ship was hers (from some secret Free Mars sympathizer on the Cobra bay's crew?). And he'd copied the information—as a backup—to her tac computer. Hidden in with all the other files, where no one would ever be likely to notice its existence—unless they had the keyword to search for it.

Ivanova felt a profound sense of loss and sadness. What had happened to her old flight instructor? What kind of person had he become, that he was involved in all this? "Dammit, J. D.!"

But this wasn't getting her anywhere. She had the computer transfer the data to a crystal, then slipped it into a pocket of her flight suit. Now to find out what exactly she had here.

The same old janitor was mopping the hall outside the

Cobra bays, and Ivanova stepped aside to get out of her way. She barely caught a glimpse of sudden movement in the corner of her eye before the blow struck—shock stick, not mop handle—shorting out her entire nervous system, reducing all her senses to blinding white static.

When they returned, the first thing she felt was hands on her, someone tearing at her uniform, tearing it off. And her first incoherent thought was rape—some maniac had attacked her. But then the voice came clear, and she recognized it.

"Where is it? I know you've got it! I knew it all along! Ms. Perfect Record! Ms. Full Commander at twenty-eight! Ms. Hero, capturing raiders single-handed! He passed it on to you! I knew he did! I knew—

"Yes! This is it! This is it, isn't it! The crystal! You knew the code, I knew you did! I knew it!"

Ivanova forced open her eyes. For a moment, she thought her brain wasn't functioning right after the shock, because the voice was Miyoshi's—it had been in so many of her recent nightmares—but the face was the little old cleaning woman from the ready room. Then they merged, the old woman's face and Miyoshi's, and she could see through the fake wrinkles, the disguise, to the lieutenant from Earthforce Command standing over her, the data crystal clutched in her hand, and her eyes bright and face glowing with triumphant success.

Of course. Khatib's crime and Wallace's failure had tainted Miyoshi. Her own career was ruined—at least as ruined as Ivanova's. Finding this data crystal was the only way to redeem herself.

And Ivanova's career? There didn't seem much of a chance that Miyoshi was interested in redeeming it, too.

Up to me, then, she thought groggily. But how could she do anything now, with the effects of the shock still barely worn off? She wondered how much she could move, slowly flexed the fingers on her right hand, then her left. If she could switch on her link . . .

But Miyoshi's eyes were on her like a hawk's. She bent down, held the crystal out, directly over Ivanova's face. "*I've* got it now! I watched you! I watched you go to the telepath, I knew it'd come out, sooner or later! If you only knew how long I waited . . ."

Suddenly she straightened, snatched the crystal away, tucked it into one of the inside pockets of the Maintenance coverall she was wearing. Then, from another pocket, she took out something else, which Ivanova couldn't quite make out, a thin cylinder. Miyoshi was smiling, and Ivanova didn't like the looks of that smile, didn't like it at all.

"You know where we are, don't you?"

Wherever it was, Ivanova didn't think she was going to be as happy about it as Miyoshi was. She blinked her eyes, turned her head, trying to place the plain, utilitarian walls—of one of the heads. And she'd been on her way to the Alpha Wing ready room . . .

"Yes, I thought you did. Nice touch of irony, isn't it? And just think how much fun your friend *Mr.* Garibaldi will have, figuring out this one! He likes to play detective, doesn't he?"

Ivanova knew she had to take her chance now. She swept with her legs, not sure until the last instant if they even worked yet, and sent Miyoshi staggering. At the same time she reached for her link, to call for help, to call Garibaldi—

It wasn't there. The back of her wrist was empty, bare.

And the strength in her legs hadn't been enough to do more than send Miyoshi stumbling into the wall. The lieutenant was still on her feet, and she quickly regained her balance, spun around to turn on Ivanova, saw her still on her back on the floor, groping for her link. The smile returned. Miyoshi slowly reached into another coverall pocket, came out with another object that she held up, out of Ivanova's reach. The link.

"Looking for this?"

The missing link, and Ivanova would have broken out into laughter if she weren't so sure Miyoshi meant to kill her. But now Miyoshi frowned and put the link back away, and with a wary eye on Ivanova she bent down to pick up the cylinder from the floor where she'd dropped it as she lost her balance. An injector, Ivanova recognized it now, and she wouldn't want to take bets that it wasn't loaded with some kind of poison.

There was going to be another murder on Babylon 5, another unsolved killing, because of course Miyoshi wasn't still on the station, Miyoshi had been shipped back to Earth with her boss, so who could have done it? Sheridan would be furious, Ivanova thought with irrelevant clarity. He was sick and tired of murders.

But Miyoshi's frown deepened while she fiddled with the tube, and finally she threw it back down on the floor with an expression of disgust. "Now, that's a nuisance! It's broken."

Still carefully watching Ivanova, she picked up a shock stick where it was propped up next to a washstand. "You know," she said in a too-casual tone, "these things are supposed to be nonlethal. But you've worked in security some, I'll bet you know better. It takes some *work,* but you can do the job with this if you have to. And now it looks like you've left me no choice. Too bad you weren't carrying a weapon, you know. I could have used it."

She firmly twisted the shock stick's handle until it was turned to the highest setting. Ivanova knew with the certainty of desperation that she was only going to have one more chance. She wished she weren't still lying here on her back.

Miyoshi approached with the shock stick held like a

sword. Ivanova braced herself, knowing Miyoshi was watching for her reaction. They were both combat trained, and they watched each other like a pair of fencers, each looking for an opening, for a feint. One touch with the stick and Ivanova would be helpless again. She pivoted to keep Miyoshi in front of her. She was at a disadvantage in this position, but she knew at least that she was recovering quickly, that every minute she was regaining her strength and coordination.

But Miyoshi clearly knew it, too. She lunged forward, and Ivanova countered with a twist to the right, to get to her feet. But she was too slow, her muscles hadn't still quite recovered their quickness, and the stick jabbed her hip, the shock instantaneous, the nerves overloading all at once, seeming to explode . . .

Garibaldi heard the call come in over his link and the security channel simultaneously. "Security! Mr. Garibaldi! It's Commander Ivanova! She's in terrible trouble! You have to find her!"

"Call an alert!" he ordered. Then, recognizing the voice, "Talia? What's going on?"

"I don't know! I just know she's in danger! Please! Hurry! Find her before it's too late!"

"Get me a trace on her link," Garibaldi ordered again. "Contact the captain. Let him know what's going on."

The computer voice broke in, "Commander Ivanova traced to Alpha Wing ready room."

"That's—" He didn't complete the statement out loud. That's where J. D. Ortega had been killed. "Tac Squad B, with me! All available security to the Alpha Wing ready room. Hurry!"

* * *

Garibaldi burst into the ready room at the head of his squad, but he wasn't the first on the scene. An officer pointed to the door to the head. "They're in there."

He hurried to the door. There was the unmistakable lingering scent of a recent plasma discharge. Three security officers knelt on the floor where there were two unconscious forms. Ivanova—

He started forward in alarm, but the closest security man looked up and said, "She's alive, Mr. Garibaldi, just stunned. We've already called Medlab."

Another stood up, holding a shock stick. "She was using *this* on the commander. I ordered her to drop the stick and put up her hands. She turned on us."

From the floor the officer bending over the other inert figure straightened. "She's dead."

Garibaldi stepped closer to see who it was. "Miyoshi!" he exclaimed in shocked astonishment. "Lieutenant Miyoshi!"

The security agent who'd shot her seemed slightly uncertain of himself. "She was attacking Commander Ivanova, Chief. She didn't drop her weapon when I ordered her to."

"Good job," Garibaldi assured him. "You can put it all in your report."

He looked at Ivanova, who seemed to be having some kind of slight spasm. "Where's Medical, dammit!"

But just then the medical team rushed into the room, Dr. Franklin at their head. "Ivanova's hurt?"

"Shock stick," Garibaldi said tersely, standing back out of the medics' way with the rest of security, their job finished for the moment.

"This one's dead," the other medic reported from Miyoshi's side. "Plasma burst. Hit point-blank."

Franklin was applying an injector to Ivanova. "She's coming around," he announced. "Commander? Commander Ivanova? Can you hear me? Can you say something?"

Now Garibaldi edged closer again. Ivanova was stirring. Her lips moved. He made out, "Mi . . . yo . . . shi . . ."

"It's all right," he assured her. "Miyoshi's taken care of. You're all right now. You're safe."

"Ga . . . ri . . ."

"That's right, it's me. She got you with a shock stick, but you're going to be just fine, isn't she, Doc?"

But Franklin wasn't about to let the security department make the diagnosis for him. He pulled back Ivanova's eyelid and aimed an instrument into one eye, then the other. "Mmh," he said finally, "looks all right. But we'll just go up to Medlab for a neurological scan, just to make sure."

But Ivanova blinked, tried to lift her head. "No! Wait! Miyoshi. Data. Crystal."

"Miyoshi has a data crystal?" Garibaldi asked.

"Ortega. I. Found. It."

Now Garibaldi understood. "Don't worry. I'll find it. Here, wait a minute, don't move that body."

He knelt down, started to go through the pockets of her coveralls. They were maintenance department issue, he noticed. And the makeup on her face made her look almost twice her real age. He *hoped* he wouldn't have to make a body check. He hated that, when people swallowed data crystals and you had to get them back the hard way. But then maybe he could just leave that up to Franklin.

Nope, no need. The crystal was there in an inside pocket, and he slipped it into a pocket of his own, then hurried after the team of medics who had taken Ivanova to Medlab, to give her the news that he'd found it.

She was sitting up by the time he arrived, recovering quickly with Franklin's treatment. Captain Sheridan was there questioning her, but when she saw Garibaldi come in she almost tried to jump to her feet before the medic could restrain her. "Did you find it? Do you have it?"

"I've got it right here," he assured her. "Do you know what it is?"

"No. It's not like anything I've ever seen. I have to think it might be alien, even."

"Hmm." Garibaldi looked speculative, taking the crystal out of his pocket and turning it around in his fingers, as if he could see into the data matrix.

"Can I see it?" Sheridan asked, and Garibaldi gave it to him.

Suddenly Talia came hurrying into the treatment room, slightly out of breath. "They said you found her! They said— Susan, are you all right?"

Ivanova's head jerked back as if she'd been slapped. "I . . . I'm fine, quite fine," she said rapidly, but Garibaldi could see her face color with confusion. And at the same time Talia's face went pale.

Garibaldi took her aside, asked in a low voice, "I wanted to ask you, when you called in, just how did you know that Ivanova was in trouble?"

Talia stammered, "I don't know, I . . . She had just finished consulting me on a . . . confidential matter. I suppose the connection . . . there must have still been a connection. After we were . . . that close. I don't know, but I *knew* she needed help."

Garibaldi stared in disbelief at Ivanova. "She went to you? As a telepath?"

"I believe she was desperate," Talia said, flipping her hair back. Her tone was more detached now.

Ivanova had heard. "Yes, I did consult Ms. Winters in her professional capacity. I felt it was necessary . . . to recall the significance of Ortega's note." She hesitated visibly. "I'm grateful for Ms. Winters calling in for help when she did."

"I'm glad you weren't seriously hurt," Talia replied, her voice even more clipped and cool than Ivanova's. "But I can see there are already too many people in here."

She spun sharply around and left the room, while Sheridan questioned Garibaldi with an unspoken *Do you have any idea what this is all about?* and Garibaldi shaking his head that he didn't. Neither of them had dared interfere between the two women, and Ivanova's expression didn't encourage any questions now.

"The crystal," she insisted, "we have to see what's on it."

Sheridan looked down at it, still in his hand. "So this is what everyone was dying for," he said quietly. "I wonder what could possibly be worth it."

He popped the crystal into the nearest computer console, saw the pattern come up onto the screen, and shook his head. "Now, what's *that*?"

To the computer, "Analysis."

"Analysis underway," it replied.

"Hey!" said Ivanova, "that's my crystal! I get to see it!" Garibaldi helped her onto her feet.

Franklin, always curious about new technology, came to watch the screen with them as the analysis progressed. "What that looks like to me," he said slowly, "is an atomic diagram. Of one hell of a *big* atom!"

A few moments later, the computer agreed with him. "Most probable analysis: the information represents a schematic of an isotope of an unknown metallic element. Analysis suggests an element of Group VI b, atomic number of 156, with anomalous electron shielding and the presence of an unknown subatomic particle—"

"That can't be right!" Franklin exclaimed. "There is no element 156! And, if there were, it'd be so radioactive it'd have a half-life measured in nanoseconds. It'd be too unstable to exist! And, see there—the atomic weight is twice what it should be for an isotope of an element in that range.''

"Most probable analysis,'' the computer replied, "the element is artificial, not capable of existing in nature. This appears to be the result of the presence of an anomalous subatomic particle, an unknown nucleon, stabilizing the nucleus.''

"An unknown subatomic particle? A new, artificial element?'' Sheridan said in wonder. "This can't be anything produced by human technology.''

The computer agreed. What they had was the schematic for an utterly unknown metal, produced artificially by a technology that had to be alien.

"But what's it good for?'' Garibaldi asked, almost suspiciously. "Why is everyone murdering people left and right to get their hands on this?''

"Estimated analysis yields a probable melting point: 6,180 degrees; boiling point: 11,500 degrees; conductivity index: 0.42—''

"It's a supermorbidium!'' Ivanova exclaimed. "No natural metal can withstand that kind of heat! I'll just bet I know what it's good for—the phase coils of plasma weapons!''

Everyone in the room stared at the display in silence. "This would revolutionize weapons technology,'' Sheridan finally said in a low voice. "The strategic advantage could be enormous.'' He was recalling the admiral's words: *Vital importance to Earth's defenses.*

"The sort of information governments would kill for,'' Garibaldi added.

"And it would make morbidium obsolete for strategic purposes,'' Ivanova said slowly. "And if morbidium were your primary source of revenue . . .''

"You'd kill to keep the information from getting out,'' Garibaldi completed the thought.

But Ivanova wasn't so sure. "Maybe. Or maybe you'd

try to get in on the ground floor with the new technology. But for that, you'd need capital. And the minute word got out about this new metal, the price of your stock would fall . . . you'd want to sell out before that happened . . . snatch whatever profits you could . . .'' She shook her head. Economics wasn't a clear-cut science, like astrogation or hyperspace field theory.

A lot of things weren't clear-cut. She realized she might never know what J. D. had intended to do with the crystal. Had the temptation of fabulous wealth been too much for him? Or had he been trying to turn the information over to Earthforce and gotten caught up in the corruption surrounding AreTech's conspiracy? Or had he been a member of Free Mars all along and intended to use the discovery to support his political goals?

Captain Sheridan, however, was quite certain of one thing. ''Commander Ivanova,'' he said firmly, ''I want you to come with me to the Command Office. We're going to be making a call to Admiral Wilson of the Joint Chiefs. I think we have something they've been looking for.''

CHAPTER 30

It was quiet in the Observation Dome on Babylon 5, a rare hour when there were no ships scheduled to depart or arrive at the station. Only the skeleton crew of duty technicians sat at their consoles, intent on their work.

On the dome's upper level, Commander Ivanova stood in front of the control console, hands clasped behind her back. The glowing colored lights of the displays reflected off the curved window above them, but Ivanova was looking past them, out at the black immensity of space and the silent stars.

All her eyes could see were peace and stillness. But the instruments controlled by her console could see further, deeper, into ranges of energy inaccessible to merely human senses. There were wars out there among those stars, contesting that space. There were ships and weapons—and the weapons were always more powerful, capable of more destruction.

Now Earth was reaching out for alien power, to put alien weapons in human hands. Ivanova had the fleeting thought that she didn't know which frightened her more: the destructive potential of technology, or what humanity might do if they obtained it.

But there was no more time to wonder, because at that moment the scan technician called out, "Commander Ivanova! Getting a sharp rise in tachyon emissions! Something big is coming through the jump point!"

"I've got it!" she said quickly, turning her attention back to the main display. In command.